诺纳德·苏克尼克作品的后现代叙事研究

Research on Postmodernist Narratives in Ronald Sukenick's Works

王海燕　著

武汉理工大学出版社
·武　汉·

序

犹太文学是美国文学的一个重要组成部分。上世纪五十年代，它曾在美国文坛一枝独秀，涌现了诺贝尔文学奖得主索尔·贝娄、艾萨克·巴什维斯·辛格，美国国家图书奖得主伯纳德·马拉默德、诺曼·梅勒和诺纳德·苏克尼克等。他们一度成为美国文坛一道亮丽的风景线。

相对而言，苏克尼克有点被边缘化了。其实他既搞小说创作，又做文学评论，特别是在1969年发表的《小说的死亡及其他》轰动了美国文坛。他尖锐地指出：六十年代美国小说死了，已经到了令人无法容忍的地步。一切都得从头开始。他的呼吁得到了许多美国作家的认同，推动了美国后现代派文学的出现。苏克尼克在文学史上留下崭新的一页。

不过，对于中国读者来说，苏克尼克是个比较陌生的作家。尽管他1995年来过中国，但相关的评介很难找到，对他的作品研究几乎是空白，仅有四五篇文章。因此，王海燕这部专著《诺纳德·苏克尼克作品的后现代叙事研究》填补了这个空白，具有重要的理论价值和现实意义。

《诺纳德·苏克尼克作品的后现代叙事研究》是作者在她的博士学位论文的基础上修订而成的。它从一个全新的视角评释苏克尼克和他的小说，指出他在上世纪六十年代美国小说危机和身份危机双重困境中努力进行叙事改革，采用生存法则、"熵"的法则和镶嵌法则来应对，从而深入揭示了这位不平凡的小说家、文论家、批评家、编辑、出版商和教育家对美国文学的重要贡献。这不但有助于读者们进一步了解苏克尼克其人其作，尤其是他小说中身份的后现代叙事，而且可以让人理解作为一个犹太作家，苏克尼克在美国文学危机的年代里对后现代派小说的产生和发展所发挥的巨大作用。因此，作者先前在进行论文答辩时受到校内外专家的点赞，专家们一致认为这是一篇优秀的论著。

那么，这部专著有什么特点呢？

首先，突出重点，抓住要害，密切结合苏克尼克的创作特色来展开论述。专著没有就事论事，谈论苏克尼克写了哪些小说，小说中讲些什么，而是抓住要害，重点评论苏克尼克在文学危机和身份危机面前如何运用三个法则的内涵和特色，深刻地剖析生存法则中的同化与异化，指出苏克尼克在小说中探讨的三种异化于社会的方式：躲进象牙塔、沉迷于幻想中和创作实验小说。同化意味着放弃个性，异化则意味着边缘化。人们不得不在同化和异化之间徘徊。苏克尼克在长篇小说《向下进入:地下的生活》里有精彩的描述。

许多美国后现代派作家如托马斯·品钦、威廉·加迪斯和唐·德里罗等将热力学第二定律的"熵"引入小说,描绘美国后现代社会的混乱无序。但苏克尼克与他们不同,他提出了身份的"熵"的法则,充分显示了美国后现代社会中的"多重身份"和"身份消解"的特点。小说中的人物往往无理由、无逻辑、随意而频繁地更改他们的身份,直到"无身份"状态,即身份的完全消解。这种"身份流"和"无身份"刻意消解人物的个性,不停地变换个性特征,形成了"身份流",即频繁地变换身份。它最好的体现是"名字流"。他的小说中人物的名字随意转换,没有一个明确的身份。这一切揭示了苏克尼克对美国后现代社会身份构建的独特看法。

在评论苏克尼克的镶嵌法则时,专著指出与精神分析相反,苏克尼克提出了精神综合的新概念,即在个人成长过程中协调和综合不同阶段的不同倾向,以达到更高的层次。他采用拼缀和拼贴手法,体现了后现代叙事的特点。这些论述结合丰富的文本分析更加令人信服。

其次,专著紧扣时代特点,从文学危机和身份危机来考察苏克尼克其人其作。上世纪六十年代是美国的多事之秋。民权运动、女权运动,特别是反对越南战争的浪潮席卷美国每个角落,文坛一片凋零景象。苏克尼克深深地意识到他的创作正处于美国一个特殊历史时期,面临着小说创作危机和身份危机。二战中希特勒和法西斯对犹太人的大屠杀和战后东西方的冷战已彻底摧毁了犹太人赖以构建身份的基石,将他们推入失望的困境。作为一位正直的犹太作家,苏克尼克对于时代和社会的危机及犹太人的困境感受很深。他尤其意识到小说面临的危机。他用"小说死了"来唤起人们的关注,呼吁用全新的模式进行叙事改革,以适应发生变革的世界,努力开创美国小说的新天地。

专著以此为突破点,将苏克尼克个人面临的危机与社会和民族的危机结合起来,对其人其作进行历史的评议,这就使得专著得出的结论更加客观而公正。

再次,专著注重基本概念的阐释,理论分析细致,层层剖析,说理明确。作为一本专著,基本概念的准确性十分关键。专著对身份的定义、身份的发展史、身份的三个特点和三个变换都做了简明的阐述;对于什么是同化、什么是异化,专著都讲得明明白白,特别是对苏克尼克的独特概念,如"身份流"、"名字流"和"精神综合"等等都交待得一清二楚,让读者们好学易懂。近些年来,西方文论大量涌入我国。在一篇论文里,引用这个,引用那个,已成为一种新常态。不过,有的偏爱它的神秘和奇特,生搬硬套,结果令人费解,望文兴叹。有的则经过消化和理解,用自己的话来表达,做到深入浅出,准确无误,恰到好处。后一种态度无疑是值得提倡的。

最后，作者在评论中将苏克尼克小说中的身份危机与后现代叙事紧密结合起来，使思想内容与艺术形式的评析达到有机的统一。专著指出，政治、文化和宗教语境中的自我定义和身份构建早已成了美国文学的常见主题。叙事一直是身份构建的核心。作为一位美国后现代派犹太作家，苏克尼克深深地意识到身份危机和后现代叙事危机，并在写作生涯中不断探寻出路。他重新定义“小说”，认为小说不再是让人信以为真的思想的形成，而是与现实之间的亲密接触。所以，小说家首先要解构传统小说的种种约束。他一生创作了 9 部长篇小说、3 部短篇小说集和 70 多篇发表于报刊的短篇小说及 3 部文学评论集等。他认为他的小说的特点是无情节、无故事、无人物、无时间顺序、无逼真描写、无模仿、无讽喻、无象征、无主题及无意义。这种所谓的“新小说”完全颠覆了传统小说中的关键元素。不仅如此，苏克尼克还采用章节的倒排、间隔空白和文中插图等变换多样的排版改革和文字游戏等手段，使小说文本混乱无序，引发读者的自由联想。专著将苏克尼克小说的内容和形式这么密切地结合起来评论，充分揭示了他的大胆实验和创新精神，肯定了他对美国文学的重要作用，令人感到他在美国文学上应占有一席之地。

总之，专著结构严谨，英文流畅，立论公允，资料翔实，富有创意，充分展示了作者刻苦钻研、精心探索的丰硕成果。

杨仁敬于厦门大学西村书斋

2016 年 10 月

前　言

1968年，诺纳德·苏克尼克的第一部小说面世。苏克尼克就将他此后40余年的生命全部奉献给了文学。其足迹遍布文学的各个领域：小说创作、文学批评、文学理论、小说编辑、出版及文学教育。

作为小说家，苏克尼克出版了9部长篇小说、3部短篇小说集及散布各个文学期刊的70多篇短篇小说，为他赢得了1988年和1999年的美国国家图书奖和2003年的摩顿·扎别儿奖等奖项。同时，苏克尼克也是美国20世纪六七十年代发出最强音的理论家之一。他的文学批评主要收录在《叙事对话》《形式：小说艺术中的偏离》及《华莱士·史蒂文斯：对晦涩的思考》中。他还在不同的文学批评期刊上发表批评文章70余篇。

苏克尼克的触角还伸到了小说出版业。苏克尼克成立了小说集锦出版社，让当时许多的先锋派作家受益匪浅。1977年，在科罗拉多大学资助下，苏克尼克创建了《美国图书评论》杂志，致力于评介那些被《纽约书评》之类的主流媒体忽视的创新作家。1989年，他成为《黑冰》杂志编辑，出版了《黑冰》丛书。

苏克尼克认为他的创作正处于美国一个特殊的历史时期，面临着双重的危机：身份的危机和小说创作的危机。他在小说《镶嵌的人》的开篇提出的三个问题清晰而明确地指出了这双重的危机："故事在哪里？文字是什么？你是犹太人吗？"首先，苏克尼克认为对犹太人的大屠杀和冷战已经彻底摧毁了犹太人赖以构建身份的基石，将他们推向身份危机的困境。而且，他还清醒地认识到，这种身份危机不仅仅困扰着犹太人，而是波及所有人。他曾经感叹，"1932我出生之年，也是希特勒掌权之年，当所有人的身份都被从这个星球清除毁灭之后，人怎么还能假装个人身份的存在？人怎么还能假装自己还是一个人，还有人性？"换言之，个人应采取什么态度来应对当代美国社会的身份危机，借用其中尚存的良善？因此，身份危机成为苏克尼克小说中反复出现的主题。他的大部分小说都围绕着身份危机和身份追寻的主题展开，时时在寻找摆脱困境的出路。

同时，苏克尼克还清晰地意识到小说面临的危机。小说这种在19世纪已明确定义的体裁，在20世纪遭到了众多作家的质疑和挑战。约翰·巴思1967年发出了"小说的枯竭"的断言。苏克尼克同样用"小说之死"来唤起人们对小说危机的关注。他认为小说体现了人们看待世界的方式。当世界发生了改变，传统小说的陈旧模式就应受到质疑，新环境呼唤全新的模式。因此，面对小说的危机，苏克尼克坚持不懈地进行叙事改革，以期开辟小说创作的新天地。

正是基于苏克尼克所面临的双重危机及他为解救危机做出的种种努力，本书《诺纳德·苏克尼克作品的后现代叙事研究》从两大方面研究苏克尼克的小说：小说中的身份危机和身份构建主题及小说危机和苏克尼克的叙事改革。本书主要探讨了苏克尼克在应对这双重危机时采取的三种法则:生存法则、“熵”的法则和镶嵌法则。

本书分为六章。

第一章绪论部分概述了诺纳德·苏克尼克的文学生涯。正如他的一部小说标题所言,苏克尼克本人就是一个“镶嵌的人”——他由文学中的不同身份镶嵌而成:小说家、理论家、批评家、编辑、出版商和教育家。他的足迹遍布文学的各个领域。

但遗憾的是,无论是在美国还是在中国,苏克尼克都没有引起学者们足够的关注。通过对美国和中国苏克尼克研究现状的综述,本书指出了造成苏克尼克文学地位边缘化的种种原因。有限的研究成果、狭窄的研究视角及整体系统研究的缺乏等状况都表明苏克尼克的研究远远无法与他文学上的成就相匹配。这种现状也为本书的研究提供了极大的空间。因此,本书尝试从一个全新的视角来研究苏克尼克的小说——苏克尼克小说中身份的后现代叙事。

第二章“身份和后现代语境中的身份研究”为本书提供理论脉络,侧重回顾身份的定义、相关的理论及身份的后现代叙事。身份作为人类经验中的基本概念之一,难以简单定义。加之哲学、心理学、社会学等学科从不同视角研究定义身份,使其定义更加复杂。通过梳理身份理论的发展历史,本书通过指出身份的三个特点对它加以定义:身份是后天形成的,非生来就有的;身份是在社会环境中构建的;身份只有通过差异才能体现出来。

虽然身份的概念由来已久,但只是在现代社会里,随着传统群居生活的衰落和工业社会的兴起,身份才开始面临困境。伴随着工业化而产生的个人主义、资本主义和城市化给社会带来巨大变化,不可避免地改变了人们身份的构建模式。其中有三个变化不容忽视:“自觉”身份的增强、身份的“他者导向”及“分裂性身份”。可见,现代语境中的身份危机在于怎样构建一个身份并保持身份的坚实稳定;而后现代语境中的身份危机在于怎样消解固定的身份,并敞开接纳多种选择。后现代社会中经济、技术和文化的变化造成了这一语境中身份的动荡、分裂和多重性等特点。

本章的第二节“关于身份的后现代叙事”将身份和叙事联系起来。事实上,叙事一直是身份构建的核心。身份构建的过程正是人们讲述自己生活故事的过程。因此,身份的叙事性构成和小说的叙事性构成之间存在极为类似的关联。再者,政治、文化和宗教语境中的自我定义和身份构建早已是文学中的常见主题。通过简单梳理美国文学中关于身份的叙述,尤其是关于身份的后现代叙事,本书指出苏克尼克小说中身份的后现代叙事的独特之处值得我们进一步研究。

作为一名后现代作家和犹太作家,苏克尼克敏锐地感受到身份危机和后现代叙事危机。面对这双重危机,苏克尼克在其写作生涯中孜孜以求,探寻出路。在仔细研读了苏克尼克的小说后,本书将苏克尼克在应对这双重危机时所探寻的种种方式归纳为三种法则:生存法则、“熵”的法则和镶嵌法则。本书的主干部分就是分别论述这三种法则,并深入解读苏克尼克小说中的身份主题及关于身份的后现代叙事。

第三章“生存法则:同化或异化”从两方面论述:身份的生存法则和后现代叙事的生存法则。第一节侧重于身份的生存法则。二战后的美国历经了一系列的政治、经济、社会和文化的变迁,使战后尤其是六十年代的美国处于动荡和骚动之中。传统意义的丧失、自我迷失、角色混乱等状况频发,所有这些迫使人们重新定义自我,对于美国的少数族裔来说,更是如此。简言之,人们陷入了身份危机。怎样在变化的社会中生存并获得安全感是个人所面临的问题。“生存法则”就是指人们在身份形成和构建中采取的种种策略和方法。面对身份危机,人们采取各种方式重新定义自我。但从根本上说,他们必须在同化于与异化于主流社会中做出抉择。

“同化”指的是使自己逐渐趋同并适应美国主流社会。同化的过程是人们调整自己和接受主流社会生活方式的过程,同时也意味着人们必须放弃那些不为主流社会所接受的种种价值观。在苏克尼克看来,人们可以通过“创造”或者“出售”自己的身份来达到融入主流社会的目的。他所谓的“创造”自己的身份是指个人根据主流社会流行的媒体形象来塑造自己的身份。而“出售”自己的身份是指放弃自己原来坚持的道德和原则以谋求金钱、名誉或其他,从而被主流社会接纳。但社会中的不少人也选择异化于主流社会,甘于边缘地位,以保持自己的独特个性。苏克尼克在他的小说中探讨了三种异化于社会的方式:躲进象牙塔、沉溺于幻想中或者创作实验小说。同化或异化于主流社会对个人来说都是难以抉择的。同化意味着放弃个性,而异化意味着处于边缘。通常人们不得不在这两者之间徘徊斗争。这种徘徊和斗争在美国格林威治村的艺术家身上得到充分体现。苏克尼克在他获得美国国家图书奖的小说《向下并进入:地下的生活》中记录了这些徘徊和挣扎。

在 20 世纪,不仅人们面临着身份危机,小说这种文学体裁也同样面临身份危机。不少作家纷纷宣告“小说的死亡”。苏克尼克就是其中之一。他认为,历经了简·奥斯丁、乔治·艾略特及海明威而成就的小说的种种模式已不足以刻画现代社会的经历,如不改革,小说就面临着死亡的结局。可见,小说本身也面临着身份危机。因此,第二节侧重于后现代叙事的生存法则。首先,苏克尼克指出了造成小说死亡危机的种种因素,并针对这些因素,开始了他的叙事改革之路。在他看来,小说家首先要解构传统小说的种种约束。诸如情节、人物、主题和模仿等这些传统小说中的关键元素在苏克尼克看来都不再是必不可少的。苏克尼克在概括自己小说的特点时说:他的新小说是“无情节、无故事、无人物、无时间顺序、无逼真描写、无模仿、无讽喻、无象征、无主题及无意义”。

在这些改革的基础上,苏克尼克重新定义“小说”。“小说不再是让人信以为真的思想的形成,而是与现实之间的亲密接触”。换言之,小说不是折射现实的镜子,而是现实的一部分,并融入现实中,从而让现实增加了新的意义。如果说小说的目的是反省我们的经历以求事实,那么叙事就是“一种能够快速多变和灵活独特的理解形式,能让人们抓住经验之流”。因此,苏克尼克认为小说的叙事必须是不自然的、诡辩的、圆滑的、流畅的、多变的、多牵连的、感情的、不一致的,甚至互相矛盾的、即兴的、临时的。改革是小说的生存法则。

第四章讲述的是“熵”的法则。鲁道夫·克劳修斯1850年首次提出“熵”的概念，用来指在系统能量的转换中不可利用的能量的参量。这一概念成为热力学第二定律的本质。这个物理学概念也相继被引入诸如宇宙学、化学、信息科学及人类学、文学等领域。众多的后现代派作家，如托马斯·品钦、威廉·加迪斯、肯·克西、斯坦利·埃尔金、苏珊·桑塔格、唐纳德·巴塞尔姆、唐· 德里罗等纷纷将这一概念引入小说中来刻画后现代社会的混乱无序。

苏克尼克与上述作家不同，他并没有在小说中直接将“熵”作为一个主题加以描述，也没有将之转化为组织结构，而是提出了身份的“熵”的法则。这一法则让他能充分凸显后现代社会中的“多重身份”和“身份的消解”两大特点。在他看来，热力学中的熵是封闭系统中大量微观粒子无序的量度，系统越无序、越混乱，熵就越大，直至“热寂”状态——完全停止。而身份的“熵”的法则是指小说中的人物无理由、无逻辑、随意、频繁地更改他们的身份，直到“无身份”的状态。苏克尼克小说中的人物在他们的身份追寻之路上，身份中稳定和有利于交流的特征渐渐丧失。而交流中的熵——流动、多变的特征逐渐增加，直到身份的完全消解。因此，本书将从“身份流”和“无身份”这两个方面论述苏克尼克关于身份的“熵”的法则。

在传统小说中，随着故事情节的展开，故事人物逐渐获得清晰、一致的个性。而苏克尼克的身份中的“熵”的法则则是刻意消解人物的这些个性。在身份构建的过程中，身份，就像密封系统中流动的能量，渐渐丧失确定、稳固的个性特征，同时获得越来越多流动、变化的个性特征，这样就形成了“身份流”——人物不停地变化他们的身份。苏克尼克的“身份流”的最好体现是“名字流”。名字是身份的符号，指向明确的对象，代表一个特定的自我。但在苏克尼克的小说中，名字不再指向明确的对象。小说中人物和名字像粒子一样任意地移动，随意地转换，永远无法固定为一个明确的身份。

苏克尼克的“身份流”凸显了他对后现代社会身份构建的理解。在他看来，人的身份不是一个固定的存在，而是一个逐渐形成的流动的过程。后现代社会的身份更具流动和互换的特点。而“身份流”的必然结果就是“无身份”。

苏克尼克的“无身份”是对传统小说人物刻画的巨大挑战。他认为传统小说刻画固定身份的人物的做法束缚了作家的想象。在后现代社会中，既然所谓的统一体验、统一世界和完整自我这样的概念无法持久，那么就让它们时时消解。我们应致力于寻找这些消解背后潜藏的种种联系。世上一切都是相互关联的，一切都是可以想象的。因而，也就无所谓最终的固定身份。联系的可能性无限扩大，而意义和身份被消解。苏克尼克试图通过自己的写作证明“无身份”不是人物刻画的灾难，而是他努力达到的理想状态，也是身份的“熵”的法则的必然结果。

身份的“熵”的法则凸显了苏克尼克人物刻画中的“多重身份”和“身份的消解”的特点。“后现代叙事的‘熵’的法则”则是强调苏克尼克叙事的后现代特征：流动性、碎片、混乱、多变和消解，与传统叙事寻求的整体性和连贯性形成鲜明对比。

苏克尼克的叙述摆脱传统小说情节、人物和模仿的束缚，是对经验流中种种联系的表达和再表达的一个连续不断的过程。为了体现这种变化的流动，苏克尼克频繁地变化小说的情节、人物和风格，尤其是苏克尼克采用变化多样的排版改革和语言游戏来达到流动和消解的目的。

排版决定小说的页面、印刷和装订等，是小说的技术环节，一直以来被作者和读者所忽视。但苏克尼克利用这些长期被忽视的环节，挑战传统小说从左到右、从上到下的排版模式。他希望通过借用排版革新的破坏性来挑战传统模式。因此，在小说中他尝试了章节的倒排、独特的间隔空白及文中图形等方式。这些技巧极大地造成文本混乱无序的同时，又为读者提供了种种新鲜的联系，引发新鲜的意义。

语言游戏是苏克尼克达到"熵"的叙事的另一方法。在他的小说中，语言就像粒子，自由随意移动，造成混乱，但同时也形成种种新的联系和新的意义。苏克尼克采用文字游戏、双关、全字母短句等语言游戏，迫使小说的语言最大限度地传递意义。

本书第五章为"镶嵌法则:碎片和拼贴"。镶嵌，这种将碎片拼贴而成为一个整体的艺术被苏克尼克借用于自己的写作理论中。镶嵌法则指的是，当整体缺失时人们采用、处理和对待部分的方式。他提出这一法则也是来应对后现代社会的身份危机和叙事危机的一种策略。

苏克尼克敏锐地观察到后现代语境下文化的多样性和异质性造成了人们越来越难以保持文化中心和整体性。当整体和中心都缺失时，部分和碎片就陷入不断的构建和重构的过程中。所以，苏克尼克的镶嵌法则的目标不是整体性和统一性，而是部分和碎片。他探讨的是当文化的中心和整体缺失时，个人如何让部分产生意义。

为了更加准确地表达镶嵌法则，苏克尼克还引入了一个相关概念:精神综合。与精神分析相反，精神综合指的是在个人成长的过程中人们在不同阶段的不同倾向，以及如何协调综合不同的方面，以达到更高层次。

镶嵌法则同样体现了苏克尼克后现代叙事的特点。他认为小说不再是线性、有着时间顺序的整体和统一，而是碎片式的。所以，镶嵌法则是苏克尼克应对这些部分和碎片的法则。苏克尼克主要采用了两种方式:拼缀和拼贴。拼缀，指的是将不同的语言因素拼合在一起。苏克尼克将叙事片段与对话、不同文体的语言、高雅语言与市侩语言拼缀在一起。而拼贴指的是将文字与非文字的元素拼凑在一起，如语言与语言符号及语言与绘画符号等。

第六章结语部分总结了本书探讨的苏克尼克应对身份和后现代叙事危机的三个法则。同时指出，作为最富实验精神的作家之一，苏克尼克以其不懈的努力为美国小说开辟了新的天地。虽然他大胆的叙事改革让读者，甚至一些批评家对他的作品望而却步，造成了他在美国文学的边缘地位，但他为美国文学做出的贡献不应该被遗忘。我们应重新认识他对美国文学的重要性。最后，作者希望这项研究能够让更多的中国学者关注和研究苏克尼克和与他同时代的作家。

Preface

Ronald Sukenick's first novel, *Up*, appeared in 1968. Since then, Sukenick has dedicated his remaining forty years of life to literature. And his efforts extend to almost every aspect of literature. He is a novelist, critic, theoretician, editor and educator.

First of all, as a novelist, Sukenick has published nine novels, three collections of short stories and more than seventy short stories, which have brought him such awards as the American Book Award in 1988 and 1999 and the Morton Zabel Award in 2003. Sukenick is also among the most articulate theoreticians in the 1960s and 1970s. His exploration into the innovations of fiction is collected in three books: *Narralogues: Truth in Fiction*, *In Form: Digressions on the Act of Fiction and Wallace Stevens: Musing the Obscure*. He has also contributed more than seventy critical articles to different literary journals.

Sukenick's "antenna" also extends to fiction publishing. In 1974, he set up a small publishing house—the Fiction Collective from which many innovative writers have benefited. In 1977, with the help of the University of Colorado, Sukenick founded *American Book Review*, a literary journal dedicated to reviewing innovative writers whose books were ignored by such established journals as *New York Review of Books*. In 1989, Sukenick became the editor of *Black Ice* and has helped to launch *Black Ice*—series of innovative novels.

Sukenick believes that he writes in a particular period of history, in which he is faced with dual crises: identity crisis and the crisis of fiction. The dual crises are expressed clearly in three questions asked at the very beginning of his novel *Mosaic Man*: "Where's the story? What's the word? Are you a Jew?" First, Sukenick believes that Jewish people are faced with identity crisis, especially when the Holocaust and Cold War have smashed the base on which they construct their identities. However, Sukenick also understands that identity crisis is not the problem faced only by Jewish people, it troubles all human beings. Thus, all through his writing career, Sukenick has been working hard to seek the answers to the following questions: "How could one assume the arrogance of individual identity after all those identities exxed off the surface of the planet since the year of my birth, 1932, the year Hitler assumed power? How could one even presume to be a person after all that, or even a human?" In other words, with what tenable attitude may one confront the difficult circumstances of contemporary American life and avail oneself of the good possible in it? So in most of his novels, Sukenick explores the themes of identity crisis and identity pursuit both as a Jew and as a man.

Second, Sukenick is keenly aware of the crisis of fiction. The genre of fiction was well-defined in the 19th century. In the 20th century, however, many writers begin to rebel against the traditional structures imposed by this form. John Barth, in 1967, made the statement of "the literature of exhaustion", which indicates the crisis of fiction in the 1950s and 1960s. Sukenick is among the strongest voices in declaring the death of the novel. In his viewpoint, fiction constitutes a way of looking at the world. With the changes of the world, the old paradigms of traditional novels are called into question and the new circumstances demand new paradigms. Faced with the crisis of fiction, Sukenick has been making arduous efforts in opening up a new space by experimenting on narratives.

Taking the dual crises and Sukenick's efforts to deal with these crises into consideration, this book—*Research on Postmodernist Narratives in Ronald Sukenick's Works* for the first time in China makes a rather systematic study of the novels of Ronald Sukenick. The book explores Sukenick's novels from the following two aspects: the themes of identity crisis and identity construction, as well as the crisis of fiction and Sukenick's innovations in narratives. It focuses on three laws Sukenick employs to deal with the dual crises: Surviving Law, Entropy Law and Mosaic Law.

The book falls into six chapters.

Chapter 1 "Introduction" gives an overall picture of Ronald Sukenick's literary career. Just as the title of one of his novels suggests, Sukenick himself is a "mosaic man" of literature: he is a novelist, theoretician, critic, editor, publisher and educator. His efforts extend to almost every aspect of literature.

However, it is unfortunate that Sukenick has never drawn broad attention in the United States and China. Then, the book explores the factors that lead to the marginalization of Sukenick by reviewing the status quo of Sukenick research abroad and in China. The rather limited amount of research, the narrow research perspectives and the lack of holistic research all indicate that the research into Ronald Sukenick is far from being matchable to his achievements in literature. So this book endeavors to make a comprehensive study of Ronald Sukenick from a perspective seldom touched upon-postmodernist narratives of identity in Ronald Sukenick's fiction.

Chapter 2, entitled "Identity and Identity Study in the Postmodernist Context", focuses on the definition of identity, the related theories of identity and identity in postmodernist narratives. Identity, as one of the most fundamental concepts of human experience, refuses a simple definition. Moreover, the definition is perplexed since identity has been the subject of such different disciplines as philosophy, psychology and sociology, which offer definitions from different angles. By briefly tracing the historical development of identity theories, the book puts forward a tentative definition which emphasizes three characteristics of identity: identity is not being but becoming; all identities are social constructions; identity is only conceivable in and through differences.

Although identity is a term with a long history, it may have become a problem only in modern times with the emergence of large-scale society and the decline of traditional group life. The developments of individualism capitalism and urbanization brought about by modernization greatly change the society and in turn fundamentally transform the formation of identity. Three changes are noteworthy: the rise of self-conscious identity the other-directed orientation of identity and the divided identity. These changes show that the problem of identity in modernist contexts is how to construct an identity and keep it solid and stable. However, the problem of identity in postmodernist contexts is primarily how to avoid fixation and keep options open. The economic, technological and cultural changes in the postmodern era result in a condition of identity destabilization, fragmentation and pluralisation.

The second section of this chapter under the title of "Identity in Postmodernist Narratives" connects identity with narratives. In fact, narrative practice lies at the heart of identity construction. The process of identity construction is closely connected with the way we tell our life-story. There is a parallel between the narrative composition of identity and the narrative composition of fiction. Moreover, self-definition and identity construction in cultural, theological and political contexts have been common themes in literature. A brief review of identity narratives in American literature is then made, with emphasis on postmodernist narratives of identity, to highlight the necessity of research into Sukenick's postmodernist narratives of identity.

Postmodern and Jewish, Sukenick is keenly aware of identity crisis and the crisis of postmodernist narratives. Faced with the dual crises, Ronald Sukenick has made unremitting endeavors to seek a way out. After a careful study of his writing, I summarize three laws he employs in dealing with the dual crises: namely, Surviving Law, Entropy Law and Mosaic Law. The next three chapters are individual studies of identity themes in Sukenick's novels and his postmodernist way of narrating identity.

Chapter 3 "Surviving Law: Assimilation or Dissimilation" is divided into two aspects: Surviving Law of identity and Surviving Law of postmodernist narratives. The first section is devoted to Surviving Law of identity in the novels of *Up* and *Down and In: Life in the Underground*. The post-World War II era, especially the 1960s in the United States has witnessed a series of political, economic, social and cultural changes, which leave America in unrest and turmoil. Bereft of traditional sources of meaning, people have difficulties in redefining themselves in the changes, thus a state or condition of disorientation and role confusion occurs. This is especially the case for American minorities. People are pushed into identity crisis. How to survive the changed society and gain a sense of security is a question before individuals. Surviving Law of identity refers to the strategies and ways of identity formation and construction, which are critical to their survival. In the crisis of identity, the individual characters develop idiosyncratic approaches to the question of self-definition. Basically, they can choose to assimilate or dissimilate into the mainstream American society.

Assimilation refers to the ability to identify with and feel at home in the American mainstream society. Assimilation is a process through which individuals are gradually steered into the mainstream way of life. Assimilation is also a process through which individuals discard various traditions and values which are not the mainstream, and adopt those of the mainstream. To achieve this purpose, one can "invent" or "sell out" one's identity. By inventing one's identity, especially according to the popular media images, one can identify with the majority and get assimilated into the mainstream. "Selling out" identity, another way of assimilation, refers to the compromising of one's integrity, morality or principles in exchange for money, success or other personal gains so as to be accepted by the mainstream society. However, in order to keep one's uniqueness and to fight against conformism, one can also choose to dissimilate into the mainstream society and stay in a marginalized position. Sukenick mentions three ways of refusing to get assimilated into the mainstream society: retreating into the ivory tower, staying in dreams and hallucination and writing experimental novels. Assimilation and dissimilation are hard choices to make as assimilation means sacrificing one's uniqueness, while dissimilation means marginal position. Usually individuals have to struggle between assimilation and dissimilation. The struggle is best expressed by the subterranean artists in the Greenwich Village in America. And the struggle is recorded by Ronald Sukenick in his American-Book-Award novel *Down and In: Life in the Underground*.

In the 20th century, people are faced with identity crisis, and the fiction has to fight to define itself too. This well-defined genre is challenged by many writers who declare "the death of the novel". Ronald Sukenick utters a strong voice among them. Sukenick states that the form of fiction that comes down to us through Jane Austin, George Eliot and Hemingway is no longer adequate to capture modern experience. Either the novel will change, or it will die. Obviously, fiction is also faced with identity crisis. Thus, the second section is devoted to Surviving Law of postmodernist narratives. To Ronald Sukenick, what an innovative novelist first should do is to deconstruct the conventions of traditional novels. Such key elements as plot, character, imitation and subject matter in traditional novels are no longer necessities to Sukenick. Sukenick himself summarizes the characteristics of his new fiction as fiction with "no plot, no story, no character, no chronological sequence, no verisimilitude, no imitation, no allegory, no symbolism, no subject matter, no meaning".

With these innovations, Sukenick redefines fiction. A fiction, to Sukenick, is not an ideological formulation of belief but a statement of a favorable rapport with reality. In other words, fiction is not a mirror or redoubling of reality, instead it adds itself to the world, creating a meaning "reality" that does not previously exist. If the purpose of fiction is to reflect on experience so as to arrive at truth, a narrative is "a mode of understanding that uniquely is quick enough, mutable enough, and flexible enough to catch the stream of experience, including our experience of the arts". So to Sukenick, narratives must be agonistic, sophistic, sophisticated, fluid, unpredictable, rhizomatic, affective, inconsistent and even contradictory, improvisational and provisional. To summarize, innovations are Surviving Law of postmodern narratives.

Chapter 4 deals with Entropy Law: Fluidity and Dissolution. The term "entropy", first coined in 1850 by Rudolf Clausius as a measure of the unavailability of a system's energy to do work, constitutes the essence of the second law of thermodynamics. However, entropy, one of the most fundamental concepts of physical science, is also introduced into other science fields ranging from cosmology to chemistry, from anthropology to information theory, and into sociology and literature as well. Such postmodernist writers as Thomas Pynchon, William Gaddis, Ken Kesey, Stanley Elkin, Susan Sontag, Donald Barthelme and Don DeLillo employ this term as a cultural metaphor in their novels to express the chaos and disorder of postmodern American society.

Unlike the above-mentioned writers, Ronald Sukenick does not directly employ entropy as his subject matter, nor does he transfer it into structural organization. Sukenick employs Entropy Law of identity, through which he develops a whole spectrum of presentational techniques, which allow him to project his concepts of multiple personality and dissolved identity. Just as entropy indicates that the disorder of energy moving at random within a closed system is increasing, and finally arrives at total inertia, Entropy Law of identity illustrates that the characters change their identity without any reasons or logical progression, and finally arrive at non-identity of characters—characters neither materialize as stable center of personal reference nor occupy a fixed position. When characters start their journey in the fiction, the stable traits in their identity, beneficial to communication, begin to lose in the process. At the same time, the fluid and changeable traits-the entropy in the communication, are bound to increase, which in the end leads to the dissolution of all identities. Accordingly, Sukenick's Entropy Law of identity in the novels of *Out* and 98. 6 is illustrated from two aspects: stream of identities and non-identity.

Contrary to the traditional way of characterization which develops consistent and identifiable characters with the unfolding of plots, Sukenick's Entropy Law of identity aims at a purposeful disintegration of the consistent and identifiable traits of characters. During the process of identity construction, identity, just like energy moving within a closed system, is losing more and more stable and fixed traits, and gaining more and more fluid and changeable traits, which leads to the stream of identities-characters change their identities like a stream. Sukenick's "stream of identities" is best expressed in the "stream of names". A name is the symbol of identity. A proper name, which conventionally has an unambiguous referent and represents a unified notion of self, cannot designate a person any longer in Sukenick's fiction. It is only a signifier without a concomitant signified. Moreover, names and characters are like particles moving randomly and switching freely in the novels, which will never consolidate to become an identity.

Sukenick's strategy of stream of identities is to foreground his belief that human identity is a fluid process of constant becoming rather than a fixed entity, which he believes reflects tendencies in the postmodern society. Identity in the postmodern society turns to be more fluid and interchangeable. Characters change their identities without reasons or logical progression, and finally arrive at the non-identity of characters.

Sukenick's "non-identity" is a great challenge to the traditional way of characterization. He believes that the traditional way of forming a fixed identity limits the author's imagination. In the postmodern world, the unity of experience and the unity of the world and self are neither lasting nor unambiguous, so let them dissolve from moment to moment and be content with many connections that lurk behind every dissolution. Everything is connectable, and everything imaginable, which is a way of emphasizing that no fixation is final or more meaningful than any other. Connections proliferate, and meaning and identity fall away. Sukenick wants to prove that, through his own practice, the "nothingness" or the "nonentity" of characters is not the disaster of characterization, as in the view of realistic novelists. Instead, it is the desired state he wants to achieve, and also the natural result of Entropy Law of identity.

Whereas Entropy Law of identity stresses the features of Sukenick's characterization, the Entropy Law of postmodern narratives emphasizes the entropic characteristics of Sukenick's narratives: fluidity, fragmentation, chaos, changeability and dissolution in contrary to traditional narratives that seek continuity and wholeness.

Free from the constraints of plot, character and mimetic realism, Sukenick's narratives are submitted to a continuous process of articulating and rearticulating new connections in the flow of experience. In order to pursue a notion of transformative flow, Sukenick employs many techniques, such as frequent shifts in plot, character and style. Besides "stream of identities" we have discussed before, Sukenick employs other techniques as changeable typography and language play to achieve the fluidity and dissolution.

Typography, the technological aspects in the novel-page, print and binding, is often neglected by novelists and readers as well. Sukenick, however, wants to challenge the long time ignorance. He wants to challenge traditional arrangements of fiction—a solid block of print from one margin to another running down the page from top to bottom. By innovating his fiction's typography, Sukenick wants to take advantage of the disruptive potentials of typographical variations so as to challenge the power of prevalent conventions. Sukenick employs such strategies as countdown arrangement of chapters, unusual spacing and drawn symbols to increase the fluidity of narratives. These techniques greatly increase the disorder and chaos of the text, but at the same time offer possibilities of new connections and new meanings.

Language play is another way to achieve entropic narratives. In Sukenick's fiction, language moves as particles, freely and randomly, causing disorder, but new connections and new meanings at the same time. Sukenick uses wordplay, puns, pangrams and other language games to open up new spaces with language, forcing words to yield new complexities and meanings.

Chapter 5 centers on Mosaic Law: Fragmentation and Collage. Mosaic-the art form which uses small pieces of materials placed together to create a unified whole, is borrowed and modified by Ronald Sukenick in his writing theories. Mosaic Law, he states, is the law of mosaics, a way of dealing with parts in the absence of the whole. He establishes the law as a solution to the identity problem of postmodern individuals and postmodernist narratives.

Sukenick is keenly aware that cultural diversity and heterogeneity in postmodern contexts mean the greater difficulties in keeping a cultural centre and wholeness. It is obvious that when the wholeness and center are absent, parts and fragments are submitted to the continuous construction and reconstruction. Mosaic Law put forward by Sukenick aims not at the wholeness and unification, but at fragments and parts. With the absence of cultural centre and wholeness, what an individual should do is to make meaning out of the parts.

To make Mosaic Law more exact, Ronald Sukenick also introduces a related term-psychosynthesis, the opposite of psychoanalysis. In its most basic sense, psychosynthesis is a process of personal growth: a natural tendency in each of us to harmonize or synthesize our various aspects at ever higher levels of organization. What is emphasized in psychosynthesis by Sukenick is the way how one makes something out of parts and fragments.

Mosaic Law also finds its way in Sukenick's fiction narratives. To Ronald Sukenick, fiction is no longer a linear and chronological whole and unity, but a collection of fragments. Sukenick's Mosaic Law of narratives—the law of dealing with parts and fragments when the whole is absent, offers Sukenick ways to hold particles and fragments of his stories together. Two main ways are introduced in the Mosaic Law of narratives: patchwork and collage. By patchwork, Sukenick puts different language elements together. That is to say, Sukenick pieces together narrative fragments with speeches, language elements of different genres and street language with highbrow language. Collage refers to the piecing together of word and non-word. Sukenick collages together drawn symbols and language elements, language symbols and language elements.

Chapter 6 "Conclusion" summarizes the three laws employed by Ronald Sukenick to deal with the dual crises of identity and postmodernist narratives. The book argues that Ronald Sukenick is one of the most innovative American writers who, with his strenuous efforts, tries to open a new space for American fiction. However, his bold innovations in narratives discourage readers, and even some critics, which, to some extent, leads to his marginalized position in literature. Nevertheless, his whole devotion to American literature should not be ignored and forgotten. And his contribution to American literature should be restudied.

CONTENTS

Chapter 1 Introduction

1.1 A Mosaic Man of Literature: Ronald Sukenick and His Literary Career

During the 1960s and 1970s, a group of American writers have their way into the general readers' vision: Kurt Vonnegut, John Barth, Donald Barthelme, Robert Coover, Thomas Pynchon, Ronald Sukenick and William Gass, to name just a few. They are generally called postmodern writers, among whom Ronald Sukenick—my focus in this book—is unique in many aspects.

His uniqueness lies first in his long life of creation. Ronald Sukenick has actively participated in the reshaping of American literary tradition for nearly 40 years. Sukenick started his literary career in 1962, when he completed his doctoral dissertation on Wallace Stevens, which in 1967 he published as *Wallace Stevens: Musing the Obscure*. In the new millennium, he still published two books: *Cows* (a novel) and *Narralogues: Truth in Fiction* (a short story collection).

Sukenick's Jewish origin and his devotion to the theme of identity pursuit as a Jew differ from other non-Jewish postmodern writers. However, his refusal of the designation of "American Jewish writer", and his understanding of Jewishness also differ from other Jewish writers. To him, "being Jewish is just an advanced case of being human, and being human may be a terminal disease that's run its course" (Sukenick 1999:16).

Sukenick is also an unusual figure in the American literary world, in that he is an example of what has been described as "Renaissance man". Jerome Klinkowitz, a famous critic and a life-long friend of Sukenick's, describes eight and a half different roles Ronald Sukenick plays in the literary world. Ronald Sukenick is a "critic, novelist, fictively-inclined scholar, scholastically inclined fictionist, and the publicized image of a fifth figure who does all these things and more... The sixth Ronnie is the combative figure of the 1970s; and the seventh Ronnie is a figure concerned with cultural power; the eighth and a half Ronnie finds the dynamic of narratives" (Klinkowitz 2003:251). In other words, as a novelist, critic, theorist, publisher and scholar, Ronald Sukenick has contributed to almost every aspect of postmodern scene, from its aesthetic and sociocultural debate to the development of new discursive practice.

First of all, as a prolific novelist, Ronald Sukenick constructs 12 books. His first novel, *Up*, came out in 1968, which was an immediate success. Since then, for more than three decades, Sukenick has been active in pushing traditional novels to their edges and in exploring innovative forms of novels. During his industrious writing life, he has published nine novels, three collections of short stories and more than seventy short stories in various literary journals. *Up* (1968), *Out* (1973), *98. 6* (1975), *Long Talking Bad Conditions Blues* (1979), *Down and In: Life in the Underground* (1987), *Doggy Bag* (1994), *Mosaic Man* (1999), *Blown Away* (1986) and *Cows* (a web novel) (2001) constitute his fiction writing. His three short story collections include *The Death of the Novel and Other Stories* (1969), *The Endless Short Story* (1986) and *Narralogues: Truth in Fiction* (2000). Such awards as American Book Award, Before Columbus Foundation, 1988, for *Down and In: Life in the Underground*, and 1999, for literature; Morton Zabel Award, American Academy of Arts and Letters, 2003, for innovative fiction highlight his achievements in literary creation.

Ronald Sukenick is also among the most articulate theoreticians and proponents of experimentalism in the 1960s and 1970s. His exploration into the innovation of fiction is collected in three books: *Narralogues: Truth in Fiction* (2000), *In Form: Digressions on the Act of Fiction* (1985) and *Wallace Stevens: Musing the Obscure* (1967). He has also devoted more than seventy critical articles to such journals as *American Book Review*, *New York Times Book Review*, *Partisan Review*, *Chicago Review*, *Fictional International* and *New Literary History*, etc.

His career as a publisher starts with his dissatisfaction with the state of publishing at that time. Even as a writer with some prestige, Sukenick finds himself denied access to the mainstream publishing houses. His first two works *Up* and *The Death of Novel and Other Stories* were published by publishing conglomerate Dial. And then his novel *Out* could only be accepted by the more liberal press Swallow. By *98. 6* even Swallow found Sukenick too non-traditional and non-mainstream. Disappointed with the requirements and emphases of commercial publishing houses and also realizing that other experimental and innovative writers might face the same problem, Sukenick, together with some other innovative writers as Honathan Baumbach, Peter Spielberg, Steve Katz and B. H. Friedman, founded the Fiction Collective to make new voices heard. This small publishing press opened its door to non-mainstream writers and had a distinguished record of fostering innovative fiction from diverse writers, including Raymond Federman, Clarence Major, Russell Banks and Ursule Molinaro. Sukenick became the editor of magazine *Black Ice* in 1989. Since then, Sukenick has helped to launch *Black Ice*, continuing his dedication to voices alternative to the cultural mainstream.

In 1977, with the help of the University of Colorado, Sukenick founded *American Book Review*, a literary journal dedicated to reviewing innovative writers whose books were ignored by such established journals as *New York Review of Books*. Since its foundation, *American Book Review* has been an active recourse for innovative writers and is still published today.

Sukenick's efforts with the Fiction Collective and *American Book Review* earned him the Coordinating Council of Literary Magazines Award for Editorial Excellence and the Western Book Award for publishing, both in 1985. 2004 also saw the Louis Shores-Greenwood Publishing Group Award go to Sukenick for his on-going commitment to small presses and his work as founding editor of *American Book Review*.

In addition, Sukenick also pursues an academic life. He has worked as instructor in such universities as Brandeis University (1956-1960), Hofstra University (1961-1962), City University of New York (1966-1967), Sarah Lawrence College (1968-1969), Cornell University (1969), University of California (1970-1972) and University of Colorado where he stayed until his retirement. As a full professor and the Director of Creative Writing at the University of Colorado (1975-1977), he has attracted several key writers as faculty, including Clarence Major and Steve Katz.

Sukenick's work in organizational causes should not be ignored. For a time he was the chairman of the Coordinating Council of Literary Magazines (1975-1977), working for grant support of alternative publishing venues. Sukenick was also a member of the executive council of Modern Language Association (1975-1977). He also worked in the advisory committee of the Publication of Modern Language Association (MLA) (1987-1990). He also served the directorship of the Nilon Award for Excellence in Minority Fiction (1990-1998). Sukenick joined the Board of Directors for the National Book Critics Circle in 1992, and served until 1995.

Just as the title of one of his novels *Mosaic Man* suggests, Ronald Sukenick himself is a true mosaic man of literature. He is the mosaic of novelist, critic, literary theorist and publisher. "One self, but known in a multitude of ways, with each act of knowing constituting its own story—this is the infinity of being that the truly fictive writer commands in his fiction of truth" (Klinkowitz 2003: 269).

The last but not the least, Sukenick's uniqueness also lies in his struggle between the mainstream and the anti-mainstream in his life as well as in his literary practice, which leads to his life-long concern about identity crisis in his writing.

Ronald Sukenick was born on July 14, 1932 to a Jewish professional family in Brooklyn, New York. His father Louis Sukenick was a dentist. The Sukenick's were a few Jewish families in a neighborhood that included the family of Bernard Malamud. Ronald Sukenick believed that Malamud's *Assistant* exactly described the environment where he was brought up. "If you've read Malamud's *Assistant* then you know where I grew up" (Sukenick 1984:285). Kids like Sukenick just loafed on the streets—the only playing field for them, so "it (was) easier to imagine going to jail than to college" (Sukenick 1984:286). Then, the family moved from Gravesend Avenue of working class to Ocean Parkway where middle-class families gathered. Young Sukenick was sent to Brooklyn's Midwood High School where most boys' dream was to move upward to be doctors and lawyers.

Tired of this mainstream version of success, Ronald Sukenick graduated from high school and followed his older sister Gloria to New York's Greenwich Village, where anti-mainstream artists and writers haunted.

In 1950, Sukenick entered Colgate University in New York, and transferred in 1953 to Cornell University. In Cornell, he established a campus literary magazine, *The Cornell Writer*, with other students, including David Behrens, who was later a Pulitzer Prize-winner and also Martin Washburn, later a painter. Ronald Sukenick was the major contributor and also the magazine's fiction editor. The first issue of the magazine came out in November 1953, with his short story "Indian Love Call" as the first story. Sukenick never expected that such an immature story would throw the administration into an uproar over his use of the word "birdshit", which they considered as vulgar and immoral. The university president decided to expel the related students without a hearing. Ronald Sukenick, the author of the article and also the founding editor of the magazine, was the first on the list for expulsion. Fortunately, the students did get a hearing, and the Cornell English Department, including Vladimir Nabokov, came to defend them. With their efforts, Ronald Sukenick and *The Cornell Writer* were permitted to stay in the university. The story, though immature and clumsy, was, just as Sukenick himself later pointed out, "a kind of anti-literary energy threatening to explode out of the well-made literary frame of the story" (Sukenick 1984:289).

In 1955, Sukenick received a B. A. degree from Cornell. Then he went to Brandeis University, where he stayed for five years and got an M. A. degree in 1957 and a Ph. D. in 1962. Sukenick once mentioned about his reasons of choosing Brandeis:

> I was at Brandies in disguise presumably to earn a doctorate I had no intention of getting. Actually I was there because my teaching fellowship both supported me and spared me for two years from the military efforts of an inimical regime, and more important, because this academy was dominated not by academics, but precisely by the intellectuals I assumed were the vanguard of the underground, and whom I took to be in tune with my real self. (Sukenick 1987:96)

Sukenick expected to enjoy unacademic intellectual atmosphere at Brandeis University, which was in sharp contrast to that in Cornell University. However, such intellectuals there as Herbert Marcuse, Abraham Maslow, poet J. V. Cunningham and critic Irving Howe encouraged him to play safe by becoming a good academic instead of choosing the precarious life of a writer. Sukenick considered this fighting within his mind as "identity crisis"—"it was a real issue and it will remain a real issue." (Sukenick 1987: 97). Sukenick was haunted by such questions as, "Is the American personality simply the sum of success-driven responses to the network of cultural pressures? Or is it the stubborn assertion of a virtuous independence, however unexamined? Is there such a thing as a real self, and if there isn't, what makes life worth living?" (Sukenick 1987:97)

This "identity crisis" not only haunted Ronald Sukenick in his later life, but also penetrated into his writing as a dominating theme in his novels. During most of his rest life, Ronald Sukenick navigated between the halls of academia and the alleys of the underground. Sukenick shifted between different teaching positions in such universities as Brandeis University, Hofstra University, City College (New York), Sarah Lawrence College, Cornell University, University of California, Irving, University of Colorado, L'Universite Paul Valery (France), Queens College (CUNY) and Hebrew University (Jerusalem). But now and then, Sukenick quit academia for the Lower East Side of New York, where the underground artists gathered, to work on his novels. His stay in Greenwich Village and his communication with artists there later led to his part memoir, part history and part autobiography book *Down and In: Life in the Underground*.

Sukenick published his first long fiction *Up* in 1968, which was an immediate success, bounding onto the publishing scene to critical and popular acclaim. However, his challenge to the traditional fictional forms in this novel also brought him attacks, even from his former professor Irving Howe. Despite these attacks, Sukenick continued his formal experiments on fiction. However, his experimental novels were rejected by such publishing conglomerates as Dial, and even by smaller and more liberal press as Swallow. Sukenick was pushed farther and farther away from the literary mainstream.

Sukenick's conflict between the mainstream and anti-mainstream was noteworthy. On the one hand, Sukenick gradually moved into the professional mainstream. From 1975 to 1977, he was elected a member of the Executive Council of the MLA. In 1976, he earned a Guggenheim Fellowship. In the early 1970s, he was invited to the board of the Coordinating Council of Literary Magazines (CCLM). He was also chairman of the board of directors from 1975 to 1977. On the other hand, his innovative writings were usually classified mainly as avant-garde, which Sukenick himself was reluctant to accept. In some sense, his writing never moved into the mainstream. His fading popularity among critics was the result of his refusal to accept mainstream modes of discourse. In this way, Sukenick's failure is perhaps his great success. In a culture in which rebellion is commodified, Sukenick remains himself.

1.2 Ronald Sukenick Studies in the United States and China

The research into Ronald Sukenick in the United States is far from being matchable to his achievements in literature. First, the amount of research is rather limited. There are only two book-length studies on Sukenick. It is ironic that the first book on the fiction of Ronald Sukenick published in the United States was written by a young Polish professor. In fact, the book *The Novel as Performance: The Fiction of Ronald Sukenick and Raymond Federman* by Jerzy Kutnik, then a professor of American history at a university in Lublin, Poland, devotes only half of the book to Ronald Sukenick. *Musing the Mosaic: Approaches to Ronald Sukenick*, a collection of essays edited by Matthew Roberson, is the only book-length study in Sukenick made and published in the United States. However, it didn't come out until 2003. In addition, four doctoral dissertations focus mainly or partly on Ronald Sukenick. Ten books devote sections to Sukenick. Fewer than 50 journal articles are devoted to the research into Sukenick.

Matthew Roberson points out the reasons of the imbalance between the research into Sukenick and his achievements in American literature:

> This is in part because—although revered in certain circles—Sukenick has never drawn broad attention. And this is in part because, at times, he's not only too much but way too much—too unusual, too challenging, and too contrary in his undermining of the idea of the book as traditionally conceived. His texts frequently subvert every expectation, narrative and otherwise, a reader might bring to them, as well as the very systems of rational thought, language, and categories supporting critical analysis and a wider discussion of his work. (Roberson 2003:2)

Sukenick's digression from the traditional way of fiction writing not only discourages readers and researchers from approaching him, but also limits their research perspectives. Although Ronald Sukenick himself refuses to be labeled a formalist, the research into Sukenick focuses mainly on his experiments on forms. His metafictional skills, typographic innovations and his language play are the parts mostly discussed by scholars. Larry McCaffery's *The Metafictional Muse*, Jerzy Kutnik's *The Novel as Performance: The Fiction of Ronald Sukenick and Raymond Federman*, Aaron Winkelman's doctoral dissertation "Authorial Presence in American Metafiction: The Novels of Coover, Federman, Sorrentino, and Sukenick" as well as the essays by Alfred Hornung and Timothy Dow Adams explore such metafictional skills in his fiction as the author's presence in the fiction, the formal self-consciousness, and the juxtaposition of fictional characters and real figures, etc.

Another focus of research is on Sukenick's innovations in the use of language, or his language play, to be exact. Jerzy Kutnik's essay "Postmodern Language-centered Writing and the Question of Ideology", Julian Cowley's essay "Ronald Sukenick's New Departures from the Terminal of Language", and Melvin J. Friedman's essay "Dislocations of Setting and Word" are the representatives of this kind of research.

Sukenick's typographic innovations are explored in Lance Olsen's essay "Graphiction: Technological Reality in Ronald Sukenick's *98.6*, *Doggy Bag*, and *Mosaic Man*". Olsen explores how Sukenick uses graphics in the three mentioned novels to destabilize, complicate and make self-conscious traditional reading assumptions and processes.

The above-mentioned research, though insightful and convincing, is limited in that it focuses mainly on the artistic features of Sukenick's fiction while seldom touches upon the themes.

Marcel Cornis-Pope's *Narrative Innovation and Cultural Rewriting in the Cold War Era and After* marks a breakthrough in the research of Sukenick. Cultural perspective is introduced in the study of Sukenick. Putting Sukenick's novels in polysystematic and multicultural environment, Pope links Sukenick's narrative innovation with cultural rewriting during and after the Cold War.

Published in 2003, *Musing the Mosaic: Approaches to Ronald Sukenick*, a collection of essays on Sukenick, offers a more in-depth, comprehensive and interdisciplinary study on Sukenick and his works. Cultural perspective continues to be used in the studies made by Ursula K. Heise, Campbell Tatham and Mark Amerika. More angles and perspectives are introduced into the understanding of Sukenick. Nancy Blake makes a study of Sukenick's first collection of short stories, *The Death of the Novel and Other Stories*, from the Lacanian theory. She points out that Sukenick's fiction not only poses "the question of the authority of the Other," but also in his work "art sets as its goal the construction of its own Other" (Blake 2003:72). Charles Russell conducts an interesting and comparative study of Ronald Sukenick and David Salle, a young neo-expressionist visual artist on the basis of their shared interest in making the act of creation a central subject in their works and their common effort in formal and thematic challenges to conventional meaning-making. Steve Tomasula and Charles Harris take an interest in Sukenick's aesthetic theory, elaborating Sukenick's opinions on the reality, self and culture.

To summarize, the research of Sukenick in the United States is not satisfactory in several aspects. First, the amount of research is quite limited. Second, the perspectives of research are neither broad nor adequate. The last but not the least, no holistic research has been conducted up till now.

The research of Sukenick in China is even grimmer. Although Sukenick came to China in 1995, no record about his visit can be found. Sukenick's research in China is limited to only seven articles. In 2000, Zhou Nanyi introduced Sukenick to Chinese readers by three articles in *Foreign Literatures*: a brief introduction to Sukenick's biography and his works, a translation of one short story and an essay on his writing skills. In 2004, professor Yang Renjing devoted one section of *The Selected Readings of Postmodern Fiction* to Ronald Sukenick. 2008 saw another essay by Yang Hongying on the intertextuality in a short story by Sukenick. In 2010, Yang Jingsong devoted two essays on his novel *Out*. Since none of Sukenick's novels has been translated and introduced into China, Chinese readers have no access to him, not to speak of appreciating him. No systematic and holistic comments have been available at all.

1.3 The Aim and Structure of This Book

Although it is unfortunate that certain factors have marginalized Sukenick, it also presents great opportunities for more research. This book aims at a comprehensive study of Ronald Sukenick from the perspective of postmodernist narratives of identity.

Two scholars have touched upon the theme of identity and self-pursuit in Sukenick's fiction. Manfred Putz in his book *The Story of Identity: American Fiction of the Sixties* makes an in-depth study into the story of identity, a genre lacking a formal name. He devotes one chapter to Ronald Sukenick. As the book was published in 1979, his research into Sukenick is quite limited. Only two novels *Up* and *Out* are explored in his book, which can not present an objective and a whole picture of Sukenick's writing.

Ursula K. Heise in her essay "Sukenick's Posthumans" probes into Sukenick's style of character construction and concept of ego identity. However, with the limited length of the paper, her essay only focuses on another two of Sukenick's novels: *Out* and *Mosaic Man*.

Another limitation of their research is that their research centers only on the discussion of the theme of identity while ignoring the narrative innovations of Ronald Sukenick. Exploring how Ronald Sukenick narrates identity in a postmodernist way is what this book aims at.

Sukenick believes that he writes in a particular period of history, in which he is faced with dual crises: identity crisis and the crisis of fiction. These dual crises are expressed clearly in three questions asked at the very beginning of his novel *Mosaic Man*: "Where's the story? What's the word? Are you a Jew?" (Sukenick 1999: 9-10) On the one hand, Sukenick believes that men are pushed to identity crisis when the Holocaust and Cold War have smashed the base on which men construct their identities. All through his writing career, Sukenick is trying to seek the answers to the following questions: "How could one assume the arrogance of individual identity after all those identities exxed off the surface of the planet since the year of my birth, 1932, the year Hitler assumed power? How could one even presume to be a person after all that, or even a human?"(Sukenick 1999:181) In other words, with what tenable attitude may one confront the difficult circumstances of contemporary American life and avail oneself of the good possible in it? So in most of his novels, Sukenick explores the themes of identity crisis and identity pursuit.

On the other hand, Sukenick is keenly aware of the crisis of fiction. The genre of fiction is well-defined in the 19th century. In the 20th century, however, many writers begin to rebel against the traditional structures imposed by this form. John Barth, in 1967, made the statement "the literature of exhaustion", which indicates the crisis of fiction in the 1950s and 1960s. Sukenick is among the strongest voices in declaring the death of the novel. In his viewpoint, fiction constitutes a way of looking at the world. With the changing of the world, the old paradigms of traditional novels are called into question and the new circumstances demand new paradigms. Faced with the crisis of fiction, Sukenick has been making arduous efforts in opening up a new space by experimenting on narratives.

Taking the dual crises and Sukenick's efforts to deal with these crises into consideration, this book for the first time in China makes a rather systematic study of the novels of Ronald Sukenick. The book explores Sukenick's novels from two aspects: the themes of identity crisis and identity construction, and the crisis of fiction and Sukenick's innovations in narratives. It focuses on three laws Sukenick employs to deal with the dual crises: Surviving Law, Entropy Law and Mosaic Law.

This book is divided into 6 chapters. The introductory part, as has been stated above, gives a general introduction to Ronald Sukenick and his works. On the basis of a brief description of the present status of research into Sukenick's works at home and abroad, this book points out the new area to be explored in Sukenick research: his postmodernist narratives of identity.

Chapter 2 is devoted to the definition of identity and the theories of identity, which will lay the theoretical foundation for the following research. The historical development of identity and identity-formation is traced, with the emphasis laid on identity in the modern and postmodern contexts. Specifically, a survey of postmodern literature is made with the purpose of exploring the theme of identity in it. Critical views of identity in postmodern fiction are also presented.

The next three chapters are individual studies of the identity theme and narrative innovations in Sukenick's novels. Chapter 3 focuses on Surviving Law: Assimilation or Dissimilation. Surviving Law of identity points out that in order to survive the consumerist postmodern society, one has to fight between getting assimilated into the mainstream at the cost of one's uniqueness and being alienated from the mainstream to keep one's individuality. Surviving Law of postmodernist narratives, on the other hand, spells out the crisis faced by fiction and the necessity of narrative innovations for the survival of the novel.

Chapter 4 deals with Entropy Law: Fluidity and Dissolution. Entropy Law of identity highlights the characteristics of postmodern identity: fragmentation, fluidity, interchangeability and dissolution. The identity fragments move at random in unstructured chaos at an increasing speed until they finally dissolve into non-identity. In order to present these characteristics, Ronald Sukenick challenges the conventional typography of novels with new alternatives and employs language play to increase the entropy in his narratives.

Chapter 5 centers on Mosaic Law: Fragmentation and Collage. The Law of Mosaics shows how to deal with parts in the absence of the whole. Living in the polysystematic and multicultural world, Sukenick's characters are mosaic men of cultural shards reasoning through psychosynthesis instead of traditional psychoanalysis. Accordingly, Sukenick employs the skills of patchwork and collage in his narratives.

Chapter 6, the last part of the book, summarizes the three laws employed by Ronald Sukenick to deal with the dual crises of identity and postmodernist narratives. The book also argues that Ronald Sukenick is one of the most innovative American writers who, with his strenuous efforts, tries to open a new space for American fiction. His whole devotion to American literature should not be ignored and forgotten. And his contribution to American literature should be restudied.

Chapter 2

Identity and Identity Study in the Postmodern Context

2.1 Identity: From Modernism to Postmodernism

2.1.1 Definition of Identity

Identity is arguably more fundamental to the conception of humanity than any other notion. No other questions are more important and fundamental than the identity question: Who am I? Whetten points out that "I can think of no other concept that is so central to the human experience, or one that infuses so many interpretations and actions, than the notion of identity" (Whetten 1998:17).

It's not surprising that the concern with identity is quite ancient. Philosophers like Socrates, Plato and Aristotle all have expressed their understanding of identity in their works and tried to answer the question: Who am I? Identity has been the subject of a vast literature in such disciplines as philosophy, psychology and sociology. Different definitions have been offered from different angles and in different periods of time.

The term *identity* in its meaning of sameness or unity of something with itself has been a key term of western thought from its beginning. Plato holds the view that each of us possesses a true self, which is the basis for our character, and which makes persons different from one another. He puts forward the concept of self-mastery: to be master of oneself is to have the higher part of the soul rule over the lower, which means reason over desires. Whetten and Godfrey summarize the understanding of identity in Greek philosophy: "In style and belief, ancient Greeks were the harbingers of objectivism in their views of identity: for them, identity is real. Their thoughts echo forward in time and supply the foundations for the modern positivist views of identity that found fuller manifestation in the still reverberating thought of Descartes" (Whetten 1998:18). French philosopher Descartes' famous statement "I think, therefore I am" expresses an idea of self which is permeating in western philosophy—the transcendental self. In this point of view, self is viewed as an idealized, abstract platform from which concepts and judgments originate. In other words, the self transcends society, and stands prior to and philosophically above the everyday life. Jean-Jacques Rousseau later expresses a similar idea: "Self as such, the soul of humanity... the self that he shared with all men and women the world over" (qtd. Holstein 1999:18). In other words, the transcendental self is the self—timeless, universal, and in each one of us around the globe and throughout history. This is the self we share. In modest and ordinary terms, it is called human nature. This kind of understanding of identity lays stress on moral introspection and subjectivity.

This unitary understanding of identity is challenged by later philosophers. Copernicus, Darwin, Marx and Freud have decentred the human subject. The subject is no longer unitary but split. And individual consciousness is no longer seen as the origin of meaning, knowledge and action. Ferdinand de Saussure challenges the unitary concept of identity by stressing the importance of language in the ongoing construction of identity. To be exact, it is through the acquisition of language that we become human and social beings. Through language, we know who we are. No matter where the challenges are from, they emphasize more or less the influence of the internal factors, while ignoring the social factors on identity formation.

In the early 20th century, several intellectual pioneers—William James, Charles Horton Cooley and George Herbert Mead make a significant change in their research of identity. They turn away from the concept of transcendental self, and begin to understand the self in a larger social context. Through the works of William James, the concept of identity enters the field of psychology and eventually becomes a central issue in psychiatry, modern psychology and psychoanalysis. William James makes a great advance in the concept of self by turning the concept from the purely metaphysical realm to the environment of social interaction, turning from transcendental self to the experiences of common men and women. In other words, it is a turning from the genteel tradition to the empirical world. In this point of view, experience plays an important role in the formation of self. The self should be conceived as an entity whose existence in the world, knowledge of itself and sense of well-being derived from experience.

American pragmatists Charles Horton Cooley and George Herbert Mead develop this idea and introduce the concept of social self. By "social self", Mead means "The self, as that which can be an object to itself, is essentially a social structure, and it arises in social experience" (qtd. Holstein 1999:15). By situating the self in daily life, Mead pays much attention to the interaction between the self and the society. Self is part of the process of communication. And the communication can be both inner and external communication. Self-consciousness, for example, is the inner conversation with oneself, while social interaction is an external conversation with others.

Several changes should be noted from transcendental self to social self. First, compared with transcendental self, the socially grounded self is dynamic, and will change in relation to others' responses and to social changes. Second, self acts actively and intentionally to the changing social demands and circumstances. In other words, self is socially responsive and malleable. Third, self changes from singular to plural. A man may have many social selves.

A brief review of identity study in philosophy and social psychology makes us realize the fact that the term lacks an unequivocal definition, a clear-cut delimitation of its field or fields of application, or an accepted differentiation from such related terms as I, me, self, ego, self-identity, ego-identity, self-concept, self-system, and subjectivity. Just as Brooker points out, "Paradoxically this is itself a sign that the concept is in crisis" (Brooker 2003:130). What makes the crisis even worse is that in contemporary society, more and more factors such as religion, nation, language, gender, political ideology and cultural theories intensify the subtleties of identity.

So it is neither possible nor our task here to offer a systematic sketch of various uses or a final solution to the terminological problems. Our task here is to work out a tentative definition for the later discussion. Webster's *Third New International Dictionary of The English Language* defines identity as:

> 1. Samesness of essential or generic character in different examples or instances; sameness in all that constitutes the objective reality of a thing.
> 2. Unity and persistence of personality: unity or individual comprehensiveness of a life or character.
> 3. The condition of being the same with something. Described, claimed, or asserted or of possessing a character claimed. (Gove 1993:1123)

This definition emphasizes only one aspect of identity—the unity, sameness and coherence of the quality of an individual, while ignoring another important aspect: the social aspect. Tajfel, the developer of social identity theory, defines identity as "that part of an individual's self-concept which derives from his knowledge of his membership in a social group (or groups) together with the value and emotional significance attached to that membership" (Tajfel 1981: 255). With this definition, Tajfel stresses the social aspect of identity: how individuals categorize themselves and others, how they identify with certain groups, and how they compare their groups with other groups, etc. In this understanding, identity is the set of meanings that define who one is when one is an occupant of a particular role in society, a member of a particular group. That's why we have such concepts as national identity, gender identity, ethnic identity, etc. However, an important aspect is ignored in this definition. Identity also claims particular characteristics that identify one as a unique person and distinguish one idiosyncratically from a myriad of other people. It's the identity of these three aspects that I want to work with.

Thus, three aspects should be emphasized in the definition. First of all, identity is not being but becoming. To be exact, identity is an ongoing process in which an individual develops under the dual influence of psychological development within himself and social changes outside him. Second, all identities are social constructions. Identity is criss-crossed by such social dynamics as class, ethnicity, race, religion, gender and nation. In this sense, identity gives us a location in the world and presents the link between us and the society. Third, identity also suggests the uniqueness of a person. Identity defines who a person is and how he/she relates to others and to the world. At the same time, identity also suggests what one is not—the Other. Identity is only conceivable in and through differences. Too much stress on the sameness will lead to homogeneity.

2.1.2 Identity in Modern Context

Although identity is a term with a long history, it may have become a problem only in modern times with the emergence of large-scale society and the decline of traditional group life. "In traditional cultures, identity is more or less fixed at birth and integrated into relatively stable structures of custom, belief, and ritual" (Dunn 1998: 53). However, with the dissolution of tradition brought by modernization, identity has led an agitated existence, more problematic and divided, less stable and fixed.

Modernization marks the social change from agrarian societies to industrial ones. This transition is closely related with the development of individualism, capitalism, urbanization and a belief in the positive possibilities of technological and political progress, which in turn fundamentally transform the formation of identity.

The first change that should be noted is the rise of self-conscious identity. As group ties weaken, an individual is freed from collective beliefs and attachments, and encouraged to forge his or her own identity independently of the ascribed characteristics inherited in one's placement in tradition. The individual has to receive, acquire and construct his or her own identity in an increasingly unknown, uncertain and rapidly changing world. And such values of individualism as autonomy, freedom and choice enforce a new self-conscious identity.

Another important change of identity formation is that the other-directed orientation of identity supplants the inner-directed orientation. With industrialization and urbanization, the comparatively stable society is replaced by chaotic diversity. Individuals step out of smaller communities of families, churches or ethnic groups into greater space of social interaction. With greater mobility, changes and role multiplicity, an individual is now defined as an "ensemble of social relations" (Feuer 1959: 244). The formation of identity depends more and more on the social interdependencies of individuals. So, as a social self, an individual gains a strong orientation to the responses of others in identity formation. To be more specific, the individual acquires an identity by means of self-formation within a socially interactive framework of mutual recognition and adaptation, a process occurring within a structure of community norms.

In addition to the self-consciousness and other-directed orientation, identity in modern context takes another feature: dividedness. Industrialization brings about social divisions: the division of sacred and secular life, the division of labor, the division of class, racial, ethnic relationships and the division of social roles. These divisions encourage extensive differentiation, which is a threat to the unified identity. Moreover, with urbanization, the acceleration of time and the episodic nature of urban life, an abundance of experience overloads individuals, which leads to a split between subject and object, which "created an inner subjectivity protecting the individual from the onslaughts of the outer world, producing at its extreme an 'exaggerated subjectivism' that compensated the alienating effects of this world" (Frisby 1988:80).

Despite the tendency of dividedness in identity formation, there still exists in modern context a strong desire for an idealized conception of modern identity, which is held together by four key elements: continuity, integration, identification and differentiation. Hewitt (1989) describes a picture of this ideal: "It is to maintain a balance between similarity and difference in the face of individual development and changing social conditions, so that one can assimilate to the self demands for change or adjustment, but also fulfill an inner desire for constancy. It is to be a whole and complete person... It is to be connected with others and yet true to oneself. It is to participate in a variegated and often fragmented social life and yet to maintain continuity and integrity" (qtd. Dunn 1998: 152).

2.1.3 Identity in Postmodern Context

While the problem of modern identity is how to construct an identity and keep it solid and stable, the problem of postmodern identity is primarily how to avoid fixation and keep the options open.

Postmodernity is generally used to describe the economic and/or cultural state or condition of society which is said to exist after modernity. It is marked by the fundamental changes in the scope and character of culture, which in turn exert great effects on the identity formation. So "it should be unsurprising that during a time of rapid and profound change, as has been characteristic of post-war (World War Ⅱ) Western society, questions of identity have reappeared with a new force and a new urgency" (Davis 2000:2).

The social and cultural changes in postmodern society can be summarized into three categories: the structural transformations in the capitalist system and the global expansion of consumerism; the growth of new information and communication technologies; and the globalization and the hybridity of multicultural groups. Accompanying these social and cultural changes, identity in postmodern society takes on such characteristics as fragmentation, destabilization, fragility, fluidity, pluralisation, etc.

In the first place, in postmodern society, consumption has replaced production as the central mode of social behavior. As a consequence, social roles, identities, attitudes, values, and the structures of daily life have undergone fundamental changes. Consumption becomes a mode of being, a way of gaining identity, meaning and prestige in contemporary society. Individuals in the new world of consumption are no longer surrounded by other human beings, but by objects, so they themselves are becoming functional objects. Moreover, consumption constitutes a total homogenization and organization of everyday life. Its influence is permeating every aspect of life. The individual in the society has turned into a consumer. And he is not merely the consumer of products. Baudrillard argues that in consumerist society, the individual is tempted to buy not a single commodity but an entire system of objects and needs through which one differentiates oneself socially, yet integrates oneself onto the consumer society (qtd. Dunn 1998:289). To be exact, he is a consumer of signs and images. So the individual constructs the identity not from the tangible relationships of a group, as he did in the past, but from the disembodied visual images and the manufactured images of mass culture. Just as Dunn points out: "The source of identity has historically shifted from the internalization and integration of social roles to the appropriation of disposable commodities, images and techniques, selected and discarded at will from the extensive repertoire of consumer culture" (Dunn 1998:65). So the fragmenting effects of the commodity form and the disjunctive features of mass culture thus become the major causes of the unstable, inconsistent and incoherent identity.

Secondly, the developments of new information and communication technologies also exert great influences on the formation of identity. In a commodified and technologized postmodern culture, communication and information technologies supplant older forms of associations and social roles, so the source of identity is shifted from social interaction to commodities, images and techniques. Thus, identities in postmodern context lose their interactional quality, and take on instrumental and performative qualities. So the other-directed orientation in identity formation in modern context becomes fully absorbed in the mediations of consumerism, media and advertising. Baudrillard argues that we live in a "hyperreality" of simulations in which images, spectacles and the play of signs have replaced the logic of production and class conflict. The distinction between representation and reality implodes. So individuals are now caught in a world of commodity signs, media spectacles, representations and simulations so that they have no access to the real world. In the past, the media were believed to mirror, reflect or refer to reality, while now they constitute a "hyperreality". Take television as an example. Now, television is dissolved into life, and life is dissolved in television. What is real to an individual is no longer his direct contact with the world, but what comes to him on the TV screen. Trapped in such a situation, individuals come to prefer representation to reality. Through the media, we enter a new form of subjectivity, in which we become saturated with information, images and events. The massive spread of media has given manufactured images and information a pervasive presence in culture, threatening the stability of meaning and disturbing our very sense of reality. Media systems undermine the authority of traditional socializing agencies responsible for the formation of stable identities and group memberships, leaving the individual adrift in a world of saturating images, which in turn leads to the destabilization of identity.

Thirdly, the impact of globalization and multiculturalism on identity can hardly be overestimated. In the postmodern world, with globalization, economic and technological changes have unleashed a set of forces subversive of the older cultural boundaries. Globalization is a phenomenon embracing these opposing tendencies toward homogeneity and heterogeneity. On the one hand, commodification continues to impose uniformity on countries throughout the world. On the other hand, diversified and pluralistic cultural formations appear in more and more places. As a result, there exists a threat of a complete disintegration of cultures with a loss of all authentic, indigenous cultures. Yet there also exists a new cultural openness with a prospect of a more genuine global culture.

Multiculturalism highlights the opposition between heterogeneity and homogeneity, diversity and unity, universalism and particularism. To be exact, multiculturalism is a response—or a set of responses—to diversity that seeks to articulate the social conditions under which differences can be incorporated and order achieved from diversity. So what lies in the core of multiculturalism is the attitude towards diversity.

One basic response toward diversity is assimilation. This vision deals with difference by removing it. Difference is understood as something dangerous, to be rid of or at least minimized. So the emphasis is on cultural homogeneity and conformity. Thus, individuals are expected to shed their previous markers of group identity and adopt those of the social whole. By minimizing or even losing their distinctiveness, individuals are assimilated into society. At least in America, the central metaphor for assimilation is the "melting pot"—new elements take on the characteristics of the whole.

Hartmann and Gerteris mention three distinct types of multiculturalism: cosmopolitanism, fragmented pluralism and interactive pluralism. Cosmopolitanism defends diversity only insofar as it allows and expands individual rights and freedoms. The emphasis in this vision is on tolerance and individual choice rather than mutual obligations. Fragmented pluralism focuses on the existence of a variety of distinctive and relatively self-contained mediating communities not only as a social reality, but also as a necessity and strength. Under fragmented pluralism, the social whole is dissolved into its component collective units. Interactive pluralism realizes the existence of distinct groups and cultures.

Interactive pluralism lays emphasis on mutual recognition and respect of differences. Moreover, interactive pluralism stresses groups in interaction with each other mutually constituting a substantive moral whole. Although these three types of multiculturalism differ from one another, one common belief is their tolerance and acceptance of difference and diversity.

In summary, economic, technological and cultural changes in the postmodern era result in a condition of identity destabilization, fragmentation and pluralisation, which in some sense, intensifies the identity crisis in postmodern context. More important, the characteristics of destabilization, fragmentation and pluralisation of identity decide our way of constructing identity. There is little hope for a fixed identity. The identity is subjected to a continuous process of construction and reconstruction.

2.2 Identity in Postmodernist Narratives

2.2.1 Identity in Narratives

A narrative is a story that is created in a constructive format (as a work of writing, speech, poetry, prose, pictures, songs, motion pictures, video games, theatre or dance) that describes a sequence of fictional or non-fictional events. It derives from the Latin verb "narrare", which means "to recount" and is related to adjective "gnarus", meaning "knowing" or "skilled".

Narrative, in the view of the formalist-structuralist theory, has two parts: a story (histoire) and a discourse (discours). A story, consisting of the content, the chain of events, characters and settings, objects and persons performing, undergoing or acting as a background for them, is the "what" in a narrative; while the discourse is the "how". A discourse is the expression, the means by which the content is communicated. Narrative can have different genres and various forms including novels, epic poetry, history, biography, autobiography, representational art and film. Narrative is one of the privileged forms used by humans to elaborate experience. Without narrative, "our experience of the world and of ourselves would not be intelligible: it would only be a continuous given, in the way one supposes it must be for animals" (Cave 1995:112). This is why narratives have been widely studied as windows into the analysis of human social history, psychology, sociology, etc.

Sukenick also points out that "Part of the argument in the *Narralogues* is that narrative is a mode of understanding that uniquely is quick enough, mutable enough and flexible enough to catch the stream of experience, including our experience of the arts" (Sukenick 2000:1).

Identity, from the very beginning, is closely related to narratives. When asked about our identity, we start thinking about our life-story. To be exact, we construct our identity at the same time as we tell our life-story. In other words, we construct our story, and hence our identity. Narrative practice lies at the heart of self construction. Social research is increasingly pointing to the narrative quality of lives, showing how selves are constructed through storytelling (Randall 1995, Ezzy 1998).

There is a parallel between identity and narratives. The first point to be noted is the sources of identity and narratives. In storytelling one's life, an individual artfully picks and chooses not only from what is experientially available, but also from what is culturally available. In other words, the sources of identity construction are not limited to the personal sphere, but also extended to the public sphere. As Trinh Minhha suggests, the question of identity is moving away from traditional queries into *who* am I to progressively become questions of *when*, *where* and *how* am I. Self-construction isn't one-dimensional but multi-dimensional. Take the gender identity as an example, "gender intersects with racial, class, sexual and regional modalities of discursively constituted identities. As a result it becomes impossible to separate out 'gender' from the political and cultural intersections in which it is invariably produced and maintained" (Butler 1990:3). In this sense, the construction of identity and the narrative of identity offer a good perspective to examine the cultural contexts.

In addition, there is a parallel between the narrative composition of identity and the narrative composition of fiction. Experience only provides an endless supply of storyable items, so it is the incorporation of particular items into a coherent account that gives them meaning. So in storytelling one's life, an individual not only picks and chooses from experience, but also processes (he/she will stress something and subordinate others), and then actively crafts and inventively constructs his/her stories. The whole process shows that the storytellers are not the mere narrative puppets of their actions. Holstein and Gubrium point out that "There's a persistent interplay between what is available for conveying a story and how a particular narrative unfolds in practice; it's from this interplay that both self coherence and diversity develop" (Holstein&Gubrium 1999:107).

Moreover, identity is fabricated, constructed in a slowly unfolding development process in which an individual interacts with the world and also with others. So the narrative of identity is also a process in which the individual is a fiction writer who constantly monitors, modifies and revises themes and storylines. Thus, the selves that stories convey, as well as the identities of storytellers and listeners, are thus shaped and edited as storytelling proceeds.

To summarize, the connection of identity to fictional narratives is "not only a matter of the provision of appropriate models for, or occasions for reflection on, theoretical concerns but has a direct bearing on understanding narrative identity" (Whitebrook 2001:5). In other words, it is applicable and proper to study identity in narratives.

2.2.2 Identity in Postmodernist Narratives

To start, a brief review of identity narratives in American literature is helpful to the understanding of postmodernist narratives of identity.

The attempt at self-definition and a projection of seeking collective as well as personal identity in the cultural, theological and political context has been at the roots of American literature since its beginnings. Perry Miller (1956) reveals the inwardness of identity searching among the early puritans—the early puritans look in vain to history and to theology for an explanation of themselves, so they have no other place to search for meaning but within themselves. Then in the 17th and 18th centuries, the preoccupation with the issue of identity and self-definition becomes almost a national obsession. An eagerness to establish a new national identity prevails in every aspect of social life. "What is an American?"—the question asked by St. John de Crevecoeur in his *Letters from an American Farmer*—becomes the question that lies in the heart of many American writers and scholars at that time.

Crevecoeur's eighteenth-century vision is soon challenged by the nineteenth-century vision of "Who am I? Where am I going", which is expressed in Carson McCuller's *Clock Without Hands*. This change from the general to the specific, from the national to the personal is evident in modern American literature. In the writings of major nineteenth-century writers like Emerson, Thoreau, Whitman, Melville and Hawthorne, such concepts as self-reliance and non-conformity stick out. Transcendentalists, in particular, strive for an independent entity in a religious, social or political superstructure. Later, the rise of the story of initiation shows the greater concern on self-searching and identity. The story of initiation, such as Mark Twain's *The Adventures of Huckleberry Finn*, establishes a paradigm of the protagonist's searching for identity through the loss of innocence, discovery of evil and experience of disillusionment.

In the 20th century, the literary preoccupation with identity and self-searching is intensified. The change in identity construction is suggested in the title of Wylie Sypher's book *Loss of the Self in Modern Literature and Art*. American fiction after World War I depicts the struggling and confusion of modern individuals, who strive for a definite sense of an identifiable form of personal existence but in vain. Being outsiders or marginalized men, modern individuals estrange themselves from society. Their seclusion and retreat from the outside world, together with their internal conflict—an acute sense of failure and suffering, loss of orientation, lead to their final loss of identity. Ihab Hassan best describes the struggle of modern individuals in his book *Radical Innocence*:

> ... the contemporary self... was not only born, like Little Dorrit, in a prison, and it has not only made of its prison, like Axel, a fortress and

> mausoleum. It has been also discovering the strange secrets of all prisons: that though their doors are never locked, no prisoner wishes to escape; that all avenues of escape lead to the same call; that nothing may really exist beyond prison walls; that every gaoler is merely another prisoner in disguise. The contemporary self recoils, from the world, against itself. It has discovered absurdity. (qtd. Putz 1979:37)

The identity of America and its citizens is at stake after World War Ⅱ. Saul Bellow, a typical representative, mentions in his essay "Some Notes on Recent American Fiction" (1963) that he is struck by the theme of "the loss of self". "Undeniably the human being is not what he was commonly thought a century ago. The question nevertheless remains. He is something. What is he?" (qtd. Bradbury 1987:xii) His novel *Dangling Man* (1944) displays the anxiety and struggling of an existential alienation and identity pursuit. Richard Wright's *The Outsider* (1940) and Ralph Ellison's *Invisible Man* (1952) capture the sense of namelessness among individuals. Even if America considered World War Ⅱ a victory, the massacre of the Holocaust and Hiroshima continues to haunt the literary and cultural zeitgeist. The traditional beliefs are challenged. What follows the war is the repression and conformity of the McCarthy Era and the Cold War. The conflict between the economic prosperity and the wasteland of spirit throws America and its citizens into identity crisis. Just as Orrin Klapp points out, the decade of the 1960s gives birth to a number of mass, collective movements aiming at restoring or finding new identity.

It's obvious that modernist writers, though suffering from the threat of identity loss, strive to find new identity. However, in the postmodern era, identity and identity pursuit take on new characteristics. In the 1950s and early 1960s, with the rise of the Beat Generation and later the counterculture movement, writers like Kerouac, Ginsberg, Burroughs and Norman Mailer show a changed attitude towards the personal existence in a repressive society. The self in their writings is no longer striving for an independent entity, but rather for a release of itself into ecstasy, communal action, fantasies and prophetic hallucinations. The novel *On the Road* by Jack Kerouac, the king of the Beats, serves as an example of Beat's relief in ongoing driving and drinking, etc.

Manfred Putz (1979), in his book *Story of Identity: American Fiction of the Sixties*, points out that an intense preoccupation with identity question forms the substance of some of the most remarkable works of the sixties (mainly novels by Barth, Pynchon, Brautigan, Rhinehart, Sukenick and Nabokov). Postmodern writers are not only concerned about identity, their narratives of identity and identity pursuit also take on characteristics of the postmodern world. Thomas Pynchon, for example, in his novel *Crying of Lot 49*, warns that the influence of media and simulacra supplants governmental authority as the newest threat to individual authenticity and subjective identity. E. L.

Doctorow's novel *The Book of Daniel* depicts how Daniel copes with the legacies of his family, culture as well as historical and socio-political background, in order to move towards self-understanding and identity. Daniel's construction of identity shows that identity and identity structure are fluid and responsive to its social context as identity is constructed and reconstructed along with social changes. Don Delillo later in his novel *White Noise* reflects the influence of mass media on identity construction. Philip Roth's *Operation Shylock* describes two "Roth" to reveal the uncertainty of identity. By employing such narrative techniques as unreliable narration and narrative gaps, the author shows that identity is liable to questioning, doubling, splitting or multiplicity.

Ronald Sukenick is also aware of the crisis of identity faced by Americans. As a Jewish writer, he considers the Holocaust and Cold War as "ego smashers" that "exxed off (all identities) the surface of the planet" (Sukenick 1999:181). Then, in this situation, "How could one assume the arrogance of individual identity... How could one even presume to be a person after all that, or even a human?"(Sukenick 1999:181)In most of his novels, Sukenick seeks answers to these questions. His first novel *Up* is the story of a young man named Ronnie Sukenick who is navigating an often uncooperative world on a bildungsroman-style journey in search of his real self. His second novel *Out* depicts the journey of identity searching of a group of people. These people turn out to be pseudo figures who move in and out of the story, merge with one another, come into existence at the drop of their names, and then disappear never to reappear again. The fluidity and dissolution of identity is highlighted. His American Book Award winning book *Down and In: Life in the Underground* records how the underground artists in Greenwich Village struggle between the mainstream version of success and vanguard spirit so as to be themselves. *Mosaic Man* reflects his meditation on the construction of a Jewish identity in a multicultural world. After examining Sukenick's works, Putz summarizes the characteristics of identity narratives in them as follows:

> The key idea behind Sukenick's endeavours—that forms of reality are based on forms of invention—has its effect on the concept of self and identity in his fiction. Self-definition turns into self-invention, the given identity of character into the arbitrary imputation of imaginative projection, which substitute multiplicity for singularity, diversity for unitary appearance, and both, self-definition and identity, become subject to a process of constant change instead of aim of a search for immutable qualities. (Patz 1979:177)

The multiplicity, diversity, fluidity, fragmentation and dissolution characteristics of identity in Sukenick's fiction are laid bare through his postmodernist narratives. After a careful study of identity themes and his narratives in his writing, I summarize three laws he employs: namely Surviving Law, Entropy Law and Mosaic Law. The next three chapters are individual studies of identity themes in Sukenick's novels and his postmodernist way of narrating identity.

Chapter 3

Surviving Law: Assimilation or Dissimilation

3.1 Surviving Law of Identity in *Up* and *Down and In*: *Life in the Underground*

Identity is formed and constructed under the dual influence of psychological development and social changes. So the changes of social context will definitely influence the formation of identity. The post-World War Ⅱ era in the United States has witnessed a series of political, economic, social and cultural changes. The collapse of traditional beliefs, great prosperity of products, overwhelming media images, conformist values in the Cold War era, and increasing demand for equality and rights from marginalized groups leave the postwar America in unrest and turmoil. In this changed society, "One can no longer be certain of attaining a sense of security by sticking to the straight and narrow. One can no longer be so sure that sheer unflinching dedication will guarantee the kind of future payoff it once promised" (Clarke 1998: 246). Bereft of traditional sources of meaning, people have difficulty in redefining themselves in the changes, thus a state or condition of disorientation and role confusion occurs. In a word, people are pushed into identity crises.

The identity crisis is even more intense for American minorities, especially for Jewish people. The mass killings of Jews by Hitler and Nazis destroy the very base on which they construct their identities and smash their ego identities. "How could one assume the arrogance of individual identity after all those identities exxed off the surface of the planet since the year of my birth, 1932, the year Hitler assumed power? How could one even presume to be a person after all that, or even a human?" (Sukenick 1999:181) These two rhetorical questions clearly illustrate the identity crisis of a Jew, or even a man.

How to survive the changed society and gain a sense of security is a question before individuals. Surviving Law of identity refers to the strategies and ways of identity formation and construction especially in the crises of identity. The conflicts in the society offer individuals great possibilities of identity formation. Faced with the dubiousness of their identities, the individual characters develop idiosyncratic approaches to the question of self-definition. Basically, they can choose to assimilate or dissimilate into the mainstream society. Ronald Sukenick in his novels *Up* and *Down and In: Life in the Underground*, depicts different choices between assimilation and dissimilation made by different characters in their identity construction, their different strategies of getting assimilated or dissimilated and their struggles in making the hard choices.

3.1.1 Surviving Law of Identity Ⅰ: Assimilating into American Mainstream

Assimilation refers to the ability to identify with and feel at home in the mainstream society. Assimilation is the process through which individuals are gradually steered into the mainstream way of life. Assimilation is also a process through which individuals discard various traditions and values which are not the mainstream, and adopt those of the mainstream.

Mainstream is, generally, the common current of thoughts of the majority of society. Gordon considers WASP (White Anglo-Saxon Protestant) as the mainstream of American society by pointing out that "if there is anything in American life which can be described as an overall American culture which serves as a reference point for immigrants and their children, it may best be described, it seems to us, as the middle-class cultural patterns of, largely, white Protestant, Anglo-Saxon origins" (Gordon 1964:72).

John Murry Gibbon, a Scottish writer and cultural promoter, in his book *Canadian Mosaic* (1938), attacks the exclusiveness of American culture by making a distinction between the immigrant culture in Canada and that in the United States. The American style is a melting-pot, a process by which immigrants are encouraged to cut off ties with countries and cultures of origin, while the Canadian style is a cultural mosaic in which immigrants are encouraged to keep their own cultures. In this sense, in the United States, immigrants and their descendants like Ronald Sukenick (a Jewish immigrant descendant) are encouraged, tempted and even forced to give up their original cultures for the mainstream WASP culture. Assimilation, to them, means giving up their Jewish origins and culture so as to adopt the values and principles of WASP.

It should also be noted that in different periods of history, this WASP mainstream takes on different characteristics. After World War Ⅱ, the nation emerges as a leading player in the international arena, and possesses great political power. Economically, the United States also enjoys great development. By the late 1940s, Americans have become the richest people on the globe. With 6 percent of the world's population, the United States produces 50 percent of the world's goods. All these developments greatly inspire American people's desire for power, wealth and consumption. So the mainstream WASP culture advocates the American Dream for power, wealth and success.

Another important feature of the mainstream American society in the postmodern era is that it has turned into a consumer-oriented society. "A consumer society is one in which the possession and use of an increasing number and variety of goods and services are the principal cultural aspiration and the surest perceived route to personal happiness, social status and national success" (Ekins 1991:244). One of the most important features of a consumer society is that individual identity is related to consumption. Consumption becomes a mode of being, a way of gaining identity, meaning and prestige in contemporary society. Anderson and Wadkins contrast consumption-oriented societies with production-oriented ones, noting that in the former, "[a]n individual's identity is tied to what one consumes rather than in a production culture where an individual's identity is more tied to what one produces" (Anderson & Wadkin 1991:129). So the popular images of WASP are closely linked with such commodities they consume as cars and other luxuries.

In addition, it is a society entering the information age. The influence of media can not be ignored. "The media impose manipulative paradigms on individual experience, so that it is almost as if people don't have any individual experience—they only have what they see being presented on television" (Sukenick 1985:117). Television, for example, traps individuals in a universe of simulacra in which it is impossible to distinguish the spectacle from the real. Media, in some sense, create a "hyperreality", in which it becomes increasingly difficult to tell true from false, or good from bad. Those familiar images imposed on us as an effect of manipulated text, constituting our social roles and identities as though we had freely chosen them. Baudrillard also points out that individuals are so caught up in a world of commodity signs, media spectacles, representations and simulations that there is no longer any access to the real. The images of America are the images of WASP, wealthy and healthy, fighting to achieve their American Dreams for power and wealth.

So, assimilation into the American mainstream society means becoming like middle-class Protestant whites. To achieve this purpose, Sukenick points out that one can "invent" one's identity or "sell out" one's identity. By inventing one's identity, especially according to the popular media images, one can identify with the majority of the society and get assimilated into the mainstream. "Selling out" identity, another way of assimilation, refers to the compromising of one's integrity, morality and principles in exchange for money, success (however defined) or other personal gains. It is commonly associated with attempts to increase mass appeal or acceptability to the mainstream society.

Inventing one's identity, especially according to the popular media images of WASP, then, is a good strategy to get assimilated into the mainstream. Strop Banally in Sukenick's first novel *Up* sets a model of identity invention.

When Strop Banally first appears before us, we can immediately realize that he is a WASP, "blond, tanned, well-tailored, and baritoned, football build, strength and regularity of feature" (Sukenick 1968:4). His physical appearance is just the ideal image of WASP, blond, healthy, wealthy and strong, a composite of images associated with idealized masculinity. However, he is not a man with his unique characteristics, but a man who "looks familiar, somebody seen in a tabloid, on a screen, in a cigarette ad" (4). He is the duplicate of the popular images seen in the media. And he is the epitome of consumer images.

Not only does his physical appearance fit the description of the mainstream WASP, Banally's success also reveals that he is a self-made man, the walking image of American Dream. He is the "boy genius of the communications industry or, as he is known to some, the Albert Einstein of the pornographic film" (4). He is just like "an infinitely more knowing Gatsby, Gatsby without illusions, Gatsby 'wised up' with the experience of the last forty years" (39). The secret to his success lies in his protean ability to adapt to the society in order to get what he wants. Just examine the series of jobs he has taken, we can see how he changes himself with the society. He has been "a cowboy, a flyer, a fashion model, a yacht captain, an actor, an undercover agent, a stockbroker, an advertising executive and an entrepreneur" (4). He is always at the forefront of the fashion; he changes his jobs with the needs of the society. Nothing but money, fame and power is what he is going after. He can do anything if only it can bring him money and profit. So his success makes Banally no longer an outsider of mainstream society, "he is in it; in fact he is practically on top of it" (39).

Strop Banally operates at the heart of the postmodern consumer culture. "He is known as a 'boy genius' in the communication industry—which seems to mean that he has his adroit finger in advertising, public relations, televisions, movies and publishing" (38). This talent wins him wealth, power and capacity to dominate or control others. And Banally has "an incredible competitive drive for power that he seems to indulge not for the sake of conquest but simply for the pleasure of exercising it" (38). To be exact, Strop Banally is power itself and a typical WASP.

The secret to his success is the strategy Banally employs in identity construction—identity "invention". He creates his past, crowds his history with "a wild series of comic feats, improbable coups, unbelievable conquests, and gratuitous crafty machinations" (38). "Nobody knows exactly where he came from, for [...] he makes up his past as he goes along so that by now nobody can tell the truth from the fiction" (38). We know him just by what he tells us. "We learn how Banally masquerades as a college professor, turns a sorority party into a bacchanale, seduces women of all ages and conditions, plots to corner the Persian melon market, hucksters dubious securities in a manner worthy of P. T. Barnum, peddles political influence he doesn't have, and gulls a Congressional investigating committee" (39). However, nobody can prove the authenticity of these stories, yet everybody believes in them. Moreover, this kind of self-invention is an on-going process, which involves reinvention according to the changing environment. Banally is a man without past. Or in other words, his past leaves no trace in his identity. No consistent principle or belief exists for him. From his story, we can see that there are no moral standards. For him, the only criterion is to achieve success. Banally can do anything to achieve success. "Plot and machination are most characteristic of Banally" (39).

From the success of Strop Banally, we know that identity "invention", as a strategy of identity construction, is quite effective, especially in the postmodern world. Baudrillard describes the postmodern world as "hyperreal". The distinction between the actual and what is seen to happen is blurred. It does not matter whether or not it really happened. "For Baudrillard, the hyperreal is not the unreal, but the more than real" (Kellner 1989: 82). So, identity invented by Banally just becomes his identity.

Name is one of the most important labels of one's identity. The name of Strop Banally is an interesting mosaic. According to the dictionary, a "strop" is the leather strip on which razors are sharpened. As a verb, "to strop" is to sharpen. Strop also has sonic resonance with strap, which as "strapping" means strong or healthy. But "banally" means completely "ordinary and trite", exactly the opposite of the sharpened or refined edge of a blade. "To strop banality" would mean to hone the ordinary, or perhaps to bring triteness to perfection. The special combination shows the author Sukenick's belief that within American culture banality and success are opposites but necessary conditions for each other. In a culture which values the banal, those who excel at banality succeed. Banally's success derives from his banality because it allows him to remain totally in sync with his culture. He is a walking erection, motivated by consumption and the fulfillment of desires. In a culture intent on seeking gratification, his natural commitment to the satisfaction of his own desires makes him a hero. So "the string of fabliaux which constitute Strop Banally's picaresque career could comprise a handbook to success in our society" (Sukenick 1968: 39). Strop Banally sets a model of identity construction. His identity invention makes him take to life like a duck to water.

Identity "selling out", another strategy of constructing one's identity, means to compromise one's values, integrity, morality, principles and/or artistic vision in order to gain fame and/or monetary profit. It is one of the strategies taken to increase mass appeal or acceptability to the mainstream society. A person, who does this, as opposed to continuing along his or her original path, is labeled a sellout and typically regarded with disgust and immediate loss of respect. Selling out is often seen as gaining success at the cost of credibility and morality.

Nancy, in the novel *Up*, sells out her identity by working as a nude model. Being a nude model, Nancy not only makes a lot of money, which makes her independent of men, she also feels that she becomes "a new person" (Sukenick 1968: 185). Although working as a nude model means she has to sacrifice her previous principles and morality, she believes that she has gained the power to manipulate the representations of female sexuality that has previously controlled her. In this sense, identity "selling out" is a strategy whereby women are able to survive and maintain their female identity.

Gender identity of the 1950s and 1960s is one of the key focuses of the novel *Up*. Patriarchy, in various forms, is an ancient phenomenon in western society. Before the coming of the wave of feminism in the 1960s, women in the United States are still faced with the conservatism of the postwar era and the formidable ideological and institutional constraints, which shape women's identities, weaken their limited protests and contain their activities within traditional bonds. Moreover, gender-based discrimination is intensified with the male dominance and female obedience advocated in mass media.

In addition, Ronald Sukenick is more concerned about the sickness of American culture—Sadomasochism. Sukenick points out that "power and sex, or violence and sex, are often confused in our culture—and that they shouldn't be" (Sukenick 1985: 113). In other words, male phallic identity often depends upon a projected female masochistic identity. Women are treated as erotic objects of male desire. The images of handcuffed women on desks or tables recur through the novel, indicating women's situation of slaves. Rapes or violent assaults on women are regarded as best ways to display masculinity. Strop Banally, for example, considers rape as an extension of masculinity and a manifestation of male authority over natural female acquiescence. Ronnie, though impotent himself, fantasizes several assaults on women by policemen (Sukenick 1968: 32, 230-231).

In this cultural context, the process of Nancy's identity construction is also the process of the awakening of sexual awareness and feminist consciousness. Born in a middle-class family, Nancy has a kind of sex frigidity because of the middle-class morality. "We never talked about sex, which was the only thing really on our minds" (85). In her puberty, she struggles in the disjunction between the needs of the body and the moral structures of the mind. Like most women at that time, Nancy is dutifully submissive to the dead weight of cultural conservatism represented by her father. Nancy's sticking to the middle-class morality makes Ronnie's attempt to seduce her fail.

However, Nancy is later seduced by Ronnie's friend Ernie Slade and marries him. Because, to Nancy, "Slade could have been a hero [...] I idealized him no doubt. I want to. He was strong. Physically strong" (178). He just fits in the popular images of strong males. In this sense, we can say that women willingly fall victim to male dominance. After her marriage to Slade, Nancy turns into a quite different woman. She goes from one extreme to another. Now she is open and acts as a temptress. She becomes promiscuous and exhibitionistic to satisfy her husband's unorthodox sexual needs. Slade encourages her to have an affair with other men so as to inspire his sexual desire. Nancy first reluctantly, but later willingly sacrifices herself to meet her husband's needs.

It's clear that whether acting as a virgin or temptress, Nancy occupies socially produced and historically conditioned subject positions inscribed by patriarchal myths of female sexuality. She remains as a sexual object. She just acts according to the male's needs and desires regardless of her own willingness and wishes.

More changes take place with the break-up of the marriage. In making love with men, she is no longer only concerned about the feeling and desire of men, but more about herself. When later she meets again with Ronnie Sukenick and has sex, in Sukenick's words, "a disappointing fuck" (182). Nancy says, "I'm glad you enjoyed yourself [...] I suppose this heals your ego. I'm glad it makes somebody happy" (183). This shows her disappointment with Ronnie's impotence. She has changed from an old "prudery", to an amoral existentialism in which "what we do we do" (183).

However, Nancy's awakening of sexual awareness does not finish her identity construction. It is until she becomes a nude model for photographers, illustrators and Men's magazines that she begins to gain some perspective on the ideological nature of female sexual identities. She considers it as an act of liberation, which can bring her money and a new identity as well. First of all, it is a lucrative business, which can make her independent of men. "It's better than eight hours a day in some phony office routine" (184). So it is a subsistence strategy of women. More important, being a nude model makes Nancy a new person. "Your best friends don't recognize you when they see you nude", she tells Ron. "That's the reason I like it—it's like becoming a new person... I take on a new identity in response to the feelings of whoever is there" (185-186). In the past, she submissively conformed to the socially constituted gender roles. Now she shows some revolt. She has learned to reappropriate her objectified body for subversive purposes. She refuses to identify with the fetishized female body displayed in her pictures. "It's only a photograph that people see, don't forget. The photograph isn't me. What do I care who looks at it?" (185)

So being a nude model is a kind of identity "selling out" strategy. By doing so, Nancy not only gives up her original path of a good woman and a good wife, she also discards the middle class morality. She poses not for an artist, but for commercial magazines, which are regarded by many people as sick magazines. In many people's views, Nancy sells out her identity to gain success at the cost of morality. It's a shame even to her mother that "She spends all her money surreptitiously buying up the monthly supply of girlie magazines in Gravesend so they won't stray into the hands of her friends" (185). However, to Nancy herself, she considers this as a justified way of constructing a new identity. "It's healthier than most jobs, and more honest [...] It's not girlie magazines that are sick. It's the people who look at them" (185). More important, Nancy realizes that it is her true self. "We're so used to recognizing one another by face and costume that your identity changes completely when you take your clothes off [...] it's like becoming a new person" (185). It's ironic that our everyday face is revealed as false, and our true self, or naked self, is unrecognizable to the world. The costumes and faces we wear in everyday life obscure a reality that is available to us only when we are stripped of the trappings of conventional culture and morality.

However, identity "selling out" is still a hard choice for Nancy. Nancy's struggle and contradiction are displayed in her ways of treating her name, an important label of her identity. "But they never use my real name in the captions, I always appear incognito" (185). In this sense, Nancy's identity "selling out" strategy is conducted with reservation. This reservation is also reflected in the fact that her job is still to satisfy men's desire. To be exact, she is still an unwitting victim in a male fantasy. In a word, "Nancy's strategy may be seen as an intervention, a subversion from within cultural constraints she can never wholly escape" (Harris 2003:52).

3.1.2 Surviving Law of Identity Ⅱ: Dissimilating into American Mainstream

Although assimilating into American mainstream is an effective strategy of constructing one's identity, some individuals choose to dissimilate into the mainstream society and stay in a marginalized position to show their determination of fighting against consumerism and conformism. In his novel *Up*, Sukenick mentions three ways of refusing to get assimilated into American mainstream. One can exile oneself from the mainstream society and retreat into the ivory tower. Dreams and hallucination are another way of constructing one's identity. Writing experimental novels is another self-marginalizing tool and way to seek identity.

The novel *Up* depicts "Ronnie Sukenick", a young man with the same name with the author, and his bildungsroman-style journey in search of his real self. Unlike Strop Banally, who adapts himself easily to the society, Ronnie finds the reality violent and harsh. It is a world of hostility and power. To him, it's just like a prison. The cold world destroys his desire and attempts to get assimilated into it. In order to survive, what he can do is to escape from the cold society, by retreating to the ivory tower, to his hallucination and to fiction writing.

The identity crisis of Ronnie Sukenick is highlighted at the very beginning of the novel. The novel opens with the words: **"THE WORST THING IS THE COLD"** (Sukenick 1968:1, capitalized and stressed by the author). In addition to the coldness, "Outrage, humiliation and dread have all been absorbed into this one, final petty discomfort" (1). Ronnie finds himself in a prison-like room: naked bulb, bare stone cell, heavy door, tiny grill and blinding fluorescent light. What surrounds him is coldness and loneliness. Moreover, news comes on the radio about the breaking of the tentative negotiations between the U. S. and the Soviet Union suggesting the Cold War and the intense international situation. "That lets me know where I stand. Nowhere" (3). He cannot find his place in the society, and he has no sense of belonging. In a word, he is left in identity crisis.

Name is an important label of one's identity. The difficulty or failure in claiming one's name indicates the difficulty or failure in claiming one's identity. When Ronnie claims his letter from the mailman, the mailman rejects him by saying: "How do I know that? How do I know you ain't Gomez, for example? Look, Jim, all I do is put the letters in the box" (5). Ronnie Sukenick cannot demonstrate to the mailman that he is not Gomez, nor Jim, nor any other person but Sukenick. A similar scene happens when Ronnie stays in a university. Whitebread Blackhead, the administrator, mistakes his name for "Suchanitch" and "Suckanitch". Sukenick, a name of Jewish origin, is even strange and unacceptable among his friends. Sukenick is often called by the name "Suchanitch", "Suckanitch", "Subanitch", "Sookenack", "Bookenack" or "Sacanook" and so on. The mistakes with his name show that Sukenick possesses a weak sense of existence and exerts little influence on others. In a word, his failure in defending his name is a reflection of his identity crisis.

His identity crisis reaches the summit when Sukenick, in a small bar, meets a "clean-cut straight-backed fellow with neatly clipped blond hair and an all American face, a Yale-graduate" (164). He is a typical WASP. Both claim that their names are Sukenick. In the following argument over the name and the question "who am I", the narrator Sukenick fails and loses his name of Sukenick. "I stepped out the door into the dark air, turned around, and next thing I knew I was flat on my ass in the cold street, no one in sight, and a terrific ache throbbing in the right side of my face. Who am I?" (167) Obviously, the loss of name means the losing of his identity.

In the novel, we follow "Ronnie Sukenick" as he stumbles along in the society, experiencing his setbacks, his failure and his struggles, all of which are twice of others' as he is a Jew. As a Jewish boy born and growing up in Brooklyn, Sukenick knows that the road set for boys like him is to gain a scholarship to Ivy League colleges and become a doctor or a lawyer. It is also the road leading to the mainstream society. However, Sukenick's love for writing and his ideal of becoming a writer make him a "misfit" in high school and earn him the nickname "Wrong Way Ron". The novel provides no description of Ron, but we can assume from his demeanor that he looks nothing like Strop Banally. Ronnie is described as "feckless", "innocent", "dazzled", "unlucky", "hapless", "lovelorn" and "lackluster". He is marginalized in school.

The popular construction of male identity stresses sexual power. So Ronnie's impotence in sex is also an obstacle in his identity construction. His sexual experiences and endeavors are generally unfulfilled and confused. His high school sweetheart Nancy refuses to have sex with him. He learns years later that his friend Ernie Slade seduced Nancy while she was still dating Ron. His sexual experience with Oola Wonderliegh culminates in a humiliating blunder, leaving Ron unsure "whether officially speaking [he] was still a virgin or not" (146).

Then Ronnie's journey into the world of Silverfish's connections continues his initiation into adulthood as it offers him chances to get to know the outside world, especially the mainstream society. The Silverfishes are rich relatives of Sukenick's, who are invited by Aunt Theda to help Sukenick get a scholarship to college. With their help, Sukenick meets a politician of the Democratic Party, a wealthy doctor and a Wall Street consultant. The three are chosen as the representatives of American WASP. However, they offer him no help but humiliations. The politician is rude to him and even splatters sour cream on Ronnie's face. The doctor is completely absent-minded, talking with him on contraception. And the Wall Street consultant even solicits bribes from him. In a word, they just make him realize that "I knew myself a fool. And I was mortified by a degrading illumination of the world we live in and my own callow complicity in it" (131). Through this journey, Sukenick gets to know the cold and violent essence of the so-called mainstream society. To him, society is just like a prison. The images of prison and imprisonment recur throughout the novel, illustrating the violent and harsh reality. Surviving Law Sukenick takes is to escape. He retreats to the ivory tower, to his hallucinations and at last to fiction writing.

Sukenick's first attempt is to retreat to the ivory tower, which makes him a young teacher in a university. He considers the university campus a paradise free from the rigid control of different powers, where he can enjoy some freedom, even if retreating to the ivory tower means living a poor life. "A can of sardines and coffee. I count my money. A five and three singles in my wallet plus two nickels and five pennies, eight fifteen I have and my bank book has ten twenty-seven equals eighteen forty-two from my last and final check. After which find work. I must borrow money" (21). Sukenick is willing to endure economic hardships for freedom.

However, Sukenick soon discovers that the ivory tower is by no means the promised land of freedom but just a mini-society. Whitebread Blackhead, the acting chairman, is a bureaucrat, who criticizes Sukenick for his classroom spontaneity and improvisation. Blackhead believes in strict adherence to the status quo and sticks to a more studied and prepared way of teaching. His manner of talking and his sarcasm show his bureaucratic power and influence which Sukenick cannot escape even when he retreats into the ivory tower.

The central point of the argument between Sukenick and Blackhead is the cheating and plagiarism of Mr. Moosoff, a football player in Sukenick's class. To Sukenick, cheating becomes a subversive tactic aiming at undermining rules which are seen to be corrupt. However, his defense for cheating earns him a pink slip—he is fired. Sukenick does not feel depressed, instead he considers it "an act of economic suicide for the sake of personal salvation" (25). To him, spiritual freedom is more important than material comforts.

As a misfit in the society, an outsider of the mainstream and a non WASP, Ronnie

Sukenick, an America-born Jew, is impotent, weak and powerless, so he has to seek alternative ways to construct his identity. Dreams and hallucination are the ways he tries. In his hallucination, Ronnie Sukenick is always the hero, possessing masculine power. His fantasy of making love with a French coquette best shows his change from impotence to masculinity. Sukenick's first attempt of sex ends with premature ejaculation, which shows his impotence. Then money gives him power. "Why have I always refused to learn what money can buy? All you have to do to get what you want is put down the price [...]. Just open your wallet and pay for it, simple as that" (42). With the money paid, Sukenick believes that he is the owner while the prostitute the slave. So he finishes his second sex, violently but successfully, displaying his masculinity. However, we can see that "his models for those fantasy roles derive from popular representations of masculinity that reproduce the very constructions of male subjectivity that are the source of his oppression" (Harris 2003:50). Indeed, the influence of the mainstream gender identities is so strong that it denies any escape. So later, Ronnie himself also confesses that the story with the French prostitute is an out and out lie, "pure adolescent braggadocio to assuage my delicate ego" (Sukenick 1968:169-170).

Escaping into the ivory tower and hallucination can only offer Ronnie Sukenick temporary relief and satisfaction, but cannot help him find his real self and construct his identity. So he turns to another way—fiction writing. Fiction writing exiles him further from the mainstream society. But at the same time, he gains freedom and power. In this sense, fiction writing offers him a chance to actively construct his identity.

As mentioned in the previous section, when he was in the middle school, Ronnie Sukenick holds the ideal of becoming a writer while other boys intend to be a doctor or a lawyer. His unusual ideal makes him a "misfit" in high school and earns him the nickname "Wrong Way Ron". He is exiled from the main body of the students.

When he leaves the middle school and tries to go to a college, his aunt Theda asks her rich relatives the Silverfishes to help him find a college. The conversation between Mrs. Silverfish and Ronnie goes as follows,

> "I suppose you want to be a doctor?"
> "No."
> "A lawyer?"
> "No."
> "An accountant?"
> "No." (Sukenick 1969:123)

Obviously, in Mrs. Silverfish's view, becoming a doctor, a lawyer or an accountant is the first choice for boys, because it promises the bright future of fame and money. And this opinion is indeed the one held by most people at that time. However, Ronnie's ideal of becoming a writer, especially a creative writer, is ignored and looked down upon by people around him. Later Ronnie tries to seek help from a Wall Street consultant who is said to have great power. Ronnie tells him that he wants to be a writer. He immediately takes it for granted that Ronnie wants to be a journalist. Even after correction by Ronnie twice, he is not taking it seriously. In his mind, becoming a journalist, though not a good choice itself, is better than becoming a writer. In this sense, Ronnie's insistence on his choice of becoming a writer forces him to take a path different from others.

He does choose a different road. When many of his friends, like Finch and Marsh, play in the business market and enjoy money and success, Ronnie has to stay in a prison-like room, suffering from poverty, writing his novels. Sometimes, he cannot even support himself and has to borrow money from his friends. He is considered a failure by his friends and is sneered at all around. Like his friend Hamstrung, who is also a writer, Ronnie can only "stay down here in my hole, mind my own business" (14). He has no sense of belonging to any group in the society. In a word, he is marginalized.

However, fiction writing offers Ronnie a chance to be himself. First of all, fiction writing makes him wrest control of his imagination from the image factories of the dominant culture. At that time, the media impose manipulative paradigms on individual experiences so that it is almost as if people do not have any individual experiences—they only have what is presented on television. They take it as their experience. However, writing offers Ronnie opportunities to control his imagination. In traditional novels, imagination is regarded as no more than an aid in adjusting the ego's desires to a pre-existent reality. But to Ronnie, imagination is the most important property of an individual. That is why he always urges his students, "Use your imagination, or someone else is going to use it for you" (Sukenick 1987:149).

Moreover, the power of literature just lies in its imagination. He illustrates this in a lecture on Wordsworth to students. "Poetry doesn't cure anything—except the mind. And the mind cures—through acts. It would be hard to overestimate the importance of the imagination in confronting and even creating the world in which we live... Perhaps what we need is a poetry that moves us to act, that points an accusing finger like the biblical prophets, a poetry that persuades, arouses, has its effect in the polling booths, gets us into the streets" (Sukenick 1968:308). This is the goal of literature, and the goal of his lecture. Inspired by his lecture, students rise to action and leave chanting "Free-DOM! FreeDOM" (309).

The power of fiction is further illustrated in the next bit when Ronnie accompanies Kenny, his childhood friend, as he hands out leaflets for an organization. Kenny and Ronnie have different opinions on fiction writing. As an activist, Kenny believes in concrete action, such as demonstrations, while Ronnie still believes in fiction writing.

> "I don't see why you'd want to write a novel," says Kenny.
> "In the current situation. What's needed is organization. Footwork, demonstrations."
> "A novel is a demonstration," I said.
> "I mean real demonstrations."
> "A novel is real," I said. (277)

To summarize, it is fiction that gives the weak, poor and impotent Ronnie a new self-assertiveness and power. With the gained power, he is bold to face the strong, rich and powerful Strop Banally. So later when Strop Banally coaxes him to revise his novel into a more commercial "property", and promises to publish his novel which will bring him fame and money, Ronnie refuses. Moreover, at a party when Banally dances with Marietta, Ronnie goes along and grabs Banally by the arm. "I'm cutting in", he says quietly. Banally looks at him. His green eyes glitter. Then he raises his eyebrows nonchalantly and smiles a smile that this time is more nearly a grimace. He hands Marietta to Ronnie. In this confrontation, Ronnie wins.

The novel *Up* ends with an interesting scene in which a boyish figure on the tenement roof, among television aerials, raises a long, bare pole above his head, moves it in a circle and lowers it again. When no signal comes, he repeats this procedure again and again. "The boy, of course, is the artist; the pole he waves, his imaginative power, the 'sentient consciousness' searching for data not yet tainted by the society of the spectacle, whose images flood the television antennas around him. His goal is to record the wash of data at the very moment of its convergence into new integrations" (Harris 2003: 59). Fiction writing is the continuous process to experience and form new integrations. Through fiction writing, Ronnie gets to know himself and is brave enough to be himself.

Fiction writing is not only a strategy employed by the character Ronnie Sukenick to find his real self, but also an important way for the author Ronald Sukenick to escape from the middle-class conformity, exile himself from the mainstream society and construct his identity as well. *Up* is considered as a mock-autobiography by many critics for several reasons. First, the narrator in the novel has the same name with the author. Second, fictive characters and people in Sukenick's real life mix in the novel. Moreover, Sukenick inserts a lot of autobiographic information in it. Therefore, the process of the narrator Ronnie Sukenick's completion of a supreme fiction and identity pursuit is also the process of the author Sukenick's exploration in literary career and his identity pursuit.

Born a Jew on Gravesend Avenue, Brooklyn, New York, Ronald Sukenick realizes that he is an outsider of the mainstream society even when he was young. His Yiddish grandmother was called a kike, which is an offensive term for Jews. Sukenick is familiar with two worlds: the upper-middle-class world and the underground world in Greenwich Village. What the middle-class world has is "caution, conformity, and mercenary values" (Sukenick 1987:12). But the bohemian life style in Greenwich Village promises a freedom from the conformity of the middle class. When he studies in Brooklyn's Midwood High School, getting straights A's and going to Harvard Med School is the life goal for kids like him and the promised road to middle-class life and success. However, what really fascinates him is not to become a doctor or a lawyer, but a writer. So Sukenick is struggling between the upward mobility and his interest in fiction writing. Sukenick visualizes this struggling of different life paths as the struggling between the Midwood High School and Greenwich Village.

This struggling continues in his life and Sukenick tries to strike a compromise between the two different life paths. Later, he manages to enroll in Cornell University, an Ivy-League University. However, Sukenick does not give up his writing.

After his graduation, Sukenick goes to Brandeis University where he obtains his doctoral degree. After graduation, Sukenick follows his teachers' advice and practices teaching in college. However, this kind of stable life can not satisfy him. Later he still decides that he is more suitable for the "precarious" writing life, so he drops out of college and academic life, moves to a flat at E. 12th and Avenue B in Greenwich Village and resumes his fiction. "For me, sneaking over to Greenwich Village from high school or living in the East Village in the sixties, the descent into the underground was a matter not of tradition but of an absolute need" (Sukenick 1987:6). It is the need for finding one's real self and true identity.

Jerome Klinkowitz summarizes the struggle of Ronald Sukenick, by saying,

> His [Sukenick's] life is an index to modern anti-heroics: a bright boy from Brooklyn who is the only one in his crowd to miss a ticket to Princeton, Columbia, or Yale; a Brandeis Ph. D. who scuffles from job to job, whose scholarly magnum opus, *Wallace Stevens: Musing the Obscure*, is sneered away by American Literature... And who, if his fictions are as autobiographical as he claims, has one hell of a time even making it with girls. How, in such circumstances, does one survive? (Klinkowitz 1987:73)

Thus, fiction writing, to Ronald Sukenick, is not only an escape from the pressure of worldly success of the mainstream, but also the way of surviving and actively constructing his identity. Sukenick realizes this when he starts his writing career:

> When I start writing my first novel, *Up*, a book about the East Side that is a combination of autobiography and invention, I realize that place and time is

> one in which we can in fact partly invent our autobiographies, in which life is not something imposed on us but a process in which we are creatively involved. (Sukenick 1987:149)

To him, fiction writing is a way of inventing our autobiographies, thus a way of inventing our identity. That is the reason why Sukenick does not consider fiction as a form of entertainment. "I realized that the pleasure and excitement that I derived from some novels was attributable to the way they helped me understand my experience and live my life" (Sukenick 2000:5).

So to Sukenick, fiction writing is never a way of getting assimilated into the mainstream society, nor a means to gain money or fame. Instead, Sukenick marginalizes himself through his literary creation. He never caters for the taste of the public or publishing houses; instead he sticks to his pursuit of writing. He never gives in to the mainstream standards or values. Instead, he challenges traditional literary values by boldly declaring the "death of the novel". So what he wants to do in his writing is to get rid of "old forms". His novels with "no plot, no story, no character, no chronological sequence, no verisimilitude, no imitation, no allegory, no symbolism, no subject matter, no meaning" frequently subvert every expectation a reader might bring to them (Sukenick 1985:211). They are too unusual, too challenging and too contrary in his undermining of the idea of the book as traditionally conceived. Sukenick's unconventional fiction, in turn, keeps him further in the marginalized place.

Staying in the marginalized place does not mean Sukenick is passive. He just enjoys his marginal place, which frees him from the commercial pressure. So when he realizes that the larger commercial publishing houses are refusing his best works, he helps to found the Fiction Collective, a small publishing house, with a group of writers. He mentions that Fiction Collective is "based solely on the principle of exclusion, meaning, I presume, that those excluded by the publishing industry..." (Sukenick 1979b: 468). Later, based on the same principle, Sukenick founds *American Book Review*, a magazine designed to review the books ignored by the mainstream *New York Review of Books*. Sukenick considers these efforts as "an assertion of power, a symbolic act of rebellion, a move toward realization that ideal of writer as free spirit, demiurge, critic of the zeitgeist" (Sukenick 1979b:473).

So it is clear that by exiling himself from the mainstream and working outside the publishing industry, Sukenick, together with these experimental novelists, gains the opportunity to develop styles that one can develop only with difficulty. They have the chances to write what they want to, which allows new voices to be heard and new criteria to be developed.

3.1.3 Mainstream and Anti-mainstream: Struggling between Assimilation and Dissimilation

Assimilation and dissimilation are hard choices to make. Assimilation means sacrificing one's uniqueness, while dissimilation means the marginal position. Usually individuals have to struggle between assimilation and dissimilation. The struggle is best expressed by the subterranean artists in Greenwich Village in America. In his American-Book-Award novel *Down and In: Life in the Underground*, a collective memoir of the subterranean in Greenwich Village, Ronald Sukenick observes how the habitués of the underground cope with various challenges to identity. The subterraneans have to struggle between the mainstream and the underground and to make the hard decision whether to get assimilated or dissimilated into the mainstream society. Sukenick records the split in the choices made by the subterraneans such as Allen Ginsberg, Gregory Corso, Judith Malina, Robert Creeley, and Norman Mailer, just to name a few.

New York City, the economic center of the United States, is the wind vane of fashion. Especially Brooklyn, the city's most populous borough, where Ronald Sukenick was born and brought up, represents the mainstream society. What is popular here is the "caution, conformity, and mercenary values" (Sukenick 1987:12). While just across the Manhattan Bridge is a village "where money was not important—and just as important, sex was not a commodity you traded for marriage" (Sukenick 1987:13). In this sense, Greenwich Village exists as an anti-mainstream, a sharp contrast to the middle-class mainstream society. It represents a cultural and intellectual style in resistance to the status quo, keeping a critical distance from the establishment, and sustaining an adversary power. It offers a quite different life style, thus presents a quite different construction of identity. "In Greenwich village at the time there was a strong sense of alternative identity. In the underground of Greenwich Village you not only knew who They were, you also knew who We were. America was one thing and Greenwich Village another" (Sukenick 1987:15).

It is obvious that choosing Greenwich Village means choosing anti-mainstream and dissimilation. Greenwich Village is a great temptation to those who are fed up with middle-class definitions of success and failure. It is also the best choice for the artists, who do not want to give up their artistic values to cater for the public standards of the mass market. To them, living the underground life in Greenwich Village involves a notion of the good life beyond mercenary concerns. More important, to them, life in Greenwich Village means freedom. Just as Adolph Gottlieb, one of Abstract Expressionists, points out, "During the forties, some artists were painting with a sense of absolute despair... Things were going so badly... I felt free to do whatever I wanted, no matter how absurd it might seem; what was there to lose?" (42) In Greenwich Village, they have nothing to lose. Instead, they enjoy the freedom of creation.

Thus, defining freedom is an important part of defining the subterraneans, and also an important part of defining their identity. What they most want to free from is the middle class definition of failure and success which equates success with pecuniary achievement. To most subterranean artists, worldly success is not necessarily the same as artistic success. A creative artist can make a million dollars and be considered—or feel like—a failure. They also want to fight "a war of liberation against the residual Puritanism and production-oriented austerities of American life" (33). So sexual liberation and Dionysian freedom, to them, are weapons and forms of dissent to established middle-class morality instead of merely a way of having fun. In a word, a true subterranean feels no remorse about his divorce from the middle class, which is not a matter of alienation but enthusiastic choice.

This kind of freedom is reflected in a completely mutinous attitude toward life. Just as Sukenick points out, "An underground is neither necessarily a physical place nor a particular life style, but precisely this mutinous attitude. It is an attitude conspired in by dissidents inside the establishment and those at its fringes, without participating in the dependent duet with the middle class called alienation" (240). So opposite to the active pursuit of America Dream advocated by the mainstream values, staying in the underground, one has to know how to hang out. One learns to waste time, waste life, disrupting the countdown toward death implicit in the chronology of production, with the pleasure principle, something that middle-class existence at that time does not dare permit. In Greenwich Village, Bodenheim, for example, would go around and sell a redundancy of a poem for fifty cents just to buy a drink. Some people have a talent for this freedom, others learn. "It requires a certain amount of stupidity, which for those brought up to pursue middle-class ambitions, is often hard to master" (26). This stupidity is a kind of stagnancy to money and fame. In Sukenick's view, money and fame are potential hazards to freedom. That is why when faced with the success of his first novel *Up*, Sukenick does not feel joyful. Instead he is quite worried, "I must be doing something wrong" (Sukenick 1987:198).

However, we must note that their underground life style and dissimilation of identity construction are challenged by many threats. First of all, their freedom is usually achieved at the cost of material success. So the underground does not only have a romantic aspect but also the harsh aspects of poverty, isolation, bitterness and survival. Marilyn serves as a good example. When she is young, starlet-pretty and Bohemian-sexy, "looking at her you know she's the kind of woman who can have anything she wants. Except that the way she comes on is like she doesn't want anything" (60). She plays away her life. Then "no more than fifteen years later, after the last several acid-induced institutionalizations, Marilyn would be out of friends, money, and places to live" (41). So on one vagrant night she walks up to the roof and jumps. Iris Brody also jumps off the roof. So does Sonya OD'd. Dylan Thomas died in 1954 after years of suicidal drinking. Charlie Parker died in 1955 and Jackson Pollock got killed in a car accident. It is the case for so many underground artists. Their rejection of the mass market causes the mass market's rejection of them, which limits their income and leads to their poverty. Bill Welbourn, for example, writes a novel but never gets it published. Later he died in total poverty. For many Hippies, their desperation to pay for drugs and even bread make them sell whatever can be sold. When everything is sold, their bodies become the goods.

More challenges come from the mainstream society. The temptation of the mass market and mainstream is hard to resist. Although the underground try hard to resist commercialization, commercialization still penetrates the underground life. Stanley is one of the first merchants to recognize and exploit the commercial possibilities of the underground. Underground papers like *The East Village Other*, *The Berkeley Barb* and *Los Angeles Free Press*, begin to promote the underground culture and attract more readers. An underground photographer Fred McDarrah even starts a program of Rent-a-Beatnik for five dollars an hour, and makes it a thriving business.

The pressure and temptation also come from within the underground. The success of some underground artists exerts great influence not only on the underground but also on the mainstream. The Abstract Expressionists, for example, become so famous that soon the whole America, even the whole world begins to notice them. They set the standards and become the mainstream. Their achievements help fuzz the distinction between the art underground and the commercial mainstream. The popularity of Beats also changes the underground. When the Beats draw more and more public attention, tourists, merchandisers and real estate speculators begin to pour money into Bleecker Street. However, this does not bring any benefit to the underground, but intensify their plight instead. The rise of the rents drives them out of Bleecker Street to the poorer and cheaper Lower East Side.

The success of Abstract Expressionists and the Beats and their entering into the mainstream society inspire many underground artists. Faced with the temptation and pressure, some subterraneans want to change their identity construction strategies. They do not want to stay in poverty and enjoy freedom. Instead, they want to fight upward into the mainstream society. In Ronald Sukenick's point of view, "selling out" their identity is the way most of them will choose. "Selling out" is to give up one's artistic values for money. To Sukenick, to sell out is to be a shmuck. "A shmuck is somebody with a certain way of thinking, a combination of caution, conformity, and mercenary values. An idolater of Things, a consumer at the feet of the Golden Calf" (Sukenick 1987: 12). Sukenick particularly points out the difference between "selling" and "selling out". An artist can sell one's paintings, novels, poems and songs. But it does not really mean selling out.

Selling out means a divorcing of one's real self from a false but more marketable public self, or at least disguising one's real self in order to make the sale (Foley 1995:7).

In this way, the essence of selling out, in Sukenick's point of view, is the split between the real self and public self. "In the schizoid dialogue of the American psyche, the real self is Emersonian, passive, innocent, and spontaneous, while the public self needs to be aggressive, power oriented, and politic" (Sukenick 1987:98). The conflict between the real self and the public self is especially intense for artists and intellectuals. "I did not know yet that in America artists and intellectuals are necessarily different sorts of critters, committed to the schizy split that pits the real self against the public self, even the two selves are part of the same psyche... A public self, in so far as it is divorced from the emotional life, which it puts to one side in the interests of calculation, policy, and power, can register feeling of any kind only in a limited way" (Sukenick 1987:99). The mass media exacerbate the split. The public self of the artist is split from his real self. In consequence, the artists, as public figures, are split from their works. Excessive attention is paid to the public self of the artists while their real self is ignored. At that time, "poets reading are becoming more interesting to many than reading poetry, thanks to the reading circuit, so painters are becoming more interesting than paintings in an art world where the creative act is tending to displace the object created" (209). Jack Kerouac, the king of the Beats, for example, becomes more like a super star, with public attention focused on his life style rather than on his novels.

The popularity of the Beats, in fact, is partly due to the promotion of Allen Ginsberg, who holds a quite different opinion on the issue of "selling out". "Selling out is one of those cornball ideas that people who didn't have anything to do got hung up on. I wouldn't have minded doing it if I could find what to sell out to. Geniuses don't sell out, in the sense that genius bursts the bounds of either selling out or not selling out" (122). Faced with the commercial society, Ginsberg believes the best way is to risk corruption by the world, sell out and "transform shit to gold" (82). It shows his willingness to confront the commercial culture, immerse himself in impurity, and at the same time, stick to his real self.

Allen Ginsberg's practice represents the efforts of some underground artists who want to struggle between the mainstream and the underground and play a balance between them. In other words, they want to take advantage of both. Norman Mailer serves as another representative.

"Norman has enormous ambivalence", says Ed Fancher of Mailer. "First of all, he's in opposition. Second of all, he's a multimillionaire... He's very interested in money. He's very money oriented, he goes crazy" (110). Norman Mailer stands between the worlds of mainstream and anti-mainstream. On the one hand, Mailer is always quite aware of, or he pays much attention to the mainstream society or the marketplace. Sukenick once asks Seymour Krim if "selling out" means anything to Norman Mailer. Krim answers, "After *The Naked and the Dead*, unlike the rest of us, [Mailer] was always conscious of having been a best-selling writer, and will always be conscious of it. It became some kind of standard for him. I mean you could take literature all you wanted but he was very conscious of the power, of the reality of that, which does not come to most literary writers. So he always wanted to straddle those two worlds" (113). It's obvious that Mailer's pursuit of money and celebrity cannot be disconnected from his artistic pursuit. Mailer sets a model for many underground artists who want to stand between the worlds of the mainstream and the underground. Just as his biographer Hilary Mills points out, "If Mailer the failed novelist could not move the culture with his fictional imagination, he would make his own life a story that others would have to follow. It would inspire the underground army of similar souls which Mailer suddenly envisioned around him" (Sukenick 1987: 109).

However, this balance between the mainstream and anti-mainstream is by no means easy. Mailer once expresses tensions between intellectual excellence and ambition, between justice and success by the words, "one is a rebel or one conforms, one is a frontiersman in the Wild West of American night life, or else a Square cell, trapped in the totalitarian tissues of American society, doomed willy-nilly to conform if one is to succeed" (111). Mailer is both a frontiersman and a conformist, both an explorer of the Wild West and trapped in the tissues of American society and its compulsion to success.

In summary, the journey to Greenwich Village, to Ronald Sukenick, is a chance to observe the identity crisis of the subterraneans and their different identity construction. More important, it is also maturation for Ronald Sukenick himself, for the reason that he himself is one of the subterraneans and also that he is faced with identity crisis at that time. JR Foley points out the struggle of Sukenick, "the implied challenge for Sukenick was to avoid selling out self like a Warhol 'Superstar' on the one hand; avoid reducing self to a 'bitter clown' like Bodenheim and Joe Gould on the other; enjoy personal liberation, dealing honestly with all the consequences of that, pleasant and otherwise; and still, as a determined artist, complete important, innovative work... that won't make money" (Foley 1995: 13).

3.2 Surviving Law of Postmodernist Narratives

3.2.1 Death of the Novel

In the 20th century, people are faced with identity crisis, and the fiction also has to fight to redefine itself. The genre of fiction has been well-defined by the 19th century. In the 20th century, however, many writers begin to rebel against the traditional structures imposed by this form. Since the 1920s, most of the American novels have been marked by a conservative stability of form, while in other countries, such writers as Gide, Hesse, Beckett, Robbe-Grillet, Cortazar, Borges and Gombrowicz have achieved success and gained popularity with their narrative innovation. However, in the United States, the experiments by Patchen, Hawkes, Miller and Burroughs have to stay underground at that time. So Stephen Koch concludes, "our literature is idling in a period of hiatus: the few important writers of the earlier generations are dead, silent, or in their decline, while the younger generation has not yet produced a writer of unmistakable importance or even of very great interest. Nothing thus far has been heard at the highest levels except an eerie silence" (Koch 1967:5).

This infertility causes some literary theorists to question the relevancy of the novel and even to declare its "death". José Ortegay Gasset predicted the "death of the novel" in his book *Decline of the Novel* in 1925. Walter Benjamin expressed the same worry in his 1930 review *Krisis des Romans* (*Crisis of the Novel*). In the 1950s and 1960s, more critics and writers, including Gore Vidal, Roland Barthes, John Barth, Louis Rubin, Susan Sontag, Leslie Fiedler and Norman Podhoretz joined the proponents of the "death of the novel". John Barth, a representative of this voice, declared the exhaustion of literature in his essay "The Literature of Exhaustion" in 1967. He believes that the conventional modes of literary representation have been "used up". Ronald Sukenick is another strong voice in declaring the death of the novel. In his collection *The Death of the Novel and Other Stories*, he clearly states:

> Reality doesn't exist, time doesn't exist, personality doesn't exist. God was the omniscient author, but he died; now no one knows the plot, and since our reality lacks the sanction of a creator, there's no guarantee as to the authenticity of the received version... In view of these annihilations, it should be no surprise that literature also does not exist—how could it? There is only reading and writing, which are things we do, like eating and making love, to pass the time, ways of maintaining a considered boredom in the face of the abyss. (Sukenick 2003:41)

Sukenick does not make such a shocking statement to attract attention. In fact, it is Sukenick's diagnosis of the predicament of fiction in the 20th century. In his understanding, every aspect concerning fiction is faced with challenges and threats, from the reading of fiction, the shape of fiction, the material of fiction to the meaning of fiction. That is to say, fiction itself is faced with identity crises, which are so serious that they are threatening the survival of fiction.

First of all, "the very act of reading a book, starting at the top of the first page, moving from left to right, top to bottom, page after page to the end in a consecutive prearranged manner has become boring and restrictive" (Federman 1975: 9). To Ronald Sukenick, this traditional way of reading a book must be questioned, challenged and demolished. New and fresh reading experience, resulting from innovations in the writing itself, will attract more readers.

Second, the shape or the form of the novel is faced with crisis. Sukenick starts his novella *The Death of the Novel* with the words, "Fiction constitutes a way of looking at the world" (Sukenick 2003: 41). Fiction of realism reflects the conventional way of looking at the traditional world. The key idea of realistic fiction is mimicry. And the purpose is to make believe. In Sukenick's view, "the fairy tale of the 'realistic' novel whispers its assurance that the world is not mysterious, that it is predictable—if not to the characters, then to the author—that it is available to manipulation by the individual, that it is not only under control but that one can profit from this control. The key idea is verisimilitude: one can make an image of the real thing which, though not real, is such a persuasive likeness that it can represent our control over reality" (Sukenick 1985: 3). So the realistic fiction employs chronological time as the medium of a plotted narrative, an irreducible individual psyche as the subject of its characterization, and above all, the ultimate, concrete reality of things as the object and rationale of its description. And these conventions of realistic novels have dominated fiction writing for such a long time that the novel has been identified with realism. When one says about the novel, he or she always thinks of the realistic novel.

However, in the world of post-realism, all of these absolutes have become absolutely problematic. The world has changed, so has the way of looking at it.

> Life is never linear, that, in fact, life is chaos because it is never experienced in a straight, chronological line, then, similarly, linear and orderly narration is no longer possible. The pseudo-realistic novel sought to give a semblance of order to the chaos of life, and did so by relying on the well-made-plot which, as we now realize, has become quite inessential to fiction. The plot having disappeared, it is no longer necessary for the events of fiction to follow a logical, sequential pattern (in time and in space). (Federman 1975: 10)

In a word, in a changed world, such key elements in traditional novels as plot, character and chronology are no longer necessities in postmodern context. So when he declares the "death of the novel", what Sukenick really means is that traditional forms of the novel should be put to death. "I think that in its realistic forms it's just lost its credibility... people don't believe that it tells the truth about things" (Sukenick 1985:

59). The form of the traditional novel is a metaphor for a society that no longer exists, so the mimetic traditions of fiction should be dismantled. So Sukenick argues that "there's really no division between if I write a dream and if I write what happened yesterday.—it's all what I'm writing. To put it one way, it's all make-believe" (qtd. Bellamy 1974:56-57). Thus, the death of the forms of the novel means that the novel is moving into new forms.

Third, the material of fiction is also faced with great challenges in the changed world. On the one hand, Sukenick believes that readers' awareness of the fictiveness of fiction causes one of the crises of fiction. In an interview with Joe David Bellamy, Sukenick mentions that "one of the reasons people have lost faith in the novel is that they don't believe it tells the truth anymore, which is another way of saying that they don't believe in the convention of the novel. They pick up a novel and they know it's make-believe. So who needs it—go listen to the television news, right? Or read a biography... there is no difference between fantasy and realistic action. It's completely continuous—it's all made up" (Bellamy 1974:60).

On the other hand, what happens in the real world is even more fictive than fiction. Just as Raymond Federman points out,

> [that] fiction is no longer possible because real fiction happens, everyday, in the streets of our cities, in the spectacular hijacking of planes, on the Moon, in Vietnam, in China (when Nixon stands on the Great Wall of China), and of course on television (during the news broadcasts); that fiction has become useless and irrelevant because life has become much more interesting, much more incredible, much more dramatic than what the moribund novel can possibly offer. (Federman 1975:6)

Sukenick attributes this crisis to our changed understanding of reality. Sukenick insists that reality, as the locus of a priori set of social, cultural and physical facts, does not exist beyond our subjective perception of it. The reality is no longer objective existence, but a self-created subjectivity. Thus the old distinction between subjectivity and objectivity dissolves, so do the categories such as literature, history, philosophy and science. The distinction between fiction and nonfiction becomes problematic and even dissolves, which leads to the consequence that everything becomes fiction. With the death of God and the total authority, nothing is true and so everything becomes fiction. So it does not matter what one writes about: real or not.

Last, the meaning of fiction is forced to change. Sukenick believes that meaning is produced in the process of writing (and reading), not preexistent. "The new fiction will not attempt to be meaningful, trustful, or realistic; nor will it attempt to serve as the vehicle of a ready-made meaning. On the contrary, it will be seemingly devoid of any meaning, it will be deliberately illogical, irrational, unrealistic, non sequitur, and incoherent. And only through the joint efforts of the reader and the creator (as well as that of the characters and narrators) will a meaning possibly be extracted from the fictitious discourse" (Federman 1975: 13).

Not only every aspect of fiction is faced with crises and challenges, fiction also has to face the challenges from the outside. First, fiction has to differ itself from other media so as to define its own identity. People are now surrounded by all sorts of information coming to them through all kinds of media. The novel, on the other hand, does not have anything special to say to them. They know that they can get the same kind of things out of a television broadcast and the news or something like that. Just as mentioned before, identity is only conceivable in and through difference, fiction must construct its identity through its difference from other forms of media.

Still another crisis, Sukenick points out, is the institutionalization of fiction. The institutional aspects of American writing "range from the commercial pressures of authorship through professional reviewing, university teaching and academic canon-formation" (Klinkowitz 1987: 20). In Sukenick's view, the commercial pressure, among the institutional pressures, is the biggest threat to fiction writing, especially to innovative fiction writing. First, experimental novelists find it hard to get their works published because of the limited profit. It is almost impossible for writers to support themselves and their families on writing.

Moreover, commercial pressures from publishing houses, Sukenick points out, even threaten literature as a whole. Just as Adorno once points out that the culture industry "transforms art into commodities and people into complacent consumers" (qtd. Leitch 2001:1222), Sukenick laments that publishing is no longer a cultural institution but a business enterprise. Money becomes the "language" of the publishing industry. "Publishers are not just ordinary bosses; they are word bosses. They have enormous power to decide what language is good and what language is bad, and to back up those decisions by saturating the market with millions of copies of their books" (Sukenick 1979b:473). In this sense, the mass market is not only an economic entity, but also a political entity. Publishers determine what books can be sold, and in turn affect what books will be written. They set the public taste. Consequently, market values are disguised as literary values. In order to make money, the publishing industry standardizes language and form and provides an "anesthetic formula that is familiar and reassuring in order to appeal to the largest number of people (Sukenick 1985:55). So the writers are left in a vulnerable and powerless situation, especially the unconventional writers whose works are non-profitable and thus often rejected by the mass market. The institutional pressures kill the imaginative spirit of fiction, threatening the ideal of the writer as free spirit, demiurge and the critic of the zeitgeist.

In summary, fiction is now faced with the pressures from the outside society and also within fiction itself. Realizing the pressures fiction is faced with, Sukenick points out, "the form of fiction that comes down to us through Jane Austin, George Eliot and Hemingway is no loner adequate to capture our experience. Either the novel will change, or it will die" (Sukenick 1985:241-242). Obviously, innovation is the only way out.

3.2.2 The Survival of the Novel: Narrative Innovations

Under the pressure of survival, fiction is forced to change. The crises of fiction offer great opportunities for fiction innovation, as Sukenick believes, "if everything is impossible, then anything becomes possible" (Sukenick 2003: 8). As we are in a time when all the "paradigms" of fiction are called into question, in consequence we begin to see the development of a poetics of fiction. John Barth, after declaring "the exhaustion of the literature", also realizes that when the conventions and constraints of discourse fall apart, it is also a time for "the literature replenishment" (65-71).

So for the survival of fiction, a group of novelists indulge themselves in a tireless practice of experimental writing. That is what Klinkowitz identifies as a disruptive tendency in American fiction in the 1960s. Such writers as William Burroughs, William Gaddis, John Barth, Thomas Pynchon, Kurt Vonnegut, Donald Barthelme, Ronald Sukenick, Ishmael Reed, Steve Katz, Clarence Majors, Walter Abish and Robert Coover experiment in different ways to challenge the grand narrative of modernism. William Burroughs in his novel *Naked Lunch* uses fragmentary to replace central narrative arc and employs pastiche to fold in elements from popular genres such as detective fiction and science fiction. Thomas Pynchon in particular provides prime examples of playfulness, often including silly wordplay within a serious context. Intertextuality is another feature displayed in works by Margaret Atwood, Donald Barthelme, John Barth and Robert Coover. Kurt Vonnegut in his novel *Slaughterhouse-Five* interplays popular science fiction with wartime reportage.

In summary, the new styles of narratives possess the characteristics of disjunction, simultaneity, indeterminacy, irrationalism, anti-illusionism, self-reflexiveness, exaggerated structural patterning, the absence of plot, literary parodies, temporal and spatial dislocations, blurred boundaries of discourse and pastiche, which later are put into the broad category of postmodernism.

Ronald Sukenick, after realizing the crises of fiction, starts his narrative innovation from his first novel *Up*. To him, what an innovative novelist first should do is to deconstruct the conventions of traditional novels. Sukenick points out that "one of the main purposes of really good writing is to destroy other really good writing, to destroy all the old concepts and formulas that come out of the best of the past. You should destroy them lovingly and with great consciousness and awareness of them, but always with the end in mind of getting beyond them again" (qtd. LeClair and McCaffery 1974:282). The title of his most important theoretical essay collection *In Form: Digressions on the Act of Fiction* shows his effort to digress from the established and set road of fiction. In this collection, such essays as "Twelve Digressions Toward a Study of Composition", "Thirteen Digressions", "Fiction in the Seventies: Ten Digressions on Ten Digressions", "Eight Digressions on the Politics of the Language", "Nine Digressions on Narrative Authority", "Film Digression" and "The Finnegan Digression" present his unremitting efforts in breaking through the constraints of almost every aspect of fiction writing. In doing so, he intends to open up a new space. "It's like cutting a log in a new direction: a new grain opens up, literally a new content appears when you cut something in a new way from the way it usually gets cut. You see different things; words then begin to surrender their meanings in different ways and begin to reveal all that huge amount of accumulated wisdom that language contains from the whole history of the culture" (qtd. LeClair and McCaffery 1974:283).

In his first novel, *Up*, Ronald Sukenick sets in his narrative innovation, which he carries through his entire writing career. Though still far from perfect, *Up* is an excellent example of Sukenick's pursuit of new fiction. It's a piece of parody of realism with fragmented scenes. The novel has no identifiable plot, nor story line, nor chronological events, nor causes and results. Time in *Up* is not story-time at all but is ultimately a matter of pagination. Time's passage is marked by page numbers which, in the absence of chronology, are the only identifiable reference points throughout the narrative. Reminiscences, fantasies and improvisations follow one another in an unpredictable order and merge in a logically discontinuous current. It has no discursive or logical meaning, but that is exactly what life is about. No traditional hard and fast characters. Wide ranges of writing styles are mixed in the novel, including autobiographical complications, fiction within fiction, journalistic styles and pornographic sketches. Sukenick also starts his typographical play—letters packed together or loosely scattering in the page.

Later, Ronald Sukenick himself summarizes the characteristics of his new fiction as fiction with "no plot, no story, no character, no chronological sequence, no verisimilitude, no imitation, no allegory, no symbolism, no subject matter, no 'meaning' [...] Bossa Nova is non-representational—it represents itself" (Sukenick 1985:211).

From this, we can see that Sukenick's first target of innovation is plot, the chronological development of events. In most of Sukenick's novels, such as *Up*, *Out*, *98.6*, and *Mosaic Man*, no traditional story lines such as exposition, conflict, rising action, climax, falling action and resolution can be clearly identified. In the novel *Up*, the long conversation between Bernie, a traditional novelist and Ronnie Sukenick, an experimental writer, reveals the clash between the belief of traditional fiction and narrative innovation of

Ronald Sukenick, the author himself. Accordingly, it deserves a long quotation here:

> "I don't want to discourage you, but actually I think the whole book may have been a mistake from the beginning."
> "No reason why that should discourage me."
> "Seriously, it doesn't go anywhere. I mean I'm not antediluvian to require that a novel have a plot, but this is just a collection of disjointed fragments. You don't get anywhere at all. Where's the control, where is the tension? You can do a lot better than this, Ronnie."
> "Thanks," I said.
> "For one thing, the chronology is completely screwed up... But this is just the thing you see. The reader doesn't know this. You can't do that sort of thing."
> "Why not? In books one isn't obliged to pursue the banality of chronological order. What the fuck I'm not writing a timetable."
> "You could at the very least indicate an underlying chronology."
> "What for? It's just a sequence of words. The only thing that matters is the order of revelation in print."
> "Sure. If you want to forgo verisimilitude, which unfortunately happens to be the essence of fictive writing."
> "Nuts. Why should we have to suspend disbelief? It's all words and nothing but words." (Sukenick 1968:222-223)

The conversation reveals that the traditional chronological sequence of events is no longer a necessity of fiction to Sukenick. Verisimilitude, the essence of traditional fiction writing, should also be got rid of as the purpose of fiction is no longer to suspend disbelief. Instead, Sukenick makes the creative process of writing a theme of his fiction, revealing its fictitious characteristics. Sukenick further illustrates in his collection of essays *In Form*: "Not plot, but ongoing incident; not characterization, but consciousness struggling with circumstance; not social realism, but a sense of situation; and so on" (Sukenick 1985:243).

Sukenick's conception of New Fiction also deletes the notion of character, another important element in traditional novels. Most characters in Sukenick's novels possess no consistent or identifiable traits. Sometimes they are devoid of any substantial existence or identity. Instead, they are just names on the page, "Cardboard people walking around as if they were flesh and blood" (Sukenick 1968:9). Different from traditional characters who possess distinct physiological and psychological features, characters in Sukenick's novels are textual constructs rather than representations of real-life humans.

In the novel *Up*, Ronnie observes people around him, "The people seemed indefinite, moving fluidly, fish in a tank. As they spoke their faces underwent exaggerations, deformations, their figures shrank, grew, metamorphosed, they became extensions of themselves... Objects themselves turn to molecules contained in shapes of couch, piano, table, fluid in the drift of time, allowing Ronnie to perceive for a moment the slow millenarian flow of one thing into another" (Sukenick 1968:298). LeClair and McCaffery summarize the features of the characters in Sukenick's novels as, "Like clouds, your characters are always shifting into different shapes, different beings, with different names, contradictory attributes, and so on" (LeClair & Macaffery 1974:294). Rex, the narrator in the novel *Out*, for example, changes his name to Carl, Donald, Harrold, Nick, Tomy, Henry Aldrich, Ronald, Roland, Sycamore, M. T. Focks and R. The frequent changes of names confuse the reader, which leads to the fact that proper names, which conventionally have unambiguous referents, cannot designate a person any longer. Sukenick points out that "If you drop the idea of imitation as the mainstay of fiction, then the idea that you need 'characters' drop away pretty quickly. You realize that characterization is always simply a part of the text or part of the consciousness of the writer, depending on at what point you wish you to start talking about character" (qtd. LeClair and McCaffery 1974:295).

Sukenick's deletion of the notion of character owes to his keen awareness that people nowadays are less well defined, more fragmented in comparison with people in the previous century. In modern society, people's character traits can be drastically changed by drugs, brainwashing, the interchangeability of people and also by the information that comes at us. "Maybe people are much more fluid and amorphous than the realistic novel would have us believe" (Bellamy 1974: 62). Consequently, the traditional character structure will eliminate certain possibilities that come from the character, subconscious or unconscious. So, Sukenick believes that what a novelist should do is to "be able to face all the possibilities in my own personality and come to some kind of agreement with them and then live with them, but in the meantime my drive is to dissolve character. I think that's not only a need on my part but I presume to think that that's also a cultural need for a lot of people, for the culture in general perhaps" (Bellamy 1974: 64).

In fact, Sukenick's unremitting efforts in innovating the plot, character and other elements in fictive narratives are made for the purpose of freeing experience from preformulated stories, providing a dynamic narrative space wherein author, character and reader can renegotiate a favorable rapport with reality, which, to Sukenick, is the essence of fiction.

Ronald Sukenick is not only trying to find a solution to the crises of fiction in his practice of fiction writing, he, as a theorist, also endeavors to establish a new rhetoric of narrative. His theoretical essays, gathered in two collections, *In Form: Digressions on the Act of Fiction* (1985) and *Narralogues: Truth in Fiction* (2000) show his efforts to redefine fiction and to develop a new rhetoric of narrative.

Sukenick starts from the redefinition of fiction. "A fiction", to Sukenick, "is not an ideological formulation of belief but a statement of a favorable rapport with reality" (qtd. Bellamy 1974:3). Realism considers fiction as representation and a form of make-believe, which, to Sukenick "if not palpably stupid, is certainly roundabout and, restrictive" (Sukenick 2000:3). What Sukenick wants to do is to free fiction from the obligations of mimesis. "Fiction is no longer an imitation of the supposedly real, but has a reality in itself whose purpose is to reflect on experience to arrive at truth, however contingent" (Sukenick 2000:3).

If the purpose of fiction is to reflect on experience so as to arrive at truth, then, the narrative is "a mode of understanding that uniquely is quick enough, mutable enough, and flexible enough to catch the stream of experience, including our experience of the arts" (Sukenick 2000: 1). So the characteristics of narratives, to Sukenick, are "agonistic, sophistic, sophisticated, fluid, unpredictable, rhizomatic, affective, inconsistent and even contradictory, improvisational, and provisional in its argument toward contingent resolution that can only be temporary" (Sukenick 2000:1).

In accordance with the fluid, unpredictable and improvisational narrative, the form of fiction should also be a dynamic, rather than an inert element of composition. Form is not given, but an object of invention. More important, the form is not the opposite to the content, but part of the content. The distinction between form and content falls away, since it is the process of thought that creates the experience, which otherwise could have no prior existence. So form is not pre-determined, but invented only in the process of composition itself. "Form is when you look back and you see your footprints in the sand" (Sukenick 1973:164). Sukenick believes that "the job of narrative fiction is not to record some preexisting reality but to contribute to the ongoing process of cultural building in and through the process of writing itself" (Sukenick 1985:79-80).

From this, we can see that "generation" is an essential concept in both Sukenick's novels and his theories. According to Sukenick, fiction is "generated by the activity of composition in an ongoing interchange between the mind and the page" (Sukenick 1985: 8). Unlike the realistic novels which try to reflect on "preexisting or presiding idea", generative fiction is "a form of invention, a way of bringing into being that which it did not previously exist" (Sukenick 1985:8). What is emphasized in this generative fiction theory is not the final product of discursive process, but rather process of narrative production. Victor Shklovsky points out, "in art, it is our experience of the process of composition that counts, not the finished product" (qtd. Scholes 1974:84). A writer's work is like an ongoing conversation with himself. Sukenick's generation is in common with action painting and Williams Olson's idea of composition as an open field. It is "a nexus of various kinds of energy, image and experience" (Sukenick 1985:11). In generative theory of composition, there is no priori form—form is generated by the currents of energy that interact on the page. It is the activity of writing which provokes the activity of invention in presenting it with problems, in imposing directions on it, in endlessly pushing it ahead.

If fiction is, to Sukenick, the recording of the truth of experience, then, fiction writing is the truth of the page. The term "the truth of the page", put forward by Sukenick, means that "there's a writer sitting there writing the page. There's a dictum of Burroughs' which goes something like 'the writer shouldn't be writing anything except what's in his mind at the moment of writing,' which means to me the same thing as the truth of the page... I'm not writing illusions—I'm not writing about a fantasy that I've had, if it's fantasy, but I'm having a fantasy and writing it down. In fact, the act of writing it down is part of the fantasy... like sleeping is part of dreaming" (Sukenick 1985: 25). The truth of the page implies the spontaneous and improvised moment of creation, which suggests the influence from the abstract expressionists, the Beat Generation and the Black Mountain poets. With the emphasis on the process of narrative production, fiction writing becomes continuous with the writer's experience. Moreover, the writer is clearly at liberty to use whatever material comes into his head as he is writing, including the data of his own experience.

More important, the purpose of the truth of the page is to force the reader to activate and reactivate their imagination as they are forced to recognize the reality of the reading situation as the writer points to the reality of the writing situation. The involvement of the reader is heavily demanded in Sukenick's New Fiction. The reader plays the role of co-author, which may ultimately lead to an imaginative reinvention of the world and self. Sukenick quite agrees with Robbe-Grillet's famous saying: "The main didactic job of the contemporary novelist is to teach the reader how to invent his world" (Federman 1975: 41).

To summarize, Ronald Sukenick is keenly aware of identity crisis faced by fiction, and through his writing career, he has been making protracted and unremitting efforts to help fiction seek new identity. Narrative innovation, to Ronald Sukenick is the only way to make fiction survive its identity crises.

Chapter 4

Entropy Law: Fluidity and Dissolution

4.1 Entropy Law of Identity in *Out* and *98.6*

The term "entropy" was coined in 1850 by Rudolf Clausius, a German physicist. It constitutes the essence of the second law of thermodynamics, which along with the first law of thermodynamics comprises the most fundamental laws of physics.

The first law of thermodynamics expresses the principle of conservation of energy, stating that energy can be transformed (changed from one form to another), but cannot be created or destroyed. The total quantity of energy in the universe remains constant. The second law of thermodynamics, on the other hand, concerns the principle of the degradation of energy, stating that the quality of this energy is degraded irreversibly.

In 1850, the studies of Lord Kelvin (William Thomson, 1st Baron Kelvin of Largs, 1824-1907), Carnot (Nicolas Léonard Sadi Carnot 1796-1832) and Clausius (Rudolf Julius Emmanuel Clausius, 1822-1888) reveal that there is a hierarchy among the various forms of energy and an imbalance in their transformations. It explains the irreversible change that physical, chemical and electrical energy can be completely changed into heat, but the reverse cannot be fully accomplished without the outside help or without an inevitable loss of energy. It is not the real loss of energy, but that some energy becomes unavailable for producing work. Entropy, then, is introduced as a measure of the unavailability of a system's energy to do work. Thus, the two laws of thermodynamics are closely interwoven and can actually be expressed in one sentence: The total energy content of the universe is constant and the total entropy, the non-usable energy, is constantly increasing.

Two important characteristics of entropy are noteworthy. The first is the concept of irreversibility. The entropy of a closed system always increases. The final entropy must be greater than the initial entropy for an irreversible process. That is to say, in a closed system, you cannot finish any real physical process with as much useful energy as you have to start with—some is always wasted. In any transformation of energy from one form to another, useful energy is lost irreversibly. Entropy describes the degradation of energy to perform work. It is a measure of the degree to which energy has lost the capacity to perform useful work. This irreversibility results in an important change in people's attitude towards time. The Newtonian physics believes in the continuing laws of energy in the universe and the continuing laws of cause and effect. From this perspective, the past and the future are identical in essence. With the transition from the Newtonian reversible time to the irreversible time implied by the law of entropy, the end of the world becomes inevitable from the scientist's point of view. Time can only flow in one direction: the arrow of time can only move from the dead past to the non-existing future.

Another important characteristic of entropy is disorder. As mentioned above, with every transformation there is a loss of energy, and an increase of entropy. As energy in a closed system dissipates, it moves from a higher level of concentration and order to a less concentrated, more disordered state, until the system reaches equilibrium or heat death. In this sense, entropy signifies the dilution and the randomization of energy. So entropy is also used to mean disorganization or disorder. J. Willard Gibbs, the 19th century American theoretical physicist, called it "mixedupness". Lots of disorder means high entropy, while order means low entropy. Entropy is a measure of disorder or randomness in a closed system. And entropy is always increasing. The increasing tendency of entropy is illustrated in the famous statement made by Rudolf Clausius, "The entropy of the universe tends to a maximum". In other words, if entropy is associated with disorder and if the entropy of the universe is headed towards maximum, then the universe is headed towards maximal "disorder". The statement may sound contradictory to the existence of spontaneous order in the universe. It is true that in a closed system, the entropy is in the tendency of increasing. However, locally, entropy can be lowered by external action. But this local decrease of entropy and increase of order can only be possible at the expense of an entropy increase in the surroundings, which leads to more disorder.

Lois Parkinson Zamora summarizes the two characteristics of law of entropy in a less scientific but more descriptive way,

> The law of entropy describes the gradual death of the universe... Entropy refers to the statistical probabilities of various molecular distributions in a thermodynamic system to move from the least probable to the most probable molecular distribution, that is, from a state of molecular organization capable of producing work to a state of random, disorganized, uniform molecular movement. Entropy reaches its maximum when the position and velocities of molecules are distributed uniformly and completely at random. Any spontaneous changes in the system will be in the direction of increasing entropy, of increasing randomness and disorganization: The law of entropy requires that the total amount of entropy in the system increase. At the end

> of the entropic process, heat energy will be nontransferable because everything will contain an equal quantity of energy. This equilibrium, which represents the maximum molecular disorder, the greatest molecular homogeneity, is called heat death. (Zamora 1989:53-54)

Entropy, as one of the most fundamental concepts of physical science, exerts far-reaching influence on other scientific fields ranging from cosmology to chemistry, from anthropology to information theory. More important to us is the introduction of the concept of entropy into sociology. Entropy, as a metaphor of chaos, disorder or dissipation of energy, has entered such social science fields as economy and psychology, and even the imaginative world of literature. Writers like Pynchon, William Gaddis, John Barth, Kurt Vonnegut, and Isaac Asimov have introduced the concept of entropy in their novels and broadened its meaning from thermodynamic sense to postmodern situation of all systems. Set in the year 2061, "The Last Question", a marvelous sci-fi short story by Isaac Asimov, published in November 1956, is about the development of a supercomputer called Multivac and its relationship with humanity through the course of millennia. The computer Multivac is repetitively asked the same question by different characters: "How can the net amount of entropy of the universe be massively decreased", which is the same as how can the death of the universe and the end of Humankind be averted. However, in each of the cases, Multivac falls dead and silent, unable to offer any answers.

Entropy is a more important metaphor to Thomas Pynchon. His short story "Entropy" (1958), expresses the process how Pynchon develops the concept of entropy from thermodynamic perspective to his understanding of the chaotic, disorder world of American society. Set in an apartment building in Washington D. C., on a rainy day early in 1957, the story describes two different scenes. In a third-floor apartment, Meatball Mulligan and a strange group of friends and interlopers are in the fortieth hour of a break-the-lease party, which is a scene complete with drunken revelers, much debris and loud music. In an apartment upstairs tenant Callisto lives in a kind of sealed hothouse luxuriating in plants and protected from the wintry weather outside, where it has been, the reader learns, precisely thirty-seven degrees Fahrenheit for three days running. Mulligan's effort to minimize the chaos of the party and establish the order is compared with Callisto's attempt to save the dying bird by transferring his temperature to it. Entropy, a measurement in heat transmission is extended to a metaphor of ambiguity, redundancy, irrelevance and even leakage that destroy human communication.

Entropy is not merely a metaphor in Pynchon's novels; it can be regarded as the main organizing principle and his basic philosophical assumption in his masterpiece *The Crying of Lot 49*. William Gaddis, another important postmodern American writer, has also introduced the concept of entropy in his four novels *JR*, *The Recognitions*, *Carpenter's*

Gothic and *A Frolic of His Own* to explore the conflict between order and disorder of postmodern world. Peter Freese in his book *From Apocalypse to Entropy and Beyond: The Second Law of Thermodynamics in Post-War American Fiction*, and Lois Parkinson Zamora in his book *Writing the Apocalypse: Historical Vision in Contemporary U. S. and Latin American Fiction* explore the development of entropy from a scientific concept to a cultural metaphor in the novels of John Updike, Ken Kesey, Stanley Elkin, Susan Sontag, Thomas Pynchon, Donald Barthelme, William Gaddis, Don DeLillo, Russell Banks and Charles Bowden.

Ronald Sukenick is not included in their lists, because Sukenick does not directly employ entropy as his subject matter, nor does he transfer it into structural organization. However, Sukenick has transformed the concept of entropy to suit his own philosophies, particularly in his characterization. He employs the Entropy Law of Identity, through which he develops a whole spectrum of presentational techniques which allow him to project his concepts of multiple personality and dissolved identity. His fiction, on almost every level out, denies the dictates of fixed and coherent identity, so as to create tentative interrelations between sets of random elements which dissolve before they become hypostasized as ontological unities. Just like entropy indicates that the increasing disorder of energy moves at random within a closed system, finally arrives at total inertia, Entropy Law of identity illustrates that the characters change their identity without any reason or logical progression, finally arrive at non-identity of characters—characters neither materialized as a stable center of personal reference nor occupy a fixed position. When characters start their journey in the fiction, the stable traits in their identity, beneficial to the communication, begin to lose in the process. At the same time, the fluid and changeable traits, the entropy in the communication are bound to increase. The identity possesses the characteristics of fluidity and interchangeability and finally the dissolution of all identities.

Entropy Law of identity is best illustrated by a scene at the end of the novel *Up*, when at a large party, the narrator Ronnie is observing all the people around him:

> The people seemed indefinite, moving fluidly, fish in a tank. As they spoke their faces underwent exaggerations, deformations, their figures shrank, grew, metamorphosed, they became extensions of themselves. Bernie lectures thick-lipped static finger gesture, Otis' comic face turns tragic comic tragic, Slim's bowlegged jeans from behind flexing pumping posting, Etta's pale plump cheeks twitch, dilate, Len shifts through the crowd in an aimless dance, Slade freezes in the bleak pose of a Renaissance monument, Nancy and Marietta talk earnestly within a nimbus of light, their bodies merge, coalesce in curves, Mancy, Narietta. Objects themselves turn to

> molecules contained in shapes of couch, piano, table, fluid in the drift of time, allowing Ronnie to perceive for a moment the slow millenarian flow of one thing into another. (Sukenick 1968:298)

Sukenick's concept of self, as Jerzy Kutnik points out, "has little to do with the modern idea of the individual as encapsulated ego. Personality for him is by no means stable and absolute but is indefinite, changeable, and fluid" (Kutnik 1996:70). Characters in Sukenick's novels, like particles, during the development of plot, become very loosely conceived, devoid of any substantial existence or identity. They are just names on the page. They are just "cardboard people walking around as if they were flesh and blood" (Sukenick 1968:9). Consequently these people can be shuffled like a deck of cards, as evidenced in the constant name changing game in his novels *Out* and *98.6*.

Sukenick's characterization is based on his keen observation of postmodern situation in American society. The increased speed of the society, rapid technological changes, superfluous print and media and rapid exchanging information supply too many messages about who we are. The postmodern world is full of meanings that it risks saturating the self. The self in the society is under the siege of different images and meanings, so that the self feels himself pulled in myriad directions at the same time. He feels it hard to manage a life that seems to spin out of control at great speed in all directions. So it becomes increasingly difficult to sustain a sense of unity and constancy. "For everything we 'know to be true' about ourselves, other voices within respond with doubt and even derision. This fragmentation of self-conceptions corresponds to a multiplicity of incoherent and disconnected relationships. These relationships pull us in myriad directions, inviting us to play such a variety of roles that the very concept of an 'authentic self' with knowable characteristics recedes from view. The fully saturated self becomes no self at all. To contrast with the modern and romantic approaches to the self, I shall equate the saturating of self with the condition of postmodernism" (Gergen 1991:6-7). To explain in other words, the very concept of personal essences is thrown into doubt. The essential and foundational understanding of identity is challenged and replaced by a plethora of possibilities for what we can be. "Each reality of self gives way to reflexive questioning, irony, and ultimately the playful probing of yet another reality. The center fails to hold" (Gergen 1991:7). So selves are in continuous construction and reconstruction, never completed, never fully coherent. In the process of construction, the self has to fight against the entropy that prevents a stable and coherent unity of identity.

The construction of identity, thus, involves the counter-entropic struggle. And the fight must be fought on two fronts: first against the total chaos which negates distinction, differentiation and form; and second, against the drab oneness of uniform motion and eventual homogeneity which a rigid society wants to impose on everything and anything.

Sukenick, thus, points out, "I think it's true in contemporary life that the mind of the larger social unit, the Zeitgeist, is becoming more and more cohesive, whereas the sense of individual identity is becoming more and more diffuse" (Sukenick 1985:132). People are much more fluid and amorphous.

Entropy Law of identity is best illustrated in the novels *Out* and *98.6*. Contrary to the traditional way of characterization—characters develop consistent and identifiable traits with the unfolding of the plot, characters in these two novels, can be called "stream of identities" in that they are always shifting into different shapes, different beings, with different names, and even contradictory attributes, just like clouds. In the process of their identity construction, with the increase of entropy, the consistent and identifiable traits in them are losing, and the changeable and fluid traits are increasing, which leads to non-identity—the dissolution of identity. Thus, Entropy Law of identity is illustrated from two aspects: stream of identities and non-identiy.

4.1.1 Stream of Identities

Out, the second novel by Ronald Sukenick, published in 1973, is an on-the-road novel. The main plot of the novel *Out* is a bizarre trip from New York to California, in which the main character moves west, meeting different people, having temporary associations with them. It is also his journey of constructing identity, and author's journey of exploring fiction writing.

Three strands of the plot are implied in the novel. First, a secret organization, in which the main male character is involved, is carrying out a mission which remains undisclosed to its members as well as the reader until the end of the novel. Second, the protagonist travels across the United States, in which many other characters are involved. Third, there is a biographical narrative involving scenes from a childhood, events at a college and a count-culture festival.

In the novel, Sukenick shows a sharp contrast between the journeys. On the one hand, the physical journey of the hero is clearly identifiable so that one can make a geographical reconstruction of the journey. The main character starts from New York City, moves to Indiana, across the Mississippi to Rochester, to Minnesota, to the Corn Palace in Mitchell, South Dakota, Kadoka, then to Black Hills, Harney Peak, Mount Rushmore, Red Desert in Southern Wyoming, to Dinosaur and Panguitch, Utah, to Las Vegas, Santa Anita, to Los Angeles and finally into the Pacific Ocean. The exact locations of the places in the novel offer the reader a realistic picture of the setting of the story.

On the other hand, the journey of his identity construction is not so identifiable. To be exact, "the fact that in all three of these 'strands of plot', it is difficult to say just who conspires, travels, or is initiated and how many people are involved points to the central problem of character in the novel: *Out* only has few characters that are identifiable as such" (Heise 2003:78). Contrary to the traditional way of characterization which develops consistent and identifiable characters with the unfolding of plots, Sukenick's characterization aims at a purposeful disintegration of the consistent and identifiable traits of characters. He uses Entropy Law of identity. During the process of identity construction, identity, just like energy moving within a closed system, is losing more and more stable and fixed traits which are beneficial to the communication. At the same time, the fluid and changeable traits, the entropy in the communication are increasing, which leads to the dissolution of all identities.

Entropy Law of identity is best illustrated by a strategy Sukenick employs in his fiction—"stream of identities". "Stream of identities" means that the characters in fiction change their identities randomly and freely, never consolidate to a fixed identity. In his novel *Out*, "stream of identities" is displayed through the stream of names, as names are important symbols of identities. Unlike traditional novels, in which the development of the plot reveals the essence of the characters to the reader, the novels of Sukenick, especially the novel *Out*, have the characters constitute themselves as characters by concealing who they are (even from themselves). Proper names, which conventionally have unambiguous referents and represent unified notions of self, cannot designate a person any longer. They are only signifiers without a concomitant signified.

At the very beginning of the novel, the first appearance of the protagonist begins to shake the reader's expectation of names' stable referent. "Of course we don't have real names, we have aliases. Today I'm Harrold. Two r's. Tomorrow I might be someone else" (Sukenick 1973: 2). The reader realizes that even when we get the name of the protagonist, we cannot be sure about who he is. The self-introduction of the protagonist predicts the following changes. The protagonist declares the falsity of a consistent name, or in other words, the falsity of consistent identity, and other characters in the novel also join in. Carl, for example, admits, "I have something to confess to you Carl isn't my real name. That's because I'm not real. I'm only trying to be real. Like a character in a novel.... You're real but you have no personality. It's all personality that's why you're a flop. You change all the time nobody knows where you're at not even you" (Sukenick 1973:26).

Sukenick first uses this meta-fictional technique to show the reader the falsified connections between a name and a character. Then "stream of names" is introduced to further confuse the reader the connections between a name and a character, or an identity.

The protagonist first identifies himself by the name of Harrold, and then falls into a stream of changes of names. He changes into Rex, Carl, Donald, Henry Aldrich, Ronald, Ton Sukenick, Nick, Roland Sycamore, R. Arr and at last R. The frequent changes of names confuse the reader, making it hard to follow. What is particularly interesting is that the protagonist's changing names turn out to be partial spellings, abbreviations or anagrams from Ronald Sukenick. When he first introduces himself as Harrold, he is careful to specify "Two r's" (2). The letter "r", doubled and pointed out, indicates the author's name Ronald. Also the letters "ro" and "ld" form the first and last part of Ronald. Then Harrold is changed to Rex, whose first initial of "R" again suggests the author. The third name is Carl, whose "ar" and perhaps "l" and "C/k" also indicate the author. Donald, which is similar to Ronald, appears as the fourth name. He in turn becomes Henry Aldrich, the name of a radio character. Henry Aldrich contains "r's" and "ald" which are in Ronald, and "ich"—German, which is like "ick" in Sukenick. Then Henry is changed into Ronald, who becomes Ton Sukenick and then Nick—which is part of Sukenick. Nick returns to Ron and then moves to Roland Sycamore. Roland is an anagram for Ronald, and "Syc" is similar to "Suk". The protagonist next becomes R. Arr—which suggests the original Harrold. Then he simplifies to R. R, the final name of the protagonist, together with S, the finial name of Sailor indicates the first initials of Ronald Sukenick—the author's name. In this sense, the journey of the protagonist's seeking for his identity is indeed that of the author's.

Just as the main male character metamorphoses into various names and letters, so does the main female character. President Nixon becomes Ova, who then changes into the names of Velma, Nadia, Trixie, Mary, Alma, Nada and Pixie. President Nixon joins male and female; and Nixon, Trixie, Pixie and Nick are all part of Sukenick.

Sometimes, the transformation is explicit within the span of one or two sentences: "Hi, says Rex. I'm Carl" (Sukenick 1973:15). Rex changes into Carl. Sometimes, the transformation occurs in longer passages, which poses difficulty for the reader. The changes of the protagonist, which cover the whole novel, serve as a good example. Sometimes the transformation is commented upon by observers within the novel: "You're real but you have no personality... you change all the time nobody knows where you're at not even you" (26). Sometimes, the changes are quite ambiguous and confusing. In Chapter 9, Carl meets a blond man, wearing a business suit.

> My name is Carl says the blond man. What's yours.
> Donald says Carl.
> Hi there Donald. Carl extends his hand and Donald shakes it.
> Hello Carl says Donald. (22)

Here Carl gives up his name and changes into Donald. The name Carl goes to another person. To make the names more confusing, the novel has several Ova's and Carl's. Heise calls this "nomad names" which means action is carried out by names that appear to migrate from body to body. "Sukenick's nomad names attach themselves to whatever human 'body' happens to appear, and it soon becomes impossible for the reader to remember the series of transformations that each character has undergone (which include, sometimes, transformations of age and gender) and consequently, to distinguish individuals from each other" (Heise 2003:79). Like particles that move randomly in a closed system, in which the increase of entropy leads to the increase of randomness and disorder, characters in the novel move and transform, which leads to disorder and confusion.

"The difficulty in distinguishing the characters is heightened by incidents that occur several times, but that involve—or seem to involve—different persons; secret meetings, robberies, seductions, coded messages, stays at 'New Vacancy' chain motels, hitchhikers on the road, and confrontations with the police recur in almost identical form. This replacement of well-defined figures by an inventory of proper names, incidents, and tag phrases that are frequently recirculated has led one critic to speak of a 'stream of character' in the novel" (Heise 2003:79). In Chapter 7, for example, a character named Nick driving a camper picks up a couple called Scott and Ova, makes love to Ova. Then, in Chapter 6, Carl meets a couple also called Scott and Ova. It is hard to tell whether they are the same couple or not.

Another factor that makes the distinguishing of characters more difficult is that Sukenick's characters are like comic strip characters: they are two-dimensional or flat. Most of them have no "personality" but are only names or even letters of names/words. They are lack of distinctive physiological or psychological features. Sukenick does not give any description of the protagonist, nor of other characters. We do not know their heights, weights, ages, nor do we know any of their facial features. The lack of distinguishable features makes the transformation from one name to another easier. Moreover, the absence of motivation and coherent sequences of action makes characters in the novel more indistinguishable. The novel starts with a meeting in which Harrold and President Nixon are involved. Carrying sticks of dynamite, they are supposed to carry out a mission which they themselves do not know. Nor does the author make it clear in the later development of plots. In this case, where they go, when they go and why they go are mysteries to themselves and also to the reader. No coherent sequences exist. "In fact, it is one of the puzzling characteristics of the book that almost anybody can turn into anybody else" (Putz 1979:178). In other words, characters in Sukenick's fiction are persistently described as textual constructs rather than representations of real-life humans. In this sense, the characters turn out to be pseudo-figures who move in and out of the story, merge with one another, come into existence at the drop of their names, and then disappear never to reappear again. Since they change constantly, it is impossible to tell who is who at a given moment and who he or she will be a moment later. The original pair in Chapter 9 is Rex and Ova. But soon they become Carl and Velma after they introduce themselves that way.

In Sukenick's novel, fixed identities or even overlapping identities cannot be found. Instead, characters can intermingle freely, merge with each other, or drop their tentatively fixed identities at random. To be exact, they are continuously created and recreated on the various levels implied. Sukenick's strategy of derealizing characters is to foreground his belief that human identity is a fluid process of constant becoming rather than a fixed entity. The purpose, on the one hand, is to challenge the traditional way of characterization which aims at creating fully rounded, psychological plausible human figures. Sukenick expresses his rejection of traditional characterization in an interview, "If you drop the idea of imitation as the mainstay of fiction, then the idea that you need 'characters' drops away pretty quickly" (qtd. LeClair & McCaffery 1974:295).

On the other hand, Sukenick believes that his representation of characters reflects tendencies in postmodern society. The self-saturating society makes characters less stable and less defined. Sukenick claims that the notion of "character" as a distinctive individual can no longer adequately reflect contemporary social realities,

> The other side of this... is the sense I have that individuals' personalities are becoming less and less important and less defined... It seems that people now, for better or for worse and for good reasons usually, are less defined—more "laid back," as they say, "going with the flow" and all that. I'm using these clichés on purpose to show that people think about personality, even their own, in this way. I also like to believe that you can have a more flattened out, flowing, less rigidly defined personality that is still not necessarily uninvolved on its own terms... man's most essential untouchable element—all that has been eroded by the sense of collectivity, by the sense that people's character traits can be drastically changed by drugs, by brainwashing, by the interchangeability of people in corporate slots, by the rate at which information comes at us. It's just very difficult to absorb and respond to so much information while having a hardened, brittle personality circumference, as opposed to one that is porous. (qtd. LeClair & McCaffery 1974:295-296)

The novel *Out* illustrates Sukenick's belief that identity in postmodern society turns to be more fluid and interchangeable under the influence of drugs, brainwashing and communication. The novel *98. 6*, on the other hand, centers on the character's development during the communication with environment. *98. 6* is very much a sequel to *Out*. In *Out*, the protagonist swiftly moves across the country, from east to west, leaves the land and sails out into the ocean and sky. But in *98. 6* he slows down and stops, returning to the land. Much more than in *Out*, Sukenick stresses the connections that the novelist has with the land, society and the cosmos.

98.6 consists of three parts, "Frankenstein", "The Children of Frankenstein" and "Palestine" respectively. The first part "Frankenstein" describes a dystopian nightmare of America in the 1960s and early 1970s. Frankenstein, the monster created by Mary Shelley, is employed as a metaphor for the United States to demonstrate that America/Frankenstein is a monster of cruelty, violence and murder. Sukenick collages the cruelties of various times with significant emphasis on Maya, Aztec cultures and postmodern society. He describes the life of a group of individuals in contemporary Frankenstein, a sort of fictional coastal California. They are in the grip of violent culture and lose their real self. The anonymity of the narrator, to some extent, illustrates that he is devoid of identity.

The children of Frankenstein, tired of the violent culture of Frankenstein, decide to flee the Frankenstein of their parents to seek health and life. Rising out of a sense of cultural failure, the children of Frankenstein go back to nature in an attempt to reenact the myth of Eden and return to their beginnings and innocence. They try to seek and reestablish their identity in their communication with nature. They build a commune that is integrated into nature. The commune house they build, called "the Monster", looks different from anything they have seen in its blending in surroundings. It looks like as extension of the woods. The major characteristics of the community are its flexibility and flux. The house is designed internally in a way "that disallows fixed interior walls and that allows extension of the basic structure at need or whim" (Sukenick 1975: 66). It is a combination of the randomness and order, because they believe in the philosophy that "What's crystallized is static and what's static is dead" (Sukenick 1975:65).

Their pursuit of flexibility and flux is also reflected in their identity construction. Even though these characters initially have much more recognizable identities than those of *Out*, they also fall into "stream of identities"—changing their names (some of them several times) and identities. It is noteworthy that coincidently or not, they end up with names that designate places and phenomena of nature. Joan, Dave, Al, Ron, Evelyn, Paul, another Joan, Helen, George change their names respectively into Feather, Goose, Tom, Cloud, Eucalyptus, Wind, Valley, Dawn, Lance. Ralph stays Ralph in the first wave of name changing. Later, Tom, Goose and Feather change to Branch, Bud and Blossom. The name shifting reflects their effort of seeking identification with natural phenomena.

Monster, the community they establish, is a closed system, in which characters are separated from their past (they never mention about their past), and from the rest of the society. In this closed system, they move randomly and freely, interacting with one another, seeking their identity. So Entropy Law of identity takes effect. At the very beginning, they develop a harmonious brotherhood relationship. In the potlatch to celebrate the finish of their commune house, they join one another in an improvisational song, using different languages and musical instruments. Their communication can overcome the barrier of languages. However, in their later living together, with the increase of entropy of identity, they become more and more fluid, changing their names, switching partners and developing new relationships. Entropy in the communication—factors that prevent successful communication—is increasing, which leads to their quarrels, misunderstanding and split of partnership. As many (though not all) of the characters revert to their original names at the end of the chapter, their attempt to return to nature fails, so does their pursuit of new identity.

Stream of identities—character changes identities like a stream—shows Sukenick's denial of the fixed and coherent identity and his advocate for fluid and changeable characters. Self-definition and identity are subject to a process of constant changes. Ronald Sukenick points out in an interview that by doing so "maybe what happens finally is that you open an awareness into multiple possibilities and multiple levels of personality, and you can be an infinite number of beings, at one point a mature businessman and at another point a vulnerable infant... but at either point you're aware and conscious of the other possibility, and it's not lost but just put aside for a while" (qtd. Bellamy 1974:64).

"Stream of identities" best illustrates Entropy Law of identity. Just like entropy is the measurement of the increasing disorder of energy moving at random within a closed system, Entropy Law of identity illustrates that the characters change their identities without any reasons or logical progression, finally arrive at non-identity characters—characters neither materialized as a stable center of personal reference nor occupy a fixed position.

4.1.2 Non-identity

The second law of thermodynamics states that every time energy is transformed from one state to another, there is a loss in the amount of that form of energy, which is available to perform work of some kind. The loss in the amount of available energy is known as entropy. The increase of entropy means a decrease in available energy. Furthermore, entropy in the world always tends towards a maximum until the equilibrium state is achieved—a stage where there is no longer any difference in energy level. It is the state where entropy has reached the maximum and where free energy is no longer available for work. It is also the state of inertia. Entropy Law of identity states that during the process of identity construction, character particles move randomly and change freely without any reason or logical progression. The stable traits in their identity decrease, while the fluid and changeable traits increase, which leads to the final dissolution of identities—non-identity.

To Ronald Sukenick, the concept of non-identity is a challenge to the traditional way of characterization which aims at portraying characters of stable and identifiable traits. Sukenick clearly states this opinion in an interview:

> The kind of character structure that you find in a Victoria novel, say, or as I was talking about, the hardened characters, characters in a colloquial sense, or hard character structure of the kind that a Victorian business man had to be to get through life, or almost anybody in that period had to be to get through life, is very limiting and ought to be dissolved in the direction of greater possibility. (Bellamy 1974:64)

Sukenick believes that the traditional character structure limits the author's imagination, because "character structure hides deeper levels. I mean, character structure is a choice that eliminates certain things that come from your, say, subconscious or unconscious and selects others. Now, for me, the liberating thing is to choose not from the social or from some catalog but to allow all the possibilities in your personality" (Bellamy 1974:64). In the postmodern world, the unity of experience and the unity of world and self are neither lasting nor unambiguous, so let them dissolve again from moment to moment and be content with the many connections that lurk behind every dissolution. Everything is connectable, and everything imaginable, which is a way of emphasizing that no fixation is final and/or more meaningful than any other. Connections proliferate, and meaning and identity fall away. So Sukenick states that "my drive is to dissolve character. I think that's not only a need on my part, but I presume to think that that's also a cultural need for a lot of people, for the culture in general perhaps. And I think that it is happening that modes of character are breaking down, as a matter of fact. They're becoming inadequate" (Bellamy 1974:65).

Based on this belief, Ronald Sukenick starts his practice of non-identity from his first novel *Up*. The first-person narrator in the novel is also named Sukenick, who, far from constituting a unitary, unequivocal center of narratives, always aims at deconstructing such a center. His authority of narrative and identity are called into doubt when he presents himself alternately in different roles and forms, and reduplicates himself partly in other figures of the novel. He oscillates between different roles of a young writer, a Jewish prisoner, an astronaut, a professor and a critic, and projects himself onto such figures as Slade and Strop Banally. His non-identity is revealed clearly in a scene when he meets a figure who also claims that his name is Sukenick. The narrator Sukenick is defeated in the quarrel and fight, and forced to give up his name of Sukenick. His loss of name leaves him in a non-identity situation in which he asks the basic identity question, "Who am I?"(Sukenick 1968:169)

A similar thing happens in his short story "The Death of the Novel". "There is an episode in which a certain Jim Jones attempts to find the essence of his own self in a bizarre obstacle race that finally leaves him a no-person" (Putz 1979:182). He does not know where he lives, nor does he know under what name he should look himself up in the phone book. "It seemed to him that his name began with a K. or an A. 'Axel Kassel,' perhaps. Or 'Anders Kidney.' Or 'Kid Actual.' Oh Jim Jones! Six hundred and fifty thousand words in the English language, and none of them to call you by? Except possibly 'Jock Joseph'? or 'Jimmy Jerusalem'? or 'Janek Johanssen'?" (Sukenick 2003: 68) The confusion of his own names reveals the confusion of his identity.

Another strategy Sukenick employs in dissolving his characters is to purposely make characters with characteristics that absolutely do not go together. Sparrow, a character in his short story "The Birds", for example, is described at one point as short and at another he is described as tall.

In *Out* Sukenick seems predominantly interested in the technical and representational implications of his concept of non-identity. Putz points out that in the novel *Out*, the author employs the strategies of constant semantic overdetermination and semantic underdetermination to maximize the confusion of the identity of his figures. By semantic overdetermination, he means that one personal pronoun is used to refer to several objects, which leads to a semantic indeterminacy and confusion. Nixie, for example, peering at the Vajrayogini, is actually Nick in drag, wearing a blonde wig (Sukenick 1973: 68, 72). Harrold subsequently becomes Arthur, who later morphs into Nick (37, 51). Are Nixie and Harrold the same or different Nicks? There is also a Nick who becomes Carl, who kills Tommy, who had been Nick (62). Were these all the same Nick? Several Ova's in the novel also cause confusion.

Semantic underdetermination, on the other hand, means that personal pronouns are frequently deprived of their function as "linguistic indices". This is the strategy of "stream of identities" we have discussed in the previous section. Take the main character as an example, he changes names from Harrold, to Rex, Carl, Donald, Henry Aldrich, Ronald, Ton Sukenick, Nick, Roland Sycamore, R. Arr and at last R. The frequent changes lead to the result that one can never be sure that the personal pronouns refer to this or that clearly defined figure. "Thus both, overdetermination and underdetermination, work together in creating a remarkable confusion, leading to an increase of referential ambiguity in the text, since neither the contradictory proper names (overdetermination) nor any of their possible pro-forms (underdetermination) can now establish the identity of the personal objects referred to. As a final consequence, the figures of the novel dissolve into a kind of 'nothingness' and can justly subsumed under the category of 'Nada', or as another comment has it, 'nonentity'" (Putz 1979: 183-184).

The "nothingness" or "nonentity" of characters is not the disaster of characterization, in the view of realistic novelists. Instead, it is the desired state Sukenick wants to achieve, and also the natural result of the entropy of identity. In the novel *Out*, the main character, whose name is Henry at that time, meets an old man Uncle Don, from whom Henry wants to seek the answers to several important questions. "The first question is my life is empty and my work has no meaning what should I do?" The second question is "what's the meaning of this trip?" (87) The answer given by Uncle Don is the meter of gas pump which reads "17 points 3 gallons 7 dollars 33 cents" (89). Henry says that he does not understand the meaning. Uncle Don tells him that he does not have to understand everything. The point is not finding answers, so much as asking the questions. So Henry falls asleep. When he wakes up, he cannot remember anything, even his name. "He wonders who he is it does not matter it's all geometry what does that mean. Actually he is a nonentity a vacuum a campground of conflicting tribes in uneasy truce that's what it means. It means angles and velocities and effects of effects of effects of effects it means luck he feels light buoyant he can not remember anything what a relief" (90). In this sense, the freedom from the fixed and stable personalities makes him relieved and energetic. The state of non-identity also predicts innumerable possibilities.

What Sukenick emphasizes in characterization is not stable and identifiable traits, but non-identity, which can offer innumerable possibilities for new connections and new meanings. Sukenick implies this at the very beginning of the novel. The main character and some other characters are involved in a secret mission, in which each of them carries a stick of dynamite. "The way you have meets is you take out your stick of dynamite that's your i. d. . . When we get all our dynamite together we have a bomb. Then we set it off" (1). So when people meet, and connections are made, their dynamite of i. d becomes a bomb, which is set off and blows up everything, including their identity. With the blow-up of stable and fixed identity, characters are opened to different connections and possibilities. "The stream of identities", for example, just illustrates these possibilities. Take the changes of the narrator as an example, during his connection and communication with different persons, he changes names from Harrold, to Rex, Carl, Donald, Henry Aldrich, Ronald, Ton Sukenick, Nick, Roland Sycamore, R. Arr and at last R. A new name implies a new identity. Different names suggest the possibilities of his different identities. Like particles in an entropy process, his personalities move freely, and can never consolidate to become a fixed identity.

So when he starts his journey west, the main character also starts his journey of making connections and communication with people of different ages, backgrounds, professions, holding different beliefs. The proliferation of the connections initiates his identity changes and also the identity changes of those around him which leads to the multiplication and indiscrimination of characters. Putz summarizes the entropy of identity in this novel as follows:

> In *Out* the multiplication and indiscriminate merging of people transcribes a kind of entropy of identities and leads to an unstructured chaos of

> agglomerated everything which by the same token is nothing. In this process, any potentially stable system of unity in diversity—most notably any stable self-system—as the precondition for an establishment of distinction and coherence collapses into a disparate multiplicity with the tendency towards entropic chaos. (Putz 1979:184)

The non-identity, to some extent, reflects Sukenick's belief that identity is not the result of a global nature, but the culmination of each person's singular engagement with his own experience. So in the example given before, in which Henry cannot find the meaning of his life and his trip, he wakes up and finds that he cannot even remember his name. He is not panic-stricken, instead, he feels relieved and energetic. And he also finds a piece of paper in his pocket on which three words are scrawled in pencil: "empty, fox, speeds" (90). His understanding to it is that, "If you're empty and you're smart you keep moving" (91). Thus, identity construction is a continuous process of moving. That is why Peter Currie calls Sukenick's figures the slaves of motion.

> The figures in Sukenick's *Out* are simply the victims of a vocabulary of perpetual transformation. Barely delineated, fleetingly individuated, the "characters" are closer to molecular particles in a state of agitated Brownian movement, equally likely to move in any direction, further motion seeming totally unrelated to past motion , and the motion never stopping. The corollary of their flight from stasis is a corresponding bondage to movement. Like the 'yo-yo' figures in Pynchon's work, Sukenick's evanescent characters are the slaves of motion, swapping the imperative "Sit still" for the equally prohibiting, and oddly American injunction "Keeping moving". (Currie 1987:63-64)

So, self-definition and identity pursuit become subject to a process of constant changes instead of the aim of a search of immutable qualities. Multiplicity and diversity are emphasized as the characteristics of identity. Multiple identities often turn to be non-entity. In Sukenick's fiction, the identity story changes its structural pattern from a story of self-search to an experiment in the non-identity of fictional constants.

4.2 Entropy Law of Postmodernist Narratives

While Entropy Law of identity reveals the characteristics of fluidity and dissolution in Sukenick's characterization, Entropy Law of postmodernist narratives represents the characteristics of fluidity and dissolution in Sukenick's narratives.

In the late 1960s and early 1970s, an emerging group of American novelists took up the notion that since no meaning preexists language, meaning is produced in the process of writing and reading. So their new fiction would not attempt to be meaningful, truthful or realistic according to any traditional models. Ronald Sukenick, a radical writer among them, particularly attacks the traditional opinion that fiction is a reflection of real life. To Sukenick, the more intense the novel is "about" life, the less it is part of it. So the position of fiction should be changed from the imitation of life to "an illuminating addition to its ongoing flow" (Sukenick 1975:431). What is emphasized is the feature of fluidity. The writer works not from a priori ideas about what will happen and what form it will take, but in and through the text. There is no such thing as a presiding idea or a preexistent scenario. "The text is generated by the activity of composition in an ongoing interchange between the mind and the page" (Sukenick 1975:432). That is what Sukenick calls "poetics of experience". Sukenick's definition of the novel has changed from art-as-illusion to art-as-experience. "The artist becomes the inventor of experience from mere phenomena: that is, we're confronted with phenomena and we want experience. Experience is phenomena taken in and made relevant to the individual psyche" (qtd. Meyer 1982:135).

Sukenick believes that this "poetics of experience" is what differentiates his novels from the traditional realistic ones. In his opinion, postmodern fiction is "an attempt to get the truth of experience beyond our fossilizing formulas of discourse, to get a new and more inclusive 'reality', if you will. This is a reality that includes what the conventional novel tends to exclude and that encompasses the vagaries of unofficial experience, the cryptic trivia of the quotidian that help shape our fate, and the tabooed details of life—class, ethnic, sexual—beyond sanctioned descriptions of life" (Sukenick 1988: 15). So for Sukenick, experience is not only the concern and source of narrative, but also its object.

Sukenick explores this "poetics of experience" in his book *Narralogues: Truth in Fiction*. A narralogue is defined by Sukenick as narrative plus argument. "Narrative is a mode of understanding that uniquely is quick enough, mutable enough, and flexible enough to catch the stream of experience, including our experience of the arts" (Sukenick 2000: 1). In order to catch the stream of experience, the narrative should also be "agonistic, sophistic, sophisticated, fluid, unpredictable, rhizomatic, affective, inconsistent and even contradictory" (Sukenick 2000:1). "I want to write a book like a cloud that changes as it goes" (Sukenick 1973:136). The dream of the narrator Sukenick in the novel *Out* is also what the author Ronald Sukenick works for. "The obligation of fiction is to rescue experience from history, from politics, from commerce, from history, even from language itself—from any system, in fact that threatens to distort, devitalize, or manipulate experience" (Sukenick 1975c:434).

Sukenick's "poetics of experience" suggests an older line of narrative improvisation from Rabelais and Sterne to Henry Miller and Jack Kerouac. However, Sukenick's "poetics of experience" is different from improvisation in that Sukenick believes that fiction should concern itself not only with the truth of experience, but also with "the truth of page". The combination of "the truth of experience" and "the truth of page" is what we call "entropic narratives" here. First of all, fiction involves a flow of energy. To Sukenick, "though there is not necessarily plot or story in a narrative, there is always a field of action, and in a field of action the way energy moves should be the most obvious element" (Sukenick 1975c: 435). Just as entropy law emphasizes the process of energy flow, "entropic narratives" emphasize the process of the energy movement in narration. Moreover, the narratives are endowed with characteristics of entropy: fluidity, fragmentation, chaos, changeability and dissolution. Traditional narratives seek continuity and wholeness, but with the constant threat of discontinuity and fragmentation. Entropic narratives imply discontinuity and fragmentation. Sukenick describes it in his early stories, "Start with immediate situation. One scene after another, disparate, opaque, absolutely concrete. Later, a fable, a gloss begins to develop, abstraction appear. End with illuminating formulation. Simple, direct utterance" (Sukenick 2003: 154). Despite the chaos, the important thing is to keep the flow of the energy. "In such a style you move from moment to moment and if you make a mistake, have a memory lapse, blow a wrong note, you either build on it anyway or leave it and do it better next time, or you lose the experimental flow" (Sukenick 1985:6-7).

Essentially, this kind of narrative is the process-oriented narrative, in which there is no search for a unifying center, nor any effort of keeping the coarse fabric of the story. Instead, irreducible twists and possibilities exist. Free from the constraints of plot, character and mimetic realism, Sukenick's narratives are submitted to a continuous process of articulating and rearticulating the new connections in the flow of experience. The frequent shifts in plot, character, and style free experience from formulaic stories, providing a dynamic space wherein character, author and reader can negotiate a "favorable rapport" with reality.

So Sukenick's novels pursues a notion of transformative flow in many aspects. "Stream of identities", discussed in the previous section, indicates the transformative flow of characters. Beside "stream of identities", Sukenick employs other techniques as the "split of narrator", stream language, changeable typography, to achieve the transformative flow. The presence and split of authorial figures are one of the techniques employed. Ronald Sukenick or the metamorphoses of Sukenick appear as narrators or main figures in his novels as *Up*, *Out*, *98.6*, *Mosaic Man*, etc. In the novel *Up*, for example, the narrator Ronald Sukenick is split into Ronnie, an author who is constructing a picaresque autobiography, Ron Sukenick, a character-author who is engaged in writing the "Adventures of Strop Banally", and Ronald Sukenick, a critic who is reviewing the novel *Up*. The stream changes of the narrator Ron in the novel *Out* is discussed in the previous section. The split of narrator comes to climax in his novel *Mosaic Man*. The narrator Ron

Sukenick narrates in first person his own biography: his childhood with his parents in Brooklyn in the 1940s, his stay in Paris in 1958, his visit of Venice in 1961 and last his travel to Israel. Intertwining with the first person narration is a Jewish writer Sukenick who is writing a novel. The mixture of documentary and fictional narratives makes the novel a mosaic.

If we say "the truth of experience" emphasizes more on the content of fiction, then "the truth of page" stresses the aspect of the form of fiction. If we say "the truth of experience" emphasizes more on the improvisation of the writer, then "the truth of page" stresses the aspect of the fiction itself. To Ronald Sukenick, "A novel is a developing structure that from the first word has its own influence in determining its shape, and by the last has far more influence than its author" (Sukenick 1975c:434). The next word can always be a surprise, to the author as well as to the reader. "Form is when look back and you see your footprints in the sand" (Sukenick 1973:164).

"The truth of experience" in Sukenick's entropic narratives is reflected in the "stream of identities" and "the split of narrator", while "the truth of page" is displayed mainly in two aspects: the typographic innovations and language play. Both aim at breaking the linearity of reading and disrupting the illusion of a causal plot and continuous chronology. His purpose is to question, challenge and demolish the traditional, conventional, fixed and boring method of reading a book. And new possibilities of expression, discursive and typographical, would be created. "The truth of page" makes a heavy demand on the reader to become involved in the creation of the novel, or to become "the co-author of a generative process that may ultimately lead to an imaginative reinvention of world and self" (Putz 1979:177).

4.2.1 Typographic innovations

Typography is concerned with the determination of the appearance of the printed page. The typography refers to the technological aspects of the novel: pages, print and binding, which are often neglected by novelists and readers as well. A novel is often treated as an imaginative structure, containing a record of the movements of a mind. More attention is paid to the content than to the typography. Sukenick, however, wants to challenge the long time ignorance. He declares,

> We badly need a new way of thinking about novels that acknowledges their technological reality. We have to learn how to look at fiction as lines of print on a page and we have to ask whether it is always the best arrangement to have a solid block of print from one margin to the other running down the page from top to bottom, except for an occasional paragraph indentation. We have to learn to think about a novel as a concrete structure rather as an allegory, existing in the realm of experience rather than in the realm of

> discursive meaning and available to multiple interpretations or none, depending on how you feel about it—like the way that girl pressed against you in the subway. (Sukenick 1975b:40)

Sukenick wants to take advantage of the disruptive potential of typographical variations which are traditionally neglected by both writers and readers so as to challenge the power of prevalent conventions. His typographical variations greatly challenge the traditional fixed typographical arrangements, opening up more connections and more possibilities, with the purpose of achieving fluidity and dissolution of narratives.

Sukenick's strategies for stressing the materiality of writing vary ingeniously from book to book. He starts his typographic play in his first novel: *Up*. From page 27 to 29, in a conversation between an astronaut and baseman, with the weight-loss of the astronaut, letters also lose their gravity. Letters in the phrase "alphabet soup" are strung out along the page, or swirled in looping designs, just like objects flying in the sky. It seems that the author, while writing, is also experiencing the zero gravity. And it also gets the reader involved in the same experience. This change in printing can break up the monotonous and boring mode of the traditional way of reading and achieve a communication between the writer and the reader.

uP

over

over

over

over

a l p h a

b

e

t

uP

s

o

u

p

(Sukenick 1968:28-29)

The same typographical play also appears at the end of the novel *Up*. When the narrator declares that "I'm coming down". The letters in the sentence are also coming down. By doing this, Sukenick tries to get the author and the reader involved in the experience of the narrator so as to achieve what he calls the "favorable rapport" with reality.

The typographic innovations in the novel *Up* are associated with the visual experiments, but are limited to a small part of the novel. In his second novel *Out*, Sukenick begins to fully realize the radical edges of his typographic challenges. Heise mentions that "*Out*, as is well known, stands out at first sight not so much by its topography as by its typography" (Heise 2003: 78). The outstanding typographic innovation lies in the countdown arrangement of the novel.

The novel consists of 11 chapters, which are arranged in reversed sequence from chapter 10 to 0. Each page of the novel contains three paragraphs whose lines are correspondent to the number of the chapter. To be exact, each of the paragraphs in Chapter 10 contains ten lines, then 9 in Chapter 9, 8 in Chapter 8 and so on and so forth. These paragraphs are separated by blank space. As the lines of the paragraphs decrease, the blank space in between increases, until the completely blank pages at the end of the novel, which indicates nothingness, or the zero stage of narration. It is indeed typographical entropy. As the novel progresses, there is visibly less and less of it left before the reader's eyes as the white space expands until the text is no longer there. In other words, the meaningful information that can transfer from chapter to chapter is decreasing. But at the same time, the untransferrable entropy is increasing until the heat death—or the death of the information. The countdown arrangement of the chapters is not made without any purpose. Instead, it is interwoven with the countdown of the plot in the story. At the very beginning of the story, the narrator and a group of people get together for a mission. "Everybody set his watch ahead that way we have nine minutes leeway all the time. The countdown starts with nine" (Sukenick 1973: 4). The counting down reoccurs now and then in the novel, intermingling with the countdown arrangement of chapters, rushing toward the end of the story.

The purpose of using this countdown arrangement and the spacing is to increase the fluidity of narratives. With the reduction of the lines of the text on the page, the reader will actually turn the pages faster as he gets further into the book. "Speeding along on the breaking crest of the present toward god knows what destination after the first word everything follows anything follows nothing follows the world is pure invention from one minute to the next" (Sukenick 1973:117-118). Similarly, this increasing rate corresponds to the acceleration of the pace of the action in the novel, as illustrated in the sentence: "speed increases space expands" (Sukenick 1973: 104). In the story, the protagonist travels from the east coast to the west coast at accelerating speeds. As he moves from

Washington D. C, the geographical spaces expand. He continues traveling westward, to larger and larger open spaces. As the geographical spaces expand, the blanks expand too. The reader turns the pages from right to left, which is comparable, geographically, to turning them from east to west. As the protagonist heads west, the vehicles that carry him also tend to increase in the speed of their movement. First in a U-Haul, then in a camper bus, next he hitches with Tommy, who "accelerates forty fifty sixty seventy high beams drill into dark on U. S. 90 somebody give you a shot of speed" (118). Because there are fewer and fewer lines of the text and more and more space on each page, the reader turns the pages faster and faster, even creating a small wind as in the open spaces—until getting "out" of the fiction. It is also the reason why Sukenick entitles the novel "*Out*". In an interview, Sukenick mentions the meaning of the title: "*Out* does move out: out of New York, across the country, out into the Pacific, out of the text, out of the language as the language gradually disappears and the book moves out into the blank page" (qtd. LeClair & McCaffery 1974:290).

In his short story collection *The Death of the Novel and Other Stories*, Ronald Sukenick continues his typographical innovations. In the story "Momentum", he divides the text into two columns. In "Roast Beef: A Slice of Life", he tape-records the conversation between "HE" and "SHE", which is also listed in two columns. In "Birds", capitalized letters are intermingled with small letters, separated by different spacing. In *98.6*, he combines several strategies of typography: spacing, patchwork of columns, mixture of capitalized letters and small ones. In *Doggy Bag*, he uses strings of punctuation marks. Also, in the pre-text, he exploits keyboard symbols and unusual punctuations in the table of contents. In *Mosaic Man*, he uses hand-scrawled symbols.

Among these innovations, spacing is an important way to foreground the materiality of the page. He even uses spacing to replace punctuation in a number of texts, including *Long Talking Bad Conditions Blues*. Sukenick himself describes the form of the novel *Long Talking Bad Conditions Blues*,

> The book *Long Talking Bad Conditions Blues* has an arbitrary form, very mathematical, something like *Out*, in which prose is organized into sentence fragments of certain numbers of words. There's no punctuation—only spacing between the fragments. The fragments are complete or incomplete sentences. In other words, it's agrammatical. It's perfectly understandable, however, if read in proper rhythm: that is, the spacing itself acts as a kind of organizing factor that makes the prose perfectly comprehensible. So what you get is fragments of word-counted prose rhythm—a very strict form. For example, in a certain section each fragment must be seven words, in another, fourteen words. The fragments then change into paragraph fragments, segments of prose fifteen lines long, based on

> the number of words somebody can speak per minute in normal conversation. There's another section in which the prose runs down one side of the page with a blank space in the middle and then the prose starts running down the other side of the page. The form of the first part is exactly repeated in the second part. A complete mirror image. (qtd. Meyer 1982:141)

In his novel *Mosaic Man*, Ronald Sukenick introduces drawn symbols into narration. These symbols are mainly used in the Chapter EX/ODE with lower-case boldface captions under those symbols which recite a personal narrative about the five points he lists at the beginning of Chapter EX/ODE: Jewish rules; reality; making it/losing it; reel/unreal; the true story, the word. Some symbols are also used as chapter markers at the beginning of each chapter. Besides these symbols, letters, recipes, road signs, newspaper articles, Raymond Federman's and others' notes on earlier drafts of *Mosaic Man*, and excerpts from a biography of Eisenhower and Chayim Bloch's *The Golem* are also included to interrupt the narration of the story.

"The truth of the page", Sukenick explains in an interview, "is that there's a writer sitting there writing the page" (Sukenick 1985: 25). By calling attention to writing's mechanical status before and disrupting it, complicating it, typographical innovation shows Sukenick's attempt to bring the reader's notice to the pageness of the page, and work against the conventional structure of western writing and also reading strategies. This also reminds the reader of the visual nature of language and the linguistic nature of images, which reintroduces fiction at another level of meaning-making, and more suitable to express experience. Lance Olsen believes that through these techniques of typographies, Sukenick "seeks to turn the book into a piece of architecture"(Olsen 2003: 170), which the reader can have a three dimensional feel to it.

4.2.2 Language Play

From the outset of his career as a novelist, Sukenick has been ready to confront the established power and rules. In his essay "Eight Digressions on the Politics of Language", Ronald Sukenick attacks the power in the publishing industry. "Publishers are not just ordinary bosses; they are word bosses. They have enormous power to decide what language is good and what language is bad, and to back up those decisions by saturating the market with millions of copies of their books. Language control is mind control" (Sukenick 1979b:473). Under this control, language is pasteurized and homogenized: U. S Standard English. Sukenick's experience in Cornell makes him fully realize the control of language. He is almost expelled from the university just because of his use of the single word "birdshit" in his short story contributed to a campus journal. "Birdshit" is considered as a coarse word and thus unacceptable on campus. However, to Ronald

Sukenick, this pasteurization of language rules out diversities of language and the diversities of experience as well. In this sense, "language and form are becoming more standardized and are supported by federal, state, and city tax money, as well as by commercial profit" (Sukenick 1979b: 468). Take the Beats for example, the Beats start their literary career by constantly challenging the literary establishment, and subsequently set up a new vocabulary, new rhythms, new forms and new models in writing which help prepare and support the liberation movements of the sixties. However, their potent language of dissent is disappearing when they are gaining popularity and the publishing industry starts to popularize them.

Ronald Sukenick believes that "our current language is inadequate. You might say language is always inadequate, by definition. That's why poetry and fiction are so important; they recreate the language. But we're living in a state of imagination—or—politics—in which language seems grossly inappropriate for the realities of our lives" (qtd. Meyer 1982: 133). "So what we need to do now is to break through word lines, as Burroughs says" (qtd. Meyer. 1982: 133). So, to break through the constraints of so-called standard language and find new language to express our experience is a chief task set before him.

From his first novel, Sukenick has shown obvious interest in wordplay, puns, pangrams and other language games. He believes that these devices can help him with the process of opening up new spaces with language, forcing the words to yield new complexities and meanings. Sukenick mentions in an interview,

> Language play releases the possibility of meaning that is inherent in language, that is built up in it through tradition. The wisdom of language only reveals itself, oddly, when you break it down. It's like breaking open a piece of fruit—if you can find a way of cracking it open, you can find a way of releasing its content, its energy, its suggestiveness, its possibilities. But in order to do that you have to deform it, or transform it, through puns or through arbitrary devices of the kind that Raymond Roussel uses—through the imposition of odd schemes, non sequiturs, even through improvisation. You have to do that kind of peculiar manipulation of language in order to release its peculiar power. You may, in the process, manage to startle or surprise the reader, but the important thing is to surprise yourself, to get out of the premeditated. (qtd. LeClair & McCaffery 1974: 284)

In his first novel *Up*, Ronald Sukenick starts his efforts of breaking language constraints. The most notable effort is a long paragraph that lasts 17 pages (from page 226 to 242) without any punctuation. Random caesuras break the textual flow and story references. With a reference to Gertrude Stein, it reads like a homage to modernist stream of consciousness. However, it is different from modernist stream of consciousness in that it proceeds cyclically as textual elements repeat themselves with variation. For example, the section about Gertrude Stein starts on page 226 and restarts on page 238 in a slightly different form. The reoccurrence and restatement of themes display Sukenick's belief that narrative is a process rather than a completed or a finalized statement. What he emphasizes is the fluidity of narratives.

In *Up*, Sukenick tries another language play—pun, to increase the possibilities of connections and meanings. In a scene about a space mission to Mars, when the space hero falls from the sky, the letters, "s/t/r/a," fall from the sentence and spread across one page in a form as follows:

s

r t

a

But on the next page, they are changed into:

r

s a

t

(Sukenick 1968:320)

Different ways of arranging the letters suggest different meanings. They can spell "stars", which stands for the space mission, or they can spell "rats", just as Slumski's voice brings the reader back into "reality". Different spellings increase the chaos in narratives, which is also a feature of entropic narratives.

Sukenick's effort of language play in *Up* is tentative and rather limited. In his second novel *Out*, Sukenick intensifies his language innovations. *Out* writes almost frantically toward the absence of realistic meaning and in doing so becomes more about writing and the production of meaning than anything recognizably literary. That is why in 1974 Raymond Federman reviewed it enthusiastically:

> *Out* makes a shamble of traditional fiction. It brings fiction to the brink of playful disaster. As such, *OUT* is a remarkable piece of fiction—a tour de force—because it fucks up all preconceived notions of what fiction should be. *OUT* fucks up the whole conventional way of reading a story. And above all, *OUT* fucks up the English language. No one, as far as I know, as yet so successfully, so brilliantly, so deliberately messed up the English syntax. (Federman 1975:140)

First of all, in *Out* Sukenick destroys conventional language styles by creating his own unique style. Ordinary sentence patterns are abandoned. Sukenick organizes language by word groups which are made up of one or more words. Take the following sentence as an example, "Three it's mute articulation of the conditions we live in today I mean not only us but everybody the zeitgeist you might say is not the human condition itself and keeps you in touch with reality" (Sukenick 1973: 1). From the example, we can see that the word groups begin with capital letters, end with periods, and have no internal punctuation of any sort. They are often what conventional terminology would call run-on sentences. Yet the run-on syntax is grammatical. But as the fiction progresses into the midway through the fiction, Sukenick lengthens but speeds up the language style. In other words, although many word groups are short, several are becoming much extended, and one grammatical sentence flows into another and another. For instance, in Chapter 5 in the novel, when the protagonist takes up a stone and tries to feel it, the syntax is flowing,

> I sit hunched in front of the tent I look at my stone smell the pine smell listen to the wind I look at my stone turn it over and over weigh it in my hand put my nose to it rub it against my cheek lick it bite on it look at it some more hold it up to the sun feel it warm in my cupped hands eyes closed run my fingers along its sharp edges try to remember its shapes map its facets its idiosyncrasies make it shine in the light this way and that I look up. (Sukenick 1973:148)

This sentence, though long, is grammatical and understandable. Moreover, Sukenick employs the combination of verb-object word groups, which lengthens the sentence, but speeds up the rhythm. So the reader has to speed up to follow the tempo.

As the novel moves to the ending, the syntax becomes ungrammatical and fragmented. The final chapter is composed of just one long and fast-moving word group. Though the sentence is becoming even longer, the rhythm of reading is even speeding up as there is no period, nor any stop. Not only does the reader reads faster and faster, his hand also moves faster and faster as there is only one line in each paragraph and only three lines on each page. The last word group, forming all of Chapter "1", has no periods, so it never "stops"; and the reader is catapulted "out" into the blank spaces of the final pages. In this sense, the language in this novel moves just like molecule in a heating system. With the increase of entropy—the amount of energy unavailable to work, the system at last reaches the state of heat death. The entropy in the narratives also increases, which means the factors which are unavailable to communicate increase, until the whole narratives come to total blank.

Another important change of language is Sukenick's rejection of quotation marks to delineate dialogue. Instead, a change of speaker is designated by a new paragraph.

Without quotations, the occasional "he says" or "she says" dialogue attribution becomes part of the sentence as a whole, connecting the voice of narration with the voice of the character. Everything is narration. Without quotes, the attribution becomes a false attribution in that it is not an attempt to call attention to a speaker, but a meta-fictional way to call attention to the artifice of the narration. This is, to Ronald Sukenick, an effective way to increase the fluidity of narratives, as the division line between narration and quotation is blurred.

From the examples above, we can see that in his novels, Sukenick throws some traditional language devices away, like punctuations. In his fiction, punctuation does not mark out the syntax or the grammatical units. Sukenick once explains his attitude toward punctuation in an interview:

> I use sentence rhythm in a variety of ways. Sometimes I use it against punctuation, using punctuation as a counterrhythm to get a fast, syncopated effect. Latterly I've been writing in sentence fragments without punctuation at all, not imitating but actually entering into the rhythms of the body. Rhythm, I think, is a way of getting at information without circulating it through the conscious part of the brain. (qtd. Meyer 1982:138)

Punctuation, to Ronald Sukenick, sometimes is an unnecessary burden, without which he can feel the rhythms of the body and express the rhythms of the body and also let the reader feel the rhythms of the body. Later in the novel *Long Talking Bad Conditions Blues*, Sukenick uses no punctuation so that the rhythms are indicated by spacing. He believes that this kind of rhythm is much more fluid than punctuated rhythm. And he explains,

> It approaches what I call prose measure, which is a lot like poetic measure except grosser and rougher. And the measure also is arbitrary so that you get a reflection there: the rhythm of the way you're writing, what's coming out of your mind, as against the arbitrary rhythm you set up on the page. It's only when the occult is measured against the known and arbitrary that something can emerge that can be clearly apprehended. (qtd. Meyer 1982: 138)

All through his writing career, Sukenick has been experimenting with language and exploring new ways to increase the fluidity of narratives. He clearly expresses his wish in the novel *Out*. The protagonist, also named Ron Sukenick, admits that "I want to write a book like a cloud that changes as it goes" (Sukenick 1973:136). *Out* is indeed that book, changing, developing and disappearing as it goes, just like a cloud. To write a book like a cloud also suggests writing with one's voice instead of one's pen. Empty Fox, an Indian he meets, is always writing with spoken language. He speaks to Ron in words; he composes songs and poems and then recites them. He opposes written language. Under his influence, Ron throws away his notebook and no longer writes words with pen or pencil. Eventually, the clouds blow away completely, and only the blank of the sky and of the page remains: the book is erased or "out".

However, Empty Fox wants more, "I want to erase all books. My ambition is to unlearn everything I can't read or write that's a start. I want to unlearn and unlearn will I get to the place where the ocean of the unknown begins where my fathers live. Then I want to go back and bring my people to live beside that ocean where they can be whole again as they were before the Wasichus came" (Sukenick 1973: 136). To Empty Fox, language is the barrier that prevents him from reaching an ideal state of the unity of thought and action and a mythic wholeness which his ancestors have enjoyed before the advent of white settlers. Obviously, literacy is a symptom of our inability to think without thought. Indian consciousness is shown as less tainted with the curse of intellection than which bears the burden of the West's rational, analytic inheritance.

To Ronald Sukenick, language is also a constraint from which he wants to escape. In his novel *98. 6*, he introduces a language play and tries to invent a new language. In "Frankenstein", the first part of *98. 6*, Ronald Sukenick introduces a word play, called pangram. Pangram is a game in which one tries to make sentences using all the letters of the alphabet, but only once. No one has ever composed a successful pangram though they have come close. However, the protagonist, a narrator without a name, is more interested in the letters left over "because sometimes they form interesting words words that didn't exist before and that mean nothing but for which meaning develops because now they exist. Brillig. Mojo. He believes that one day he's going to find a word this way that will be the key to The Problem a word that didn't exist before. Fork jugs vex'd nymph waltz bidq. Nymphs waltz jig fuck vex rod bq. Hymn waltz fuck vex prod big sqj. Hymn waltz fuck sex gip v. d. bjorq. Vex'd nymphs waltz jig fuck borq" (Sukenick 1973: 26). This new language, composed from the nonsensical residue of pangram-making is called Bjorsq by Sukenick.

In an interview, Sukenick tries to answer the question "What is Bjorsq? What gets spoken in Bjorsq?"

> Bjorsq is really a word I discovered doing that language game, pangrams, in which you try to make a complete English sentence using every letter of the alphabet, but each only once. Bjorsq is just the left-over letters. It points out the peripheries of language where language gets created: the edge of

> language, where there's a fresh contact between language and whatever is out there, phenomena. Bjorsq is that part of language which poets work with. (qtd. Meyer 1982:133)

From these words, we can see that Bjorsq is an effort to get rid of the constraints of language, or an effort to push the existing language to a new space and open up new possibilities.

The children of Frankenstein, who are tired of the violent culture of Frankenstein, escape from it and try to establish a commune called Monster. The Monster is built from the weathered wood from the old barn. Besides, it is erected on the improvisational design of the children of Frankenstein and so it looks different from anything they have seen in Frankenstein. The monster represents an art that arises out of the detritus and debris of culture. This is the same with the language of Bjorsq, which is created from the waste language. So to celebrate the near completion of their house Ron makes up a song:

> Bjorsqi poppamomma
> Wocky wocky
> Plastic jam
> Iron blintzes
> Fill the inches
> Sooky buby nishtgedeit (Sukenick 1973:75).

From this song, we can see that Bjorsq is a personal, private language, as disassembled and different as to be indecipherable to anyone but its creator. "This language that people don't understand is extremely stupid and nonsensical and is the language the Lunk speaks. This language is called Bjorsq. While Bjorsq is obviously inconvenient for many purposes it has one great advantage when two Lunks meet and speak in Bjorsq they understand one another perfectly... Of course Bjorsq isn't very exact you couldn't write a textbook in it it expresses nothing with any definition but that's the price you pay. It defines little but it says everything [...] it's not this or that object floating the stream it's the whole force and direction of the stream the power that moves everything" (Meyer 1982:161). Bjorsq represents new possibilities of language. Though indecipherable, incomprehensible, untranslatable and nonsensical, Bjorsq is the process one has to go through so as to achieve a completely new language. It is the price one has to pay. At least, it marks changes: "Bjorsq is a vertical language all others are horizontal. Bjorsq is a deep language all others are flat. Bjorsq is a window language all others are mirrors. Bjorsq is rhythmic the rhythm of your pulse the rhythm of the surf. All others are clop-clop" (Meyer 1982:161-162).

Sukenick's language of Bjorsq demonstrates his ostentatious attempt to violate the rules of grammar, spelling, punctuation and other normal language habits in order to illustrate, as Bernstein contends, "experience is not inextricably linked to representation, normative syntax, images, but rather, the other way around, is synthetic, generative activity" (qtd. Bernstein 2001: 35). To Sukenick, the constraints of language, which come from the grammar, spelling and punctuation, draw the attention of both the writer and reader from experience and into an aesthetic formula that is familiar and reassuring. Thus his language innovations can free the writer from these constraints and establish a favorable rapport with experience. As the experience is not fixed and stable, the language should also resist stability and fixation. Indeed, the fluidity and diversity of narratives do achieve the purpose Ronald Sukenick advocates—establishing a rapport with reality. The reader, attracted by the changes in typography and language of fiction, is actively involved in deciphering and creating meaning of fiction, which leads to the desired communication between the narrator, the author and the reader. Yet, we should also note that, his innovations in typography and language, to some extent, digress the reader from the content of fiction to its form. Moreover, too bold innovations usually discourage the reader, which leads to a limited readership of his novels.

Chapter 5

Mosaic Law: Fragmentation and Collage

5.1 Mosaic Law of Identity in *98.6* and *Mosaic Man*

Mosaic is the art of creating images with an assemblage of small pieces of colored glass, stone or other materials. It is among the most durable forms of art. Its history can be traced back to 1500 BC. However, it is not until the Hellenistic period (323 BC-146 BC) that mosaics were introduced into the decorations of floors, surfaces of walls and ceilings. It became one of the hallmarks of luxury in Roman times. Mosaic pavements have been found in hundreds of buildings of the Roman period from northern Britain to Libya, from the Atlantic coast to the Syrian Desert. The mosaics of the Villa Romana del Casale near Piazza Armerina in Sicily are the largest collection of late Roman mosaics in situ in the world, and are protected as a UNESCO World Heritage Site.

The art of mosaic is later introduced mainly in Christian buildings. Mosaics of Santa Constanza and Santa Pudenziana, both from the 4th century, still exist. In the 5th century Ravenna, the capital of the Western Roman Empire, became the center of late Roman mosaic art. Mosaic art was exuberant in the Byzantine Empire from the 6th to the 15th century. Byzantine church interiors are generally covered with golden mosaics. Mosaic, as an art, is later brought to other cultures as well. Under Roman and Byzantine influence, Jews also decorated their synagogues with classical floor mosaics. The remains of a 6th-century synagogue have been uncovered in Sepphoris. During the reign of the Umayyad Dynasty mosaic making remained a flourishing art form in Islamic culture and it continues in various parts of the Arab world.

The art of mosaic continues in modern times. A modern example of mosaic is the Museum of Natural History station of the New York Subway. Today, among the leading figures of the mosaic world are Emma Biggs (UK), Marcelo de Melo (Brazil), Sonia King (USA) and Saimir Strati (Albania).

John Murry Gibbon, a Scottish Canadian writer, first introduces the term "mosaic" into the field of sociology and uses it to refer to Canadian society, which is different from the melting-pot of American society. In his book *Canadian Mosaic*, Gibbon attacks the American melting-pot, a process through which immigrants and their descendants are encouraged to cut off ties with countries and cultures of origin so as to get assimilated into the American way of life. While in Canada, cultural mosaic is the co-existence of different ethnic groups, languages and cultures. The distinction between the melting-pot and cultural mosaic reveals the different relations between the parts and the whole, which is one of the concerns of Ronald Sukenick.

Ronald Sukenick is acutely aware of the crisis of postmodern identity construction—the absence of the center and the whole. Robert Dunn states that "the postmodern condition begins with the cultural density and heterogeneity resulting from structural transformations in the capitalist system of production and marketing, the impact of media technologies and aesthetics and a massive expansion of private consumption" (Dunn 1998: 143). The cultural diversity and heterogeneity mean the greater difficulties in keeping a cultural centre and wholeness. Cultural fragmentation is the inevitable result, as "social and cultural experience is shattered, disconnected, and incoherent" (Dunn 1998: 144). Robert Dunn continually points out that these fundamental changes in the scope and character of culture in the moment of postmodernity "not only transform but more importantly problematize processes of identity formation. This can be seen in the ways that the commodity works to reduce culture to highly dispersed, market-based systems of semiotic exchange and their disunifying effects on the self" (Dunn 1998: 81). In the postmodern world, the wholeness and the centre are destroyed. What is left is "Interruption. Discontinuity. Imperfection. It can't be helped. This very instant as I write as you read a hundred things. A hundred things to tangle with resolve ignore before you are together. Together for an instant and then smash it's all gone still it's worth it. I feel. This composure grown out of ongoing decomposition" (Sukenick 1975a: 167).

In the face of the absence of cultural centre and wholeness, Sukenick believes that what we should do is to make sense of parts. In this sense, mosaic—the art form which uses small pieces of materials placed together to create a unified whole is borrowed and modified by Ronald Sukenick into his writing theories. His first mention of Mosaic Law appears in his novel *98.6*: "The Mosaic Law is the law of mosaics a way of dealing with parts in the absence of wholes" (Sukenick 1975a: 122). From the statement, we can see that Sukenick's concept of mosaic is quite similar to Gibbon's cultural mosaic in that when the wholeness is non-existent, and what we should do is to make sense of parts.

The Mosaic Law put forward by Sukenick aims not at the wholeness and unification, but at the fragments and parts:

> It's a division of the whole into a dialectical fragment. The whole consciousness breaks up into its parts, and various energies can begin to

> flow because of that polarizing among the parts. The fragmentation can then alter the parts, or the parts can be combined into different ways, and the final consequence can be that an alteration can take place in the whole consciousness or the whole text. (qtd. LeClair & McCaffery 1974:295)

Mosaic Law of identity is put forward by Sukenick to deal with the identity crisis of the absence of cultural centre and wholeness. When the cultural centre and wholeness are demolished, individuals in postmodern society are only cultural shards. So they have to seek ways of piecing these shards together and make them meaningful. His novel *Mosaic Man* depicts a young man's cryptic search for individual identity, as an artist and a Jew, across a half-dozen countries and in many decades. As the title of the book suggests, Sukenick does not find what he is looking for in one piece. Instead, he tries to show that one, in the postmodern context, is cultural shards and hybridity. The novel tries to answer the question how "could one even presume to be a person... or even a human" after being submitted to the "ongoing ego smasher" of twentieth-century history (Sukenick 1999:181), especially in the post-Holocaust/post-Cold War era. The unity of identity is no longer possible, so "Sukenick offers the idea of Mosaic Man, the self built up of discrete and relatively unchanging parts. Some of those parts are fragments of the past, memories of events and people, as well as past imaginings of self. Others are imaginative self-projections" (qtd. Roberson 2003:131). So, the self of the protagonist in the novel is the mosaic of different cultural shards: European, Jewish and American. Mosaic Law is the principle how he recognizes his cultural shards and deals with them.

To make Mosaic Law more exact, Ronald Sukenick also introduces a related term—psychosynthesis. "Psychosynthesis is the opposite of psychoanalysis" (Sukenick 1975a:122). As we know, psychoanalysis (also called Freudian psychology) is a body of ideas developed by Austrian physician Sigmund Freud in the 1890s and later continued by others. Freud bases his theory on the observation that childhood experiences and unconscious desires influence later behavior and develops a theory that describes development in terms of a series of psychosexual stages. According to Freud, conflicts that occur during each of these stages can have a lifelong influence on personality and behavior. In this sense, we can see that psychoanalysis emphasizes a cause-and-effect relationship between what has happened to a person in his stages of development and how he behaves and how he looks at himself.

Psychosynthesis, on the other hand, was developed in 1910 by Roberto Assagioli, an Italian psychiatrist. Although he is a colleague of Sigmund Freud and C. G. Jung, and an early pioneer of psychoanalysis in Italy, Assagioli becomes dissatisfied with psychoanalysis because he believes that psychoanalysis neglects the healthier and "higher" aspects of human nature. He seeks not only "psycho-analysis" but also "psycho-synthesis"—an understanding of how the psyche becomes whole. He puts forward two major models: the "oval-shaped" diagram of the basic model of the human personality ("egg" diagram) and the diagram of the stages of psychosynthesis to help us understand the various components of the self. In its most basic sense, psychosynthesis is a process of personal growth: the natural tendency in each of us to harmonize or synthesize our various aspects at ever higher levels of organization.

Ronald Sukenick believes that psychosynthesis replaces the rigid cause-and-effect relationship with moments of "Luminous... coincidence" between reality and invention. What is emphasized in psychosynthesis is "A way of things happening without happening. A way of dreaming without dreaming. A way of going mad without going mad. We deny nothing. We incorporate the negation in the affirmation" (Sukenick 1975a:180). Unlike the psychoanalysis which emphasizes the permanent effect of traumatic experience on one's personality, "in the process of psychosynthesis as in the subconscious as in the laws of physics there is no negation" (Sukenick 1975a:179). So the point of psychosynthesis is to "pick up the pieces and make something of them" (Sukenick 1975a: 122). What is emphasized in psychosynthesis by Sukenick is the way how one makes something of parts and fragments. Sukenick gives a vivid description of how psychosynthesis makes a difference in identity construction,

> Let me ask you something I'm very curious about you. What are you feeling now what is your life like. Can you describe it in a series of equations? Each equation should include the term fear thus failure plus fear equals despair love divided by fear equals hate now drop the term fear. Thus failure does not lead to despair love does not lead to hate you can look at your life this way even though it is not this way. But once you begin to look at life this way it begins to change do you follow a change in the field of consciousness is a change in the field of fact in one of the crucial factors in the field of fact." (Sukenick 1975a:179)

To Ronald Sukenick, different attitudes of treating one's parts and fragments can greatly influence one's life and one's identity construction. Thus, psychoanalysis and psychosynthesis suggest different ways of dealing with parts and fragments and also different ways of constructing identities.

5.1.1 Cultural Shards and Hybridity

As a Jewish writer, Ronald Sukenick cannot avoid Jewish themes in his works. However, it is not until his tenth work *Mosaic Man* that he begins to touch upon the theme of Jews and Jewishness. *Mosaic Man* depicts how a Jewish kid named Ron Sukenick seeks for his identity.

> Exiting Brooklyn as a kid Ron too is looking for something, though he doesn't know what it is... whatever it is, he thinks it may be rooted in Europe. He thinks maybe they'd left it there. Or brought it with them in the exodus and lost it en route. Or maybe Ron lost it when he was a kid. He doesn't know what it is but he knows he's going to have to trace the root. (Sukenick 1999:16-17)

Exiting Brooklyn, Ron starts his journey of identity pursuit, trying to find answers to such questions: what does it mean to be Jewish? What does it mean to be a Jew and a writer? A Jewish writer? A writing Jew?

However, the author Ronald Sukenick does not limit the identity seeking only to Jews. In "Genes", the first chapter of the novel, the protagonist Ron repetitively asks the questions: "Am I a Jew?" "Are you a Jew?"(Sukenick 1999:15) By quoting an article from *New York Times*, Ron shows that the research of scholars and descendants proves that Catholics in Spain and the mountains of New Mexico were converted from Jews under the threat of expulsion by Spainish monarchs in 1492. What he wants to prove is that whether a Christian or a Moslem, if one goes back far enough, he will find his Jewish root. Then, he clearly points out that "Being Jewish is just an advanced case of being human" (Sukenick 1999:16), which reminds the reader of the famous statement made by another Jewish writer Bernard Malamud, "Everyone is a Jew". In this way, Ronald Sukenick extends the theme of the novel to: What does it mean to be a human being? Just as Heise points out, "Pointedly, he [Sukenick] translates the issue of the Jew living in non-Jewish societies into the question of human identity in the midst of multiple nonhuman forms of life" (Heise 2003:92). Thus, the identity seeking journey of Ron, a Jew, is also the journey of a human to seek for his identity.

More important, the exploration of identity is made after the "ego smasher of history"—the Holocaust and the Cold War. "How could one assume the arrogance of individual identity after all those identities exxed off the surface of the planet since the year of my birth, 1932, the year Hitler assumed power? How could one even presume to be a person after all that, or even a human?" (Sukenick 1999:181) In other words, how could one be a human being in a most inhumane world? How could one search for identity in a "bankrupt modern world" (188), especially when the Holocaust and the Cold War smash the traditional ego?

In order to find answers to these questions, the protagonist Ron searches in different countries in Europe, America and the Middle East. He traces the history of his family as well as other Jews'. Finally, he arrives at the conclusion: Mosaic Man. As the title of the book suggests, Sukenick does not find what he looks for in one piece. Instead, he realizes that he wants to be and he has to be a Mosaic man: a man of hybridity of different cultural shards—his Jewish, European, American shards. He believes that modern man must be a patchwork mosaic in which the parts are the wholes, when the original wholes are destroyed.

For a Jew to seek the things he has lost, the best way undoubtedly is going back to the Holy Book of the Jews—Old Testament. Being a Mosaic man, first, means being the man of Moses, the follower of Moses and the Law of Moses. The Law of Moses is the law delivered from God through Moses to the Israelites during their Exodus from Egypt. "Behold, my soul delighteth in proving unto my people the truth of the coming of Christ; for this end hath the law of Moses been given; and all things which have been given of God from the beginning of the world, unto man, are the typifying of him" (2 Nephi 11:4). From this, we can see that the Law of Moses, which emphasizes obedience and sacrifice, is the foundation of the gospel, intending to bring the Children of Israel to knowledge of the Messiah. The Law of Moses refers to everything that Moses writes, and is divided into three parts: the Commandments, the Ordinances and the Judgments. The Commandments mainly contains the moral laws; the Ordinances, also called the spiritual code, includes the doctrine of Christ; the Judgments, the social code, is the divine laws of establishment applied to social living. Ronald Sukenick hopes that the Mosaic Law—the law of Moses, the Judeo-Christian tradition—which establishes God's wholeness as a solution to the fragmented character of contemporary culture to define one's being.

So the novel starts with the chapter entitled as Testimony (also read: Testament), which is the modification of the Old Testament's five books of Moses: Genesis as Genes, Exodus as EX/ODE, Leviticus as Umbilicus, Numbers as Numbers, and Deuteronomy as Autonomy. Indeed, this is Ron's self-mythology after the Old Testament, in which he mainly traces his roots in his familial history. "EX/ODE" for example, is a tape-recording of his conversations with his parents before his father's death, with gaps and missing words due to water-damaged tapes. The discontinuous recording fragments reveal the family history: the family comes from Bialystok, Poland, where they own a cloth mill. Ron's grandfather is the richest man by his sewing machine business. The family goes through pogroms (massacre of Jews) in Bialystok, and flees to the United States, where they are discriminated against and called "Dirty Jews". Then the death of his father means his breakage with his Jewish tradition, so he turns to his uncles for spiritual support. However, his uncles, under the influence of American culture, are giving up their Jewish beliefs and faith to materialistic comforts and pursuits. They no longer keep kosher, nor do they go to synagogue, nor do they keep the Sabbath custom. "The Uncles ate all the time whatever they were doing and they were all fat, as if they believed in the survival of the fattest" (Sukenick 1999:40). What they care about is only money. "American values are like Jewish values. The American dream is our dream" (45). A rabbi, to them, is an idiot, a dream, a person living in another world, and also a person who can't make a living. Under their influence, Ronnie no longer keeps such Jewish customs as Sabbath, kosher, going to synagogue and circumcision. Obviously, the Jewish traditions can no longer offer enough support to Ronnie's identity construction.

Just like the ancient Israelites, who exit from Egypt, take a journey onwards from Sinai towards Canaan—which is called Exodus, Ronald Sukenick in the part EX/ODE, exits from Brooklyn and heads for Europe as he believes that what he has lost may be rooted in Europe. The long history of European civilization can offer him answers. The chapter "Numbers" depicts the journey of identity searching of Ron Sukenick, now a college-age student and an American Jewish writer in such European countries as Germany, Poland, and France in the 1950s.

However, the bankruptcy of European culture completely disappoints him. "He goes to Europe to find it, but that's where he loses it completely" (73). In Germany, Ron observes that many people hold distorted opinions towards the defeat of Hitler and the Holocaust of Jews. Anti-Semitism is still popular. A Maltese once even says to Ron, "The one thing about Hitler is that it's too bad he didn't kill the rest of them. The Jews" (74). When he hears it, Ron realizes that "maybe this is when Ron loses it" (74). In Warsaw, Ron is told by a distinguished poet that "anti-Semitism continues in Poland, even though all its Jews have been annihilated" (75). To make things even worse, "victims become executioners" (76). In Paris, Adek, a Jew, whose father died at Auschwitz, joins an atelier consisting largely of right-wingers and anti-Semites. Moreover, the atelier is supported by a neofacist Le Pen. An unexpected encounter between the atelier and Jean Paul Sartre and Simon de Beauvoir reveals the direct confrontation between the young fascists and the country's leading left intellectuals. The aggression, vulgarity and corruption of the atelier—representatives of the young generation, make the West's greatest post-war philosopher become "sufficiently disillusioned with western culture to turn down, some years later, the Nobel Prize" (80). Later, his visit to the ghost ghetto in Venice—the most terrible living quarter for Jews—intensifies Sukenick's problems of identity: he realizes his own invisibility and reminds him of the same question by Kafka, "What have I in common with the Jews when I have nothing even in common with myself?... What self?" (160).

His visit to Berlin offers Ron chances to closely observe the fate of Jews in World War Ⅱ. The scene described by Erica, in which a torpedoed ship filled with refugees is sinking, makes Ron realize that "we no longer talk so much about the end of the world because at heart we realize the world as it used to be has already ended" (184). Moreover, the Jewish cemetery Ron visits is devoted to two kinds of death, that of individuals and that of a community—"a whole culture disappeared into a black hole" (189). What he experiences and witnesses in Europe makes Ron declare the bankruptcy of European civilization, "the great tradition of Humanism wasn't worth shit in chateau, a fox hole, a death camp, a stately state palace" (197).

To make things even worse, Ron finds that the post-war Europe infested with more insidious versions of "virus". From the neofascists' attacks on "Blacks, Arabs, and other foreigners in the metros of Paris" (12) to "anti-Semitism without Jews" (76) in Poland, and to a more general sense of "dead-ended" history experienced in the "ghost ghettoes" (189) of Europe, Ron feels the spread of the virus. And he is sad to realize that this virus has spread in America where "the civic philosophy, sickening, fell victim to epidemic self-interest" (107). Moreover, "European artistic culture is likewise contaminated, offering the American novice only varieties of decadence: from the 'inhuman' fiction of Celine (Louis-Ferdinand Céline, an anti-Semitic French writer) to the sadomasochistic Parisian avant-garde of the late 1950s; from the self-absorbed Lacanian 'auto-fiction' to the obsession of the contemporary German intelligentsia with the work of Holocaust survivors (as fellow writer Federman explains to Ron, they are trying to 'conduct a sort of autopsy. Now that they've killed off the Jews, they're interested in finding out what Jews were' (187)" (Cornis-Pope 2001:204).

Ron, after the bankruptcy of European culture, turns to American culture for the possibility to stake out a new cultural-aesthetic. American popular culture, represented by pop singer Elvis Presley, presents different features from highbrow culture in Europe with the art of speaking in "conundrums, riddles, nonsense, stupidity, slapstick, wordplay, clowning, quips" (Sukenick 1999:224). Though the great energy of American popular culture is an attraction, it is also infected by the European virus. Both Ron's Brooklyn childhood and his struggling youth in New York are marked by traumatic encounters with anti-Semitism, sexism and social discrimination. Moreover, the post Cold-War America is now craving for shallow materialism, represented by the Golden Calf.

Since he cannot find what he is looking for in Europe, nor in America, Ron decides to trace his family origin and also the origin of the Jews. His root-seeking journey first takes him to Bialystok, Poland, where his family came from. At the beginning, Ron is doubtful about his journey since the Holocaust in World War II has taken away the lives of 48,915 Jews, and the anti-Semitism after the war drives almost all remaining Jews out of the country. So when Jews are almost extinct in this country, "Why bother going back to Bialystok, or anywhere in Poland for that matter? There is nothing to go back to" (109). However, Bialystok surprises Ron with a few "luminous coincidences". Marta, a Jewish writer, translator and editor of an underground publication, first cooks him a Jewish meal. "We want to know what Jews were like. What their culture was, what they ate. How they thought" (116). More important, the rebellious tactics she adopts in harsh situations make Ron recognize a "Siamese twin" in her. "Stupidity is our means of survival... But sometimes it takes some really stupid people to change a situation the smart people know is hopeless" (113). The statement "Marta is a sukiennik" clearly demonstrates his identification with Marta, and with the Jewish beliefs represented by Marta.

His journey to Jerusalem—the Holy Land of Jews—is the highlight of the novel. Israel (much like in *98.6*) is not the real geo-cultural location of a country. Instead, it is a metaphor of paradoxical inclusiveness and mosaics. "Jerusalem, especially is a place where everything seems to happen at once" (120) "Because in Israel the past is the present" (136). This historical co-presence and co-existence give the country "hard definition, redefinition over-definition" (146). In Israel, languages from all over Europe, North Africa and the Middle East are spoken. Looking from Mount Scopus, the city looks like "gems heaped on a pale table refracting sharply but differently from different perspectives" (146). It's also a place "with too many gods, too many tribes, each obsessively drilling its own tunnel to the light... It's full of holes tunneling toward our missing whole" (146). Three major religions—Judaism, Christianity and Islam resemble the "jewel-like birds that inhabit its parks—bulbul, hoopoe, sunbird—each monopolizing the attention in turn with its dazzling, singular and dominating brilliance" (146). In this sense, Israel is a mosaic place of all languages, all religions and all peoples. The peaceful co-existence of different parts offers Ron the answers to the questions of identity he asked at the beginning of the novel. "Being Jewish is an art. You got to have talent" (204). He realizes that "He's a dummy. A manikin. An android. An alien cyberpod. Slapped together. Mosaic man, the man of parts. Ceramic. Or silicon. Prick him he doesn't bleed. He who? The Jew" (Sukenick 1999:205). It's obvious that when cultural centre is destroyed, one has to be a mosaic man, making meaning of his different cultural shards.

We should also note that Ron seeks his identity not only as a Jew, but also as a writer, as a Jewish writer. So the journey of seeking "who he is" is also the journey of finding "how should he write". In fact, at the very beginning of the journey, Ron displays his rebellion against the established literary principle—fiction is to make things up. "It's not until Ron starts writing his first novel, *Up*, that he realizes he doesn't want to be a novelist. It's then that he realizes he finds the whole idea of what's called a novel boring. He realizes that he simply does not like the idea of making things up" (Sukenick 1999: 96). To him, this dislike is deeply rooted in his Jewish tradition. "The Jewish tradition has a long history of struggle against imitation" (96). Moreover, Ron believes that the old tradition of composition of making things up gives one a false liberty. Indeed, it is not real liberty, but libertine instead. Libertine cannot be called Art. Moreover, libertine leads to idols that are always cheap imitations of treacherous gods. The Golden Calf—the idol made by Aaron to be worshipped by Israelites—is an example of such cheap imitations. That is why God gets furious and nearly destroys the Jews because of their worship of the

Golden Calf.

According to Ron, "books should be literally true. It is only the literally true that is fundamentally mysterious" (105). So he puts his ideas into practice and works on a book entitled *Wholly Book*, in which he combines reality and illusion.

> This book would be the book that is wholly book (doven).
> This would be a book that Ron believes in wholly (doven).
> This would be and is the wholly book of books. (106)

His realization that fiction is not something made up but a literally true reflection of his experience is the first step to his answer of identity seeking as a Jewish writer. Then his visit to the post-1989 Berlin inspires a meditation on ideas frozen in concrete and prepares him for his Mosaic Law. The mutilated Berlin Wall suggests to Ron the collapse of ideological discourse. "The page... crammed with multicolored multilingual writing, the writing on the wall an incomprehensible babel of symbols, slogans, signs, messages, epigraphs, hieroglyphs, riddles, runes, alphabetic jocularities, plays on words and words playing on themselves... what you might call concrete poetry, all hacked and pocked and pitted and peeled through layers of painted and petrified pal" (184). Fragments of different forms are collaged into a hybridity and mosaic, which manages to challenge the traditional monologic discourse.

At last, his journey to Jerusalem makes him settle down on Mosaic Law because Jerusalem makes him realize that different parts can co-exist peacefully to form a new whole. More important, Mosaic Law makes him realize that the post-Holocaust/post-Cold War writer finds his home not in a particular geocultural location (ancestral Poland, Venice, Paris, Berlin, Jerusalem, Boulder or New York), but in the re-creative "mosaic" of his fiction that honors the visionary "unworldly" as much as the "worldly-wise" (qtd. LeClair & McCaffery 1974:180).

Ronald Sukenick is a new Moses who is writing a new "scripture"—fiction—and leading us to a new "promised land"—the land of fictive invention. Furthermore, mosaic—coming from the Latin Musa for muse—is like *98.6*, an artwork of disconnected pieces that an artist puts together to make a whole.

5.1.2 Psychosynthesis vs. Psychoanalysis

To clearly illustrate the term Mosaic Law—the law of mosaics or the law about how to deal with parts in the absence of wholes, Ronald Sukenick introduces another term psychosynthesis. Psychosynthesis is the opposite of psychoanalysis in that the former connects, and the latter separates. Psychosynthesis connects the disparate pieces of our experience. And in Sukenick's understanding, it also connects letters to make words,

words to make sentences, and sentences to make fiction—and all through the power of imagination.

Psychoanalysis, referring to a psychological theory and a method of treatment of psychological disorders, is first put forward by Sigmund Freud, and later developed by other psychoanalysts as Melanie Klein and Jacques Lacan. The core of psychoanalysis is the theory of the unconscious and the structural model of the psyche. The unconscious comprises ideas that are usually unacceptable, either because they are experienced as internally threatening to the existence of the individual, or because they are experienced as threatening to society. Thus, these ideas are repressed, only to be released and fulfilled in dreams. Freud's account of dreams provides the most elaborate analysis of the workings of the unconscious. These unconscious factors may create unhappiness, sometimes in the form of recognizable symptoms and at other times as troubling personality traits, difficulties in work or in love relationships, or disturbances in mood and self esteem. Thus psychoanalysts try to understand the troubles and difficulties in identity construction by tracing back to one's past trauma and experience.

Freud's psychology divides the human mind into three elements: the id, ego and superego. The id contains everything that is inherited, everything that is present at birth, and the instincts. The ego, the link between the id and the external world, is responsible for controlling the demands of the id and instincts. In addition, the ego responds to stimulation by either adaptation or flight, regulates activity and strives to achieve pleasure and avoid displeasure. At last, the superego is responsible for the limitation of satisfactions and represents the influence of others as well as the impact of racial, societal and cultural traditions (Freud 1949:15). By dividing a man's sexual development into four main phases: the oral phase, the sadistic-anal phase, the phallic phase and the genital phase, Freud tends to view the man's higher values and achievements from the angles of the lower instincts and drives.

Roberto Assagioli, an Italian psychiatrist, a colleague of Sigmund Freud and C. G. Jung, and first a follower of psychoanalysis, shows his move away from Freud's psychoanalysis towards what he calls psychosynthesis in his doctoral dissertation. By developing psychosynthesis, Assagioli seeks to address not only the resolution of early childhood issues—a focus on what he calls the lower unconscious—but to give attention to the sphere of aesthetic experience, creative inspiration, and higher states of consciousness—which he calls the higher unconscious or superconscious. The higher unconscious (or superconscious) denotes "our higher potentialities which seek to express themselves, but which we often repel and repress" (Assagioli 1965:22). In this way, psychosynthesis believes that although the past experience is worth exploring, it is a shortcoming for us to assume that an individual is purely the result of nature or nurture. For psychosynthesis, "the deepest reason for our pain and suffering is that we have forgotten who we really are. The true source of our suffering may lie in this 'forgetting', the betrayal, the loss of contact with our essential nature of Self and the meaningful journey life is meant to be for each of us" (Whitmore 2004: x). So Assagioli maintains that the purpose of psychosynthesis is to help integrate, to synthesize, the multiple aspects of individual's personality into the increasing wholeness.

Two major differences lie between psychoanalysis and psychosynthesis. First of all, psychoanalysis focuses on the isolated individual struggling with inner drives, while psychosynthesis focuses on personal growth, self-actualization and the higher unconscious. Moreover, psychoanalysis focuses on personal psychology, while psychosynthesis emphasizes transpersonal. Stretching beyond the boundaries of personal psychology and individuality, Assagioli's psychosynthesis recognizes the individual's need for meaning, both the meaning of our own individual existence and the meaning of the world in which we live. Diana Whitmore summarizes psychosynthesis in the following way,

> It does not seek to explain away the mystery of life and human development. It values times of darkness as much as periods of joy; it encourages us to embrace the unknown with no guarantees of security; it respects the creativity of confusion, rather than ready-made certainty; and most importantly it welcomes the unexpected which shatters our attachments and fixed models. (Whitmore 2004: X)

Sukenick first introduces the term psychosynthesis into his novel *98. 6*. "Psychosynthesis is the opposite of psychoanalysis but apart from that Cloud refuses to define it. Cloud feels that life is a lot like a novel you have to make it up. That's the point of psychosynthesis in his opinion to pick up the pieces and make something of them" (Sukenick 1975a: 122). Cloud, whose original name is Ron (the same as the author Ronald Sukenick) believes that one has to construct one's life story by picking up the pieces and making something of them. It is what he means psychosynthesis and also the strategy of identity construction in postmodern American society.

The novel *98. 6* consists of three parts: Frankenstein, The Children of Frankenstein and Palestine. In "Frankenstein", by piecing together fragments from books and newspapers, all describing incidents of monstrosity, such as torture, rape, sadomasochism and murder, the author describes Frankenstein (the metaphor for America) in the 1960s and early 1970s as a monster of cruelty, violence and murder. Especially the bloody ceremonies of sacrificing girls and boys to gods in ancient Maya and Aztecs civilization are traumas which influence the later civilization in the same way the childhood traumas affect later behavior and personality. They are the roots of the "sadism + masochism" (7) in modern civilization. These traumas, together with the trauma like the Great Depression, are hard to get rid of. "Joy doesn't get rid of it. Dope doesn't get rid of it. Sex doesn't get rid of it. Freedom doesn't get rid of it. Murder doesn't get rid of it. Give up and die. Emptiness is the best you can hope for" (67). Moreover, the trauma results in the loss of identity, which is displayed by the namelessness of the narrator and the anonym of the character.

Though hard, ten children of Frankenstein still try to get rid of the traumas, and escape from Frankenstein to seek their new identity. They establish a Garden-of-Eden-like commune called Monster, where they live together, work together and grow together. In their new life, "the only rule they have is not to talk about the past" (65). They do not believe that the psychoanalyst way of exploring and understanding the past traumas can help solve the current emotional and behavioral problems. Instead, they turn to psychosynthesis. Actually they unconsciously follow the four stages of psychosynthesis put forward by Assagioli: thorough knowledge of one's personality; control of its various elements; realization of one's true Self—the discovery or creation of a unifying center; and at last psychosynthesis—the formation or reconstruction of the personality around a new center (Assagioli 1965:21). Away from the violent culture of Frankenstein, living in the beautiful harmonious Garden-of-Eden-like environment, the children of Frankenstein begin to know their own personalities. Paul, for example, who used to be a civil rights lawyer, now finds himself a handyman. "There seems to Paul nothing better in life that you could do than to be able to work with your hands repairing things patching things together making useful things out of whatever happens to be at hand" (Sukenick 1975a: 71). Moreover, the communication between them begins to change them. In the beginning, two share a tent. Later, "Feather comes often now to Al's tent to make love. She still lives with Dave. Al and Dave are developing a kind of intimate comraderie... The three of them together are quite charming... Generating a lot of energy... Dave feels so changed by his new relation with Feather that he too changes his name. His new name is Goose" (82-83). The new name declares the new identity.

The new life offers them opportunities for personal growth, self-actualization and new-identity construction. Paul's way of identity construction is by making things up. "He feels a need to make things up to fill the emptiness to fill it with themselves their dreams and their nightmares the fantastic shape of their house" (84). Ralph, on the one hand, believes that he needs a kind of breakthrough. "I had too much going on inside me the pressure was too much. I sort of broke open. I was kind of a bundle of parts that didn't go together anymore. I need another way now. I need to put myself back together again. That's why I came out here" (112). This kind of making a new whole and unity out of old parts is just the practice of psychosynthesis. So after living together, each of them assumes a new name, which is a symbol of their new identities.

However, this ideal state does not last long, nor do their new identities. The past they want to escape keeps coming back and exerting influence on them. Moreover, their relationships get confused. Triangle relationships become quadrangles. Quadrangles become hexagrams. The confused relationships generate such negative mood as jealousy, which in turn causes problems in emotions. The threat from Frankenstein and other tribes causes more and more damage to them. At last, the death of the coming baby of Valley and the fire of the Monster completely destroy the commune and their newly-established identities.

With the failure of the children of Frankenstein, Ronald Sukenick continues his search for an effective way of identity construction in the third part "Palestine". He comes to realize the importance of imagination in achieving psychosynthesis.

"Palestine", the third part of the novel, depicts how a character, named Ronald Sukenick, is seeking his identity both as a writer and as a Jew. He, at last, achieves what he wants in Palestine. Palestine, under the pen of Sukenick, is turned into an ideal state. It has perfect weather and perfect harmony, even between Arabs and Jews. Its ocean rhythms repeat in the bodily rhythms of blood and breath. The city is the joint work of architects and artists. However, it is no longer Israel in the real sense. Noel points out that "Israel is a state of mind more than a particular geopolitical entity" (Noel 1976:128). Since Israel is no longer a geopolitical entity, the only way to enter the place is through psychosynthesis. Noel points out that "At all events, Psychosynthesis is Sukenick's way back to the Holy Land" (Noel 1976:129). To be exact, the only way back to Palestine is through imagination. Sukenick emphasizes the importance of imagination to psychosynthesis. "Only the mind can deal with the mind only the imagination can deal with the imagination thus Psychosynthesis. A way of curing the disease without catching it. A way of things happening without happening. A way of dreaming without dreaming. A way of going mad without going mad" (Sukenick 1975a: 180). So it is a way of employing imagination to deal with the disorder of our imagination. Just like we connect letters to make words, words to sentences and sentences to fiction, psychosynthesis connects the disparate pieces of our experience, through the power of imagination to make a new whole of self. Psychosynthesis, in fact, in some way, emphasizes the centrality of imagination in the construction of reality.

"Psychology was the trademark of a previous era" (Sukenick 1975a:123). To Ronald Sukenick, psychoanalysis is not enough to deal with the problem of fragmentation we meet in identity seeking and construction in the postmodern world, as psychoanalysis forces us to shatter experience. So in the postmodern context, "What we have instead of psychology is imagination. In any case psychology was always the science of imagination but as a medical science was obliged to treat it like a sickness" (Sukenick 1975a: 123). Only imagination can restore that lost synthesis which analysis has forced us to shatter.

In the postmodern world, the whole and the unity are destroyed, what we have now is

"Interruption. Discontinuity. Imperfection. It can't be helped" (Sukenick 1975a:167). This is where Mosaic Law can be realized. This is where the psychosynthesis can be practiced—to compose out of ongoing decomposition, to synthesize out of fragments. This is the new Torah of postmodern novel creation. This is the solution proposed by Ronald Sukenick to the problems of identity construction: when the whole and unity are absent, the principle is to make meaning of out parts and collage parts.

Mosaic Law of identity illustrates identity construction in the postmodern context from two perspectives: culturally and psychologically. Sukenick's keen diagnosis of identity crisis—the absence of cultural centre and wholeness makes his solution to the crisis effective: when the centre, wholeness and unity are destroyed, what an individual can do is to make sense of parts and fragments.

5.2 Mosaic Law of Postmodernist Narratives

Ronald Sukenick introduces Mosaic Law both into the principle of identity construction and into his principle of fiction writing. According to Ronald Sukenick, postmodernist works operate in the absence of wholes. The overwhelming information ceaselessly saturates the individual with new data and new experiences that he cannot keep up with. So "the closure sought in the traditional text also symbolizes a closing off of experience, a death of possibility, a false sense of mastery of life" (qtd. LeClair & Mc Caffery 1974:121). In this sense, Sukenick believes it is impossible for a writer to find a formal structure that can contain the fullness of experience. Moreover, the fragments, though uncompleted, suggest different possibilities and mark a richer and more complex world. "One cannot have control 'over' that of which one is a part, or even to formulate it completely—one can only participate more deeply in it" (Sukenick 1975c:4).

Denied totality, wholeness and unity, and in the presence of so many fragments and particles, what the character and the writer have to do is to choose and compose. This process of creating a new whole from fragments of disparate discourses is just like the modernist strategy of collage. In an interview with Patrick Lavalle, Sukenick mentions the collage used in T. S. Elliot's *The Waste Land*, Ezra Pound's *Cantos* and James Joyce's *Ulysses* and *Finnegan's Wake*, stressing that the collage is "a way of pulling in a lot of new material, recombining it in a new form that create[s] something unpremeditated" (Sukenick 1985:130). Sukenick believes that collage can generate unforeseen connections and create unpredictable meanings. However, Sukenick does not simply borrow the technique of collage from modernism. Instead, he creates the Mosaic Law of postmodernist narratives: the law of dealing with parts when the whole is absent.

Charles Russell points out the difference between the modernist collage and the Sukenick's postmodernist mosaic:

> But unlike the modernists who assumed the individual writer's subjective power to substitute the overarching authority of art for debased or rejected cultural codes that provided the fragments for their collages, the postmodernist has little faith in the transcendent or totalizing power of the artwork (or, for that matter, even the authority of the creative subject). (Russell 2003:119)

In other words, postmodernist mosaic never aims at a coalescence of meaning into a new whole, because the wholeness is rather fragile. Fiction writing, as a self-reflexive process and an improvisational flow, constantly deconstructs the stable structure of the text. What is left is "Interruption. Discontinuity. Imperfection. It can't be helped. This very instant as I write as you read a hundred things. A hundred things to tangle with resolve ignore before you are together. Together for an instant and then smash it's all gone still it's worth it. This composition grown out of ongoing decomposition" (Sukenick 1975a:167). In the process of composition and decomposition, the full and stable structure of the text is smashed. What we have are just fragments. In postmodernist mosaic, no fragment is more essential than others. The purpose of postmodernist mosaic lies in that "the interplay of semiotic elements rather calls attention to the interstices of discourses, the gaps within meaning systems, as well as the competition of invading discourses that intrude on and subvert other meaning systems" (Russell 2003:119).

Mosaic Law of postmodernist narratives—the law of dealing with parts and fragments when the whole is absent—offers Sukenick skills to hold the particles and fragments of his stories together and make them interchangeable parts of mosaics that come into existence as the stories move along. Sukenick points out the importance of Mosaic Law of postmodernist narratives to his innovation of fiction writing:

> The kind of sequence developed by linkage of disparate fragments might seem lunatic, but it might be argued that this kind of organization is one of the mind's most formidable methods of organizing the disparities of experience. It has the virtue of generating unforeseen connections, and is particularly useful in a time when traditional causes no longer seem adequate to account for observed effects. It may produce new systems of order when traditional ones no longer seem persuasive. Since it starts beyond system it is capable of including kinds of experience that given systems might exclude. Or if such a method of organization is considered as a system, then it is an open system. (Sukenick 1985:14)

So in order to achieve the purpose of breaking the stable structure of traditional novels and generating new, unpredictable connections, Sukenick pieces together fragments of different kinds, some of which seldom appear in past novel writing. In order to illustrate Sukenick's unique use of Mosaic Law of postmodernist narratives, I divide it into two kinds: patchwork and collage. Patchwork refers to the putting together of different language fragments, while collage refers to the piecing together of words and symbols.

5.2.1 Patchwork

Patchwork, or "pieced work", is a form of needlework that involves sewing together pieces of fabric into a larger design. The larger design of patchwork is usually based on repeat patterns built up with different geometric shapes, carefully measured and cut, straight-sided, making them easy to piece together. Patchwork is most often used to make quilts, but it can also be used to make bags, wall-hangings, warm jackets, skirts, waistcoats and other items of clothing. This term is introduced here for the purpose of emphasizing Sukenick's different and diversified use of mosaics. A key difference between patchwork and collage lies in that patchwork pieces together pieces of the same kind, while collage assembles pieces of different kinds.

Patchwork, the technique of sticking various pieces into a whole, is employed by Ronald Sukenick in his fictional writing from his first novel *Up*. "This is just a collection of disjointed fragments" (Sukenick 1968: 222). Bernie, a character in the novel makes such comment on the novel being written—*Up* exactly. This, in some sense, points out a very important feature of Sukenick's novels: fragmentation. And his Mosaic Law of narratives is the way Sukenick finds to make sense of fragments and make them into a new whole. Throughout his fictional writing practice, Sukenick experiments with different forms of patchwork: patchwork of narratives and speeches, patchwork of language of different genres and patchwork of street language and highbrow language.

The patchwork of narratives and speeches is a practice quite common in Sukenick's fiction. In his third novel *Out*, Ronald Sukenick experiments with the forms of fiction. The unique arrangement of chapters—the countdown from Chapter 10 to 0, the different lengths of the paragraphs within each chapter—the decrease from nine lines in each paragraph in Chapter 9 to one line in Chapter 1 and to a complete blank page in Chapter 0, and the blank space separating paragraphs all challenging the traditional fiction writing and reading. More unique than the arrangement of chapters is Sukenick's treatment of characters' speeches in the novel. All the direct speeches in the novel are presented without quotation marks so that the narratives and speeches are patched together. The blurring of the voice of narration with the voice of characters erases the separating lines between these two different voices and turns everything into narration.

No quotation marks are used to delineate dialogue. Instead, a change of speaker is designated by a new paragraph. In this way, without quotations, the occasional "he says" or "she says" dialogue attribution becomes part of the sentence. And also without quotes, the attribution usually becomes a false attribution. Moreover, sometimes, the dialogue goes on without quotation marks and also without the attribution, which causes the confusion. The confusion, sometimes, is intensified by the stream of identities we have discussed in the previous part, in which the character changes his names frequently. Just as when two Nicks meet together:

> What do you mean says Nick.
> So you're Carl says the guy.
> What makes you think I'm Carl.
> I got a thing with names I never get em wrong.
> That's remarkable.
> Yeah ainit. Well glad to know you Carl my name's Nick a terrifying yowl tears out of the back of the car my god what's that says Carl.
> Nothing I got a cat in the trunk says Nick he touches a switch a soul thudding rock number buzzes Carl's eardrums ah heard it though the gape vine ah heard it through the grape vine.
> Open the glove apartment Nick yells Carl opens it you wanna take out that baggie in there Carl takes it out unroll it Nick yells Carl unrolls it it's filled with skinny little cigarettes you wanna hand me one of those joints yells Nick Carl hands it to him. (Sukenick 1973:58-59)

So when the first Nick meets the second Nick, he is forced to change into Carl. The long sentence in the last paragraph quoted pieces together the voice of narration with the voices of Nick and Carl. No quotation marks, or other punctuation marks, can help the reader to make proper stops so as to understand the meaning. Clearly, the author's purpose of doing so is not to call attention to a speaker, but a meta-fictional way to call attention to the artifice of the narration.

Moreover, by blurring narration with speeches, Sukenick blurs the present and the past, dissolving time to the point of the present. In his short story "The Death of the Novel", Ronald Sukenick, through a conversation between two characters, explains that his non-use of attributions is a formal way of forcing the narration into the present tense:

> Well, in general, I mean, wait a minute. Since this is a story you have to say "she said" after everything you say.
> Do I really?
> Yes. Because how are people going to tell, right?

> Oh I don't like that.
> She said.
> I don't like that.
> She said.
> Because that's like living at a distance from your own body.
> She said.
> That's like the character in "A Painful Case" in *Dubliners.*
> What's that? She said I mean I said.
> Everything he thought he appended a pronoun and a verb in the past tense, to every thought.
> For example.
> Well he would think, um, "The world works in mysterious ways, he said."
> Oh, really? I said. Would you rather I said I said, since I'm writing the story I'll say, okay since I'm writing the story I'll say I said. And she said. Fine. I'm your character. Except for the dialogue.
> ...
> But you're also in the story. I said.
> What do I do?
> She said. You talk like you're talking now. I said. And also you occupy the place where the story is being composed, namely here. (Sukenick 2003:82-83)

The conversation reveals Sukenick's improvisation principle of fiction writing: since I'm writing the story, I have the right to say. The cover page of the collection of short stories just reveals this principle. Instead of the traditional "*The Death of the Novel and Other Stories* by Ronald Sukenick", the cover page says

> RONALD
> SUKENICK
> Author of "UP"
> WRITES
> THE DEATH
> OF THE
> NOVEL
> AND OTHER
> STORIES

The present tense used here, and also the present tense used in the novel show that fiction writing is a communication between the author and his character, the author and his experience. The patchwork of voice of narration and voices of characters also brings the reader into the communication.

Patchwork of language of different genres does not begin with Ronald Sukenick. As early as in the 1930s, John Dos Passos first introduces in his trilogy *U. S. A.* the skill of Newsreel: extracting newspaper headlines into his stories. Rather than using only headlines of the news in the fictional text, Sukenick inserts whole articles in newspaper into his novel. In his first novel *Up*, Ronald Sukenick inserts a newspaper article by Bernie into his narrative. Noteworthily, Ronald Sukenick formats the article and makes it just like the way it appears in the newspaper. Bernie's article, which is entitled "Liberation to What", is printed down the center of a newspaper page, next to ads for underwear and pet treats, as well as a portion of an article on military expansion in Latin America.

One more reform and innovation Sukenick makes here is that the quotation is interrupted by Ronnie's comment and his conversation with Nancy while reading. The patchwork of narrative and journalistic genres with the interruption of conversation shows that the text is a developing object of itself over which even the author has little control.

In his later writing, Ronald Sukenick continues his practice of patchwork of language of different genres. However, he does not simply repeat the practice. Instead, he always experiments with new ways of patchwork of different genres.

In *98. 6*, from page 45 to page 50, Ronald Sukenick patches pieces and fragments from different genres of books: a novel of new journalism, articles from magazines and a historical book. To be exact, fragments from Tom Wolfe's *The Electric Kool-Aid Acid Test*, articles by Lucian K Truscott, Maharibi Muntu, Bob Kuttner, Dore Ashton and Joanna Russ from magazines of *Village Voice*, *The Los Angeles Times* and *Los Angeles Herald Examiner*, and clips from the historical book *The Hummingbird and the Hawk: Conquest and Sovereignty in the Valley of Mexico 1503-1541* by R. C. Padden are put together. The piece from Tom Wolfe's novel depicts a scene of gang rape. Truscott reports the Manson Family murder case. Muntu's article covers the inhuman treatment to the prisoners. Kuttner reveals the terrible facts that the American government and a university cheat the poor patients in an experimental treatment. Padden describes the Aztec custom of sacrificing virgins to gods. Although they are taken from different sources, factual or fictive, reportorial or commentary, realistic or historical, these fragments centre on common themes: blood, violence and monstrosity. So, the author's purpose of putting them together is to indicate that contemporary America's obsession with violence and death can be traced back to a legacy of cultural violence.

Noteworthily, all these clips are appropriated, repunctuated and juxtaposed, just like the cloth which is carefully measured and cut, straight-sided. More important, this kind of patchwork is a Cubist patchwork, with each piece a block, put together like the toy bricks. All the pieces are pieced together in two columns in a jigsaw pattern. As Lance Olsen points out,

> The consequence of all these visual displays is the development of an intricate piece of textual architecture akin to the assemblage-house called The Monster built at the commune or a kind of graphictional Frankensteinian patchwork stitched together in a proto-avant-pop gesture out of the detritus of our culture to mimic a multidimensional polyverse, or what Foucault calls a HETEROTOPIA, the linking together of things that are inappropriate; I mean the disorder in which fragments of a large number of possible orders glitter separately in the dimension, without law or geometry of the heteroclite. (Olsen 2003:158-159)

So the patchwork of language fragments of different genres brings a result of multicolor, polyverse in which each fragment keeps its own feature. But at the same time they form a whole, adding new meanings by the new connections.

Ronald Sukenick goes farther in his practice of patchwork of different genres in his novel *Mosaic Man*. Just as the title suggests, Ronald Sukenick attempts to achieve mosaic narratives. Instead of the traditional linear chronological narrative, Sukenick aims at a multivocal and polyphonic narrative. For this purpose, he quilts narratives of different genres. Basically, the novel is an autobiographical narrative of Sukenick's search for his identity as a Jew and a writer. Among the autobiographic narratives, Sukenick pieces together other narratives as the popular stories of Captain Midnight, tape-recording of conversations and criticism of others.

The "EX/ODE" part narrates the life story of Sukenick's father. His father, as a Jew, has to ruin one of his eyes so as to escape from Russia where they want him to serve in the army. Then, as a descendant of the owner of a cloth mill, Sukenick's father makes a fortune in the United States by inventing Singer Sewing Machines, which brings him money to enjoy the life of wine, women and songs. Yet he is discriminated against in Brooklyn because he is a Jew. Among the narratives of his childhood memory, tape-recording conversations between Sukenick and his mother, Sukenick and his father, Sukenick and his grandmother are inserted. These untagged dialogues function as complement, offering the clues for the reader to understand the suicide of Sukenick's father, from another perspective. The exodus of Sukenick's aged mother—her move to another unit in the same apartment building does play some role in the suicide of Sukenick's ailing father.

From page 48 to page 72, a story of Captain Midnight is inserted into the autobiographical narrative. The story depicts the secret mission of Captain Midnight and his group—to save the Jews in Germany from Hitler's death machine by bombing the Nazi concentration camps. The character Captain Midnight is a comic hero in the 1940s radio series. And Sukenick is also in the mission group. The tense and exciting development of the plot and the frequent exchange of secret codes give the story the style of a detective or war story. The style of the Captain Midnight story, though not fit in the style of the autobiographical narrative, offers a different voice about the fate of Jews. The whole insertion is a black humor, to be exact. Their mission is "denazification" (Sukenick 1999: 52)—using American germs again German germs so as to have a world where there are no Nazis. However, who they really destroy are not Nazis, but Jews. Then "What about the Jews? Aren't afraid of hitting the Jews?" "Jews? In Germany?" "The Jews are already chosen. They're chosen to live in the other world" (Sukenick 1999:52-53). The dialogue reveals the essence of their mission—they destroy the Jews as well as the Nazis. This, in some sense, also reveals the hypocritical attitude of the American government towards Jews.

The part "After the Fact" records Sukenick's trip to Berlin where he meets other writers and shows them his early drafts of *Mosaic Man*. This part, in fact, concentrates on one of the important themes of the novel—the Jew's pursuit of identity in the period of fascism—"ongoing ego smasher of the history" (Sukenick 1999: 181). To be exact, it records Sukenick's pursuit for his identity as a Jewish writer in the period when the fiction is dead. The conversations between Sukenick and two other writers Raymond Federman and Serge Doubrovsky, reveal the communication and clash between the traditional writers and innovative writers and also the communication within the group of innovative writers. To vividly display different voices of fiction writing at that time, in the narrative of their communication in Berlin, Sukenick inserts in this part Federman's and Doubrovsky's notes on the drafts of *Mosaic Man*, respectively on pages 181, 183, 181, 192, 194, 195 and 200. These notes, to some extent, predict the possible responses of different critics to the novel *Mosaic Man*, both attack and praise.

More important, the three writers—Federman, Doubrovsky and Sukenick, all Jewish—display different pursuits of identity. Doubrovsky, a French autobiographical writer, graduates from the elite school for French intellectuals, "looks like the complete European Jewish intello" (Sukenick 1999: 194). As a conventional writer, Doubrovsky innovates in a limited scope. Federman, on the other hand, shares more common ideas with Sukenick in such fiction innovations as characterization and form innovations. However, they still show great divergence in identity pursuit. In Sukenick's point of view, Federman's ambition in life is finding the Golden Calf—the symbol of material wealth. What he is running after is fame and money, to which Sukenick disagrees. So the insertion of Federman's and Doubrovsky's notes into the narration directly illustrates the different voices in identity pursuit and in fiction writing.

Sukenick also inserts in the novel *Mosaic Man* other language pieces that usually do not appear in fiction. For example, the exact recipes of such traditional Jewish foods as prune soup, kreplach and cholent are inserted into the narrative of the story respectively on pages 107, 114, 115, 115 and 124. Newspaper clipping is also used in this fiction. Clippings from the French newspaper *Le Monde*, reporting the archaeological discovery of Golden Calf (131), from *New York Times* (141) and *Jerusalem Post* (143) are inserted into the development of the plot. The purpose is to achieve the multivocal and polyphony paradigm of narratives so as to replace the traditional linearity and chronology of narratives.

To Ronald Sukenick, a major feature of the postmodern society is the cultural communication and clashes. Individuals, in communication and clashes, have more difficulties in constructing their identities. To illustrate these difficulties and problems, Sukenick employs the patchwork of street language and highbrow language to illustrate the clashes between cultures.

Doggy Bag (1994) is a collection of interconnected short stories. All the stories collected centre on a common context: Americans in a spiritually exhausted Europe. In a sense, *Doggy Bag* is an answer to T. S. Eliot's *The Waste Land*: Don't waste anything; recycle it, cut it up and engulf it down. The design of the cover just reveals the theme: "The cover design—representing a wolf dog holding a green bag with a skull-and-crossbones drawing—suggests that recycling within and between cultures resembles a process of cannibalization" (Cornis-Pope 2001:185).

Doggy Bag explores the theme of identity pursuit in the context of communication and clashes between European and American cultures. Characters in different short stories seek and construct their identities in the clashes of European high culture against American pop culture. To illustrate the clashes and hybridity of cultures, Sukenick mixes the street language of America with the highbrow language.

The first story "Who are these people?" depicts an American waiting outside the Uffizi—the famous museum and a symbol of European culture. About two-thirds of the people waiting in long line in front of the museum are Americans. Americans of different ages, different colors and from different walks wait to pay their worship to European culture. Among the conversational, causal and everyday American English of "woodja", "gonna", and "sheez" etc., Sukenick inserts the highbrow language of Henry James. "I'm heading for the Uffizi yesterday in a leisurely way, expecting to 'do' it, as Henry James might say, for the third time after a lapse of twenty-odd years, when as my 'companion', as Henry James might call her, and myself turn into the piazza in front of the entrance" (Sukenick 1994:9). Other words like "interlocutor" are also inserted in the text.

The mosaic of street language and highbrow language, in a sense, vividly displays the clashes and hybridity of cultures. Olsen points out one important difference of this kind of patchwork: "unlike Eliot's serious, even nostalgic shoring up of fragments against the ruins, however, Sukenick expresses a devious joy in toying with the cultural shards, often citing them for no other purpose other than to cite them, to riff on them, conflating pop material with that of high art to a degree *The Wasteland* finds it impossible to contemplate" (Olsen 2003:162).

Sukenick's novel *Mosaic Man* is another example of the patchwork of street language and highbrow language. The book's title itself is a pun. It refers not only to Moses but its mosaic-like construction. Ronald Sukenick adopts and adapts books from the Old Testament for his own purpose. "Genesis" becomes "Genes", "Exodus", "EX/ODE" and so on. At the very beginning of the part "Genes", Sukenick elaborates the beginning of fiction:

> In the beginning was the WORD which is unspeakable, unreadable and unintelligible. Beyond human perception. Sublime. Writing not yet language. Dazzle. Pure information. Generative. Algorithmic. Digital, i.e. DNA. Digital Not Analog. Helical. The master code. Orginal. The first person. Iconoclastic. Always beginning. (Sukenick 1999:9)

We can see that the first paragraph of "Genes" is indeed, an imitation of the beginning of "Genesis" in the Old Testament. "Genesis" narrates the beginning of human beings and the world, while "Genes" is Sukenick's reflection on the beginning of the word and the beginning of the story. The language used in this part is rather highbrow and serious.

However, under the title "EX/ODE", which is also adopted from the sacred book of the Jews, Ronald Sukenick presents the untagged and untailored dialogues from the transcripts of tape-recorded interviews and family gatherings. All these dialogues are causal, daily and colloquial. These dialogues of American street language are collaged with the highbrow language at the very beginning of the part "Genes", forming a sharp contrast to each other.

In summary, the patchwork of different language fragments, especially the fragments that usually do not go together, is a good way, to Sukenick to shake off the bondage of conventions of fiction writing and to open up new possibilities to the author as well as the reader.

5.2.2 Collage

Collage, the term coined by both Georges Braque and Pablo Picasso in the beginning of the 20th century, is a distinctive part of modern art. Artists assemble different forms to create a new whole. For example, a collage may include newspaper clippings, labels, ribbons, colored papers, photographs, wood, bottle tops and other objects, glued to a new piece of work. "By analogy, collage is applied in literature to works incorporating quotations, allusions, foreign expressions, and nonverbal elements" (Harmon 1999: 103). What I want to emphasize about the collage of Sukenick is his piecing together word with non-word.

In the novel *Mosaic Man*, Sukenick (the narrator) pays a visit to the Berlin Wall, where he finds the cement crammed with multicolored multilingual writing. Moreover, the writing is a mixture of symbols, slogans, signs, messages, epigraphs, pictograms, hieroglyphs, riddles, runes, alphabetic jocularities..." (Sukenick 1999: 184). These Wallpeckers, a coined word for the chippers of wall cement, to Ronald Sukenick, are an ideal of mosaic. His fiction *Mosaic Man*, represents his effort to achieve this ideal. Beside the patchwork of different language elements we just mentioned, Sukenick also collages language and symbols.

Just as Lance Olsen points out: Sukenick's fiction is "a play and interplay between and among these graphic and verbal elements that allow them to interpenetrate, reminding us of the visual nature of language and the linguistic nature of images" (Olsen 2003:155). More important, by "bringing words and other opticals to the surface of the page, treating them as non-allegorical entities of design, signaling their existence as objects and therefore signaling their immediate connection to other tangible items in the extrapaginal world, while at the same time quoting, paraphrasing, and alluding to similar uses of graphication in synchronic and diachronic texts" (Olsen 1999:155).

Sukenick mainly uses two kinds of collage. First, many hand-drawing symbols are inserted into the language fragments mainly in Sukenick's novel *Mosaic Man*. Second, Sukenick also arranges words and punctuations and makes them into graphs so as to better reveal the visual nature of language.

The novel *Mosaic Man* is not a coherent, plot-centered narrative but a conglomerate of fragments. The fragments are of different forms, language elements and non-language elements. All these fragments, just like particles, are moving in different directions. Sukenick, just like a skillful craftsman, patches up all these particles and fragments of his stories together and makes them interchangeable parts of mosaics that come into existence as the stories move along.

In the part "EX/ODE", Ronald Sukenick inserts 5 hand-drawings symbols at the very beginning of this part and attaches meanings to each symbol. Then he further illustrates these symbols and meanings in the later language elements. So the ordinary words of narrative, symbols and lower-case boldface captions beneath those symbols are collaged and arranged to make the whole page just like a collage painting. The following page serves as a good example:

EX/ODE

Annotated Family Annals
Analog recorder-transcription and analysis
Legend:

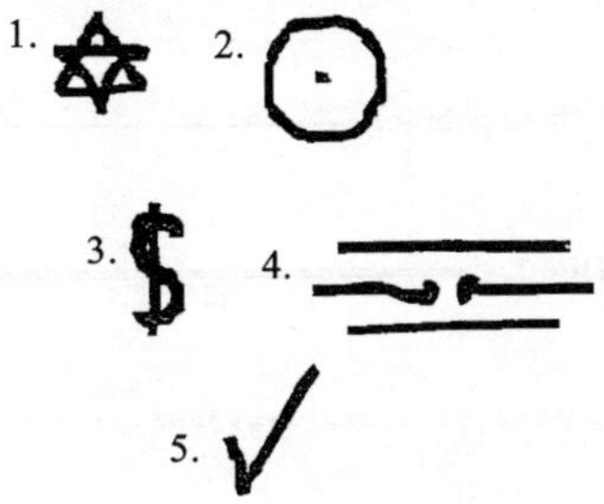

1. Jewish rules; 2. reality; 3. making it/losing it
4. reel/unreal; 5. the true story, the word

—>

(Sukenick 1999:19)

From the example, we can see that the symbols, narrative and lower-case language fragments under the symbols complement one another, elaborating the theme from different angles and perspectives. Symbols are the direct way to picture the theme to the reader. While the lower-case explanations under symbols reflect the author's meditations on five themes Sukenick lists at the beginning of this part: Jewish rules, reality, making it/losing it, reel/unreal and the true story, the word. And the narration of the main body of the story connects the five themes together and makes them into a whole: the identity seeking as a Jew and a writer.

Sukenick experiments with the collage of different elements which are not usually put together: symbols and graphs. In this way, Sukenick jumps from one combination to the other and then reverses the logic of the sequence. For the fragments and particles, everything can develop out of everything; there are endless possibilities of arrangements and rearrangements. Just as Putz points out, "Sukenick's specific use of the collage technique plays upon a possibility which has not often been explored by its practitioners. In his works the collage becomes increasingly dynamic: contracting, expanding, miscegenating its parts, moving in the direction of what Richard Kostelanetz once described as 'an imaginative work whose parts can be interchangeably ordered, like cards in a pack'" (Putz 1979:190).

Ronald Sukenick also collages language with language graphs. To Sukenick, language itself not only transmits meaning, but also possesses the visual nature. In a word, to him, words themselves are also symbols. So in his fiction, he experiments with different ways to turn words into graphs. The first way he experiments with is the use of punctuations.

In his short story collection *Doggy Bag*, punctuations are not merely used in their usual ways to help express the meaning. Punctuations are also changed into symbols to suggest a context very different from conventional writing. On the page of the contents of the collection, no pages are listed; instead, punctuations are introduced together with other symbols.

who are these people?}-->

nameofthedog}==>

doggy bag}##########################::::::::::::::------------->

a mummy's curse}**************************+++++++++====--->

50,010,008}}}}}}}}}}}}}))))))>>>>>////////%%%%%%%%%::::====>

the wondering jew and the black widow murders, or the
return of the planet of the apes}"""""""""" ''''' ~~~~~~~~~--->

the burial of count orgasm}||||||||||::::::::...... . . . . .

death on the supply side}_______________-------------~~~~~~~~~~

(Sukenick 1994:7)

These symbolic punctuations not only appear on the page of contents, but also serve as intermission between two stories in the novel. They give the reader a fresh reading experience, calling their attention to the physicality of the page. In other words, it is a way of transforming language into a tangible entity.

Other combinations of punctuations and symbols also appear in the stories, suggesting different meanings. Some combinations suggest a musical rhythm of the words. Some combinations suggest the ancient writing that people can not understand now, while some times the combination can refer to something belonging to the future. Some serve as the endings of the stories. No matter where they appear, they just serve the purpose of breaking the boredom of reading and attracting reader's attention to the truth of the page, as the page offers great possibilities for them to guess and to read from different perspectives.

oOOOo

-o+O+o-

v^^* #+#* %%% @&<.> #~~@#* <<-{&+* ::
|.|=~~ _-·_ ~+|++/+='=''==* \\/'-% ../@//\~)&[^
/%\%|: -_-'^#//=]<*>{:*
' " '%% ='=/+ (^~~~\\|-_-":+* }""_-/='* }{.%/--*

50,010,008}}}}}}}}}}}}}))))))>>>>>////////%%%%%%%%::::===>

You know what I hate? People who wear trade marks on their clothes. As if to say you are what you buy. But hey, do it yourself. Make up your own mark. Make a statement. Write yourself in to the book of life.

It's happening. I see signs everywhere. They are signs that say, "Hey, I'm me. Pay attention." And the reason is is that nobody is.

It's true I'm sensitive to style. Especially in clothes. Even for a woman, I mean. Because I'm in modes. But this is not a fad. This is a movement. I call it Egoslogan. A movement about persons. But it's not exclusive. It includes second persons and third persons as well as first persons. It's just, like, intensely personal.

I saw a T-shirt the other day that said, "I'm On Hold." It was on an older woman, maybe pushing sixty, which gave it a kind of twist. Then I saw one on a young woman that said "Handle With Care." That was over her breasts, which were big and bouncy. On her back it said, "This Side Up." She was with a big, strong guy whose chest said, "Agile."

(Sukenick 1994:88)

"How could you expect people to understand it?" the survivor said. "Or even believe it? I was there and even I don't believe it. Much less understand it. Less than you."

of every positive, the negative without which we can't even see the positive. outside a little town in Italy, Rimini I think it was, after a hard day of hitch hiking. It was a long time ago, I can date it precisely from

down from the cab of the truck at a small bridge into town. They were selling peaches by the road side, it must have been

bought a bag and sat on the stone wall of the bridge, thinking to rest and eat a peach before going into town for lunch. So I ate a peach, I can still remember the taste. It was a perfect peach, I remember thinking it was the best peach I ever ate. I threw the pit off the bridge and bit into another. I ate that one, threw the pit off the bridge and ate another. Threw the pit off the bridge and ate another. Threw the pit off the bridge and ate another. There must have been twelve or fourteen peaches in that bag and before I knew it I'd eaten them all. They were big peaches too. The Byzantine mosaics in Rimini, said to have inspired Dante, are in fact sublime.

../@//\~)&[^ v^^* #+\#* %%%* @&<.> #~~@#* |.|=~~ _-·_

/'-% v^^* #+#* %%%* @&<.> #~~@#* ^\<<-{&+* :: |.|=~~

|=~~ '==* ~+|++/+='=' '==* \\/'-% . ./@//\~)&[^ /%\%|:*

-_-'^#//=]<*>{:* ' " '%% ='=/+ (^~~~\\|-_-":+* }""_-/='*

}{.%/--* %%%* _-·_ ~+|++/+='=' '==* \\/'-% . ./@//\~)&[^

/%\%|:* -_-'^#//=]<*>{:* ' " '%% ='=/+ (^~~~\\|-_-":+*

}" "_-/='* }{.%/—* %%%* _-·_ v^^* #+#* %%%* @&<.>

#~~@#* ^\<<-{&+* : : | . |=~~ \\/ '-% ~+|++/+='=' '==*

_-·_ v^^* #^\+#* %%%* @&<.> #~~@#* #^\+#* ~+|++/

+='=' '==* \\/'-% . ./@//\~)&[^ #^\+#* %%%* @&<.>

#~~@#* ^\<<-{&+* :: |.|=~~ _-·_ ~+|++/+='=''==* \/'-% ..

/@//\~)&[^ }" "_-/='* }{.%/—* %%%^* _-·_ ^\<<-{&+*

: : | . |=~~ _-·_ |=~~ . . /@//\~)&[^ /%\%|:* -_-'^#//=]<*>{:*

the wondering jew and the black widow murders, or the return of the planet of the apes}""""""""" ' ' ' ' ' ~~~~~~~~~~~>

I get a strange feeling in Europe, when I go to Germany, especially, I understand that I'm already dead. In Europe I'm detached from the human race. I no longer care about sex, money, career, prestige, fun, the love of women, the admiration of men, even current events. If you come and tell me your troubles I'll sympathize, if you want to brag I'll applaud. But it's all at a remove, that is, because it moved me before,

(Sukenick 1994:102-103)

Ronald Sukenick not only uses unusual combinations of punctuations and symbols to call the attention of the reader to the physicality of the page, he also fully develops the symbolic nature of the language. He starts his practice of exploring the symbolic nature of the language from his first novel *Up*. At the end of the novel, when Sukenick, an imaginative space hero, comes down to the earth, the words also come down:

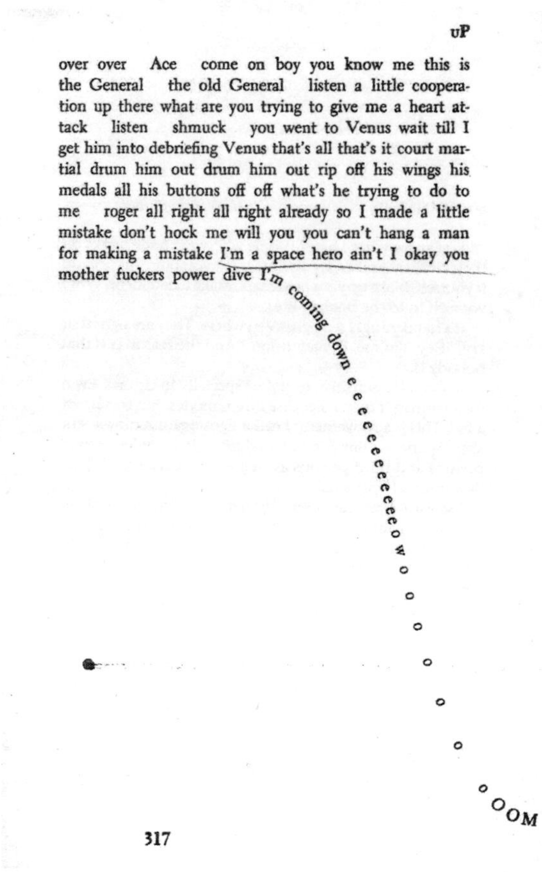
uP

over over Ace come on boy you know me this is the General the old General listen a little cooperation up there what are you trying to give me a heart attack listen shmuck you went to Venus wait till I get him into debriefing Venus that's all that's it court martial drum him out drum him out rip off his wings his medals all his buttons off off what's he trying to do to me roger all right all right already so I made a little mistake don't hock me will you you can't hang a man for making a mistake I'm a space hero ain't I okay you mother fuckers power dive I'm coming down eeeeeeeeeeeeow o o o o o o ooOM

317

(Sukenick 1968:317)

The graphicalization of language is to get the narrator, the author and the reader involved in the ongoing experience so as to establish a rapport with reality, and also to call the reader's attention to the fact that fiction writing is an ongoing process of composition and recomposition.

The change of capital form and small letters is another way Sukenick employs to make the language visual. At the end of his novel *98. 6*, his skillful changes between the capital forms and small letters leave a deep impression on the reader. The purpose of doing this is not for the clarification of meaning. Instead, it means to bring a new reading experience to the reader. "You don't have to understand it do you understand everything you remember. You have to love it and feel it" (Sukenick 1975a:187).

Sukenick plays with words, making changes as he wishes. To him, words are no longer to be lined from left to right, from top to bottom on the page. Instead, he tries to make the reader treat the page as a mirror which provides a three dimensional surface for the spatial displacement of words. So the page, which formerly consists of solid blocks of line-by-line print with fixed margins, is turned into a playground for words which are set free to perform themselves. This free play releases language from its conventional meaning.

In *Doggy Bag*, for example, on pages 17-18, Sukenick widens the space between the letters of the words:

i s

?

t h e

t h e t e x t

t h e t e x t o f l i f e

name of the dog}===================================>

(Sukenick 1994:18)

This kind of word play highlights the visual nature of language. And at the same time, it catches the attention of the reader and beats back the boredom in reading.

Beethoven appeasing wart hogs
Beethoven pleasing the hippopotamus
Beethoven
boring the rhinoceros
Beethoven goes to a Masai
cattle raid
Beethoven watching a flamingo flap
Beethoven amazed at the hyrax call
Beethoven
reacts to the oryx horn
Beethoven blinks at the vulture dance
Beethoven menaced by mild monkeys
Beethoven
protests the turaco's squawk
Beethoven gawks as the ibis soars
Beethoven blubbers in Bantu

Z
i
Z i Z i Z
i
Z

L
a
L L
La La
L
La La

l
disintegration of
b
e
r
jackal
l

e
p w
history's music
s h l
r d
u
s d
t o
g
o
f

b
l
a
dark of bush
e e
r
d

s
w
terminal olduvai turkana express
l n
l o
maribou stork l
a

g
a
hyena

(Sukenick 1986:118-119)

uP

over

over

over

over

a l p h a

b

e

t

uP

s

o

u

p

(Sukenick 1968:28-29)

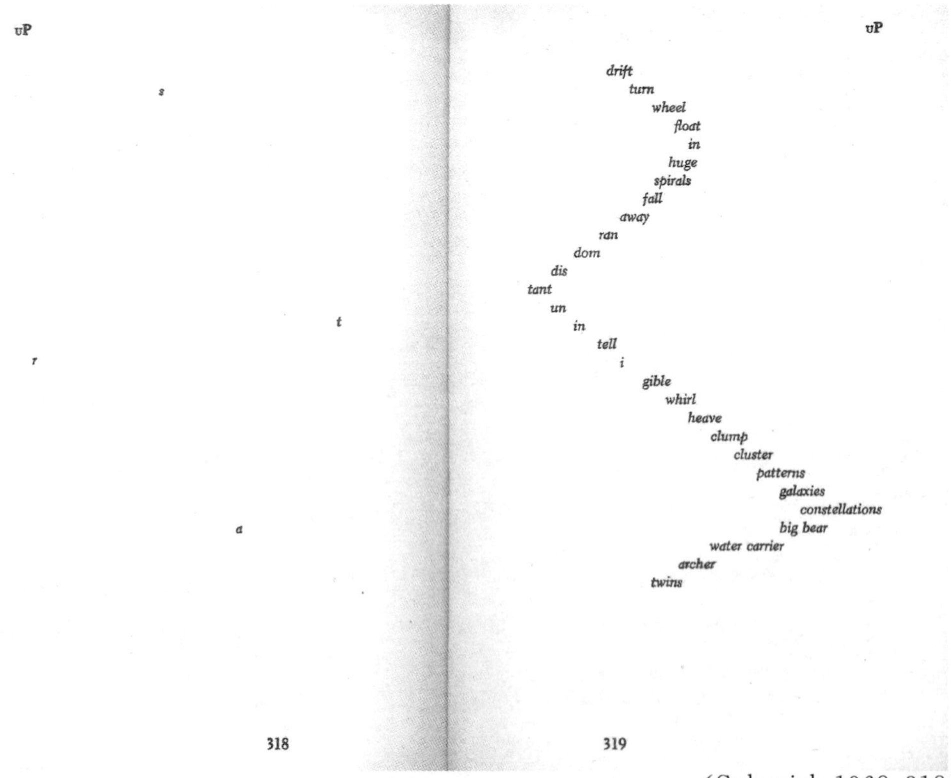
uP

s

t

r

a

318

uP

drift
turn
wheel
float
in
huge
spirals
fall
away
ran
dom
dis
tant
un
in
tell
i
gible
whirl
heave
clump
cluster
patterns
galaxies
constellations
big bear
water carrier
archer
twins

319

(Sukenick 1968:318-319)

In the above three examples, we can see that Sukenick plays with words, just as children play with toy bricks. He has been exploring different ways to let the language produce different possibilities of meanings. To summarize, by exploring more possibilities of language, Ronald Sukenick tries to make the form of fiction release new and often unexpected contexts and open up new possibilities to the experience. Sukenick once points out the purpose of doing this, "by breaking the language code when you break the language code you get a new language" (Sukenick 1979a: 102). Moreover, Sukenick's Mosaic Law of Postmodernist Narratives elaborates his ways to hold the particles and fragments of his stories together when the whole and centre are absent.

Chapter 6 Conclusion

I want to bring my research into Ronald Sukenick to a conclusion by quoting the ending scene of his first novel *Up*, which I think best summarizes his writing career:

> On the tenement roof above the corner, among television aerials, a boyish figure raises a long, bare pole. He holds it above his head, moves it in a slow circle, and lowers it again. No sequel in the vacant air, no signal comes. He raises the pole, moves it in a circle, and lowers it again. The light is emptying from the sky. He raises the pole, moves it in a circle, lowers it again. The light is emptying from the sky. He raises the pole, moves it in a circle, lowers it. He raises the pole, moves it in a circle, lowers it. He raises the pole, moves it in a circle, lowers it. Again. Again. Again. The light empties from the sky. (Sukenick 1968:330)

Ronald Sukenick is just like the boy in this picture, who uses his imaginative power (the pole he waves), with his unremitting efforts, searching for data from experience and reality, especially those not yet tainted by the society of the spectacle, whose images flood the televisions around him. His goal is to record the wash of data at the very moment of its convergence into new integrations. However, such moments are rare, and the integrations themselves only briefly meaningful. But such moments stand between a life of calcified experience and the possibilities for meaningful experience, so that they are worth the efforts made by Ronald Sukenick.

The picture clearly depicts Sukenick's efforts in two aspects. On the one hand, Sukenick tries to record the experience of postmodern Americans and make meaning out of it. He explores the post-trauma identity crises and individuals' struggles in a harsh and violent culture. He studies and diagnoses American culture and tries to catch the Zeitgeist. On the other hand, Sukenick has been probing into experiments of the forms of fiction. By purposely digressing from the established conventions in fiction writing, Sukenick tries to open new space and offer new possibilities.

Ronald Sukenick's efforts in these two aspects are provoked by his diagnosis of the dual crises of American culture in the 1960s and 1970s. Sukenick believes that he writes in the dual crises of the "death of God" and "death of novel". "Death of God" reveals the abyss of contemporary experience in the culture void created by the existential death of God. The Holocaust and Cold War add more confusion and sense of loss to the people already at the bottom of the ocean, and push individuals to difficult situations of identity confusion and loss. The hunger for Golden Calf (money) and the "sadism + masochism" essence of culture intensify their identity crisis. Moreover, the identity crisis is even doubled for American Jews and Jewish writers, who have experienced the massacre, which destroys all the base on which they construct their identities.

Faced with the identity crisis, individuals seek different ways out. Ronald Sukenick, in his fiction, explores different strategies individuals employ in their identity seeking journeys. After carefully studying the strategies used, I summarize three laws he employs in dealing with identity crisis: Surviving Law of identity, Entropy Law of identity and Mosaic Law of identity.

Surviving Law of identity reveals Ronald Sukenick's keen awareness of the identity crises of postmodern Americans after traumatic historical events and their struggles between assimilation and dissimilation into the mainstream society when constructing their identities. The post-World War II era in the United States has experienced a series of political, economic, social and cultural changes. To survive the changed society and gain a sense of security, individuals either choose to assimilate or dissimilate into the mainstream society. By "inventing" or "selling out" one's identity, one can get gradually steered into the mainstream way of life. However, in order to keep one's uniqueness and to fight against conformism, one can also choose to dissimilate into the mainstream by three strategies proposed by Sukenick: retreating into the ivory tower, staying in dreams and hallucination and writing experimental fiction. However, assimilation and dissimilation are hard choices to make, so that many individuals struggle between them.

Entropy Law of identity deals with the fluidity and dissolution characteristics of identities. Unlike traditional novels, which aim at developing consistent and identifiable characters with the unfolding of plots, Sukenick's Entropy Law of identity presents a purposeful disintegration of the consistent and identifiable traits of characters. With the disintegration of these traits, characters change their identities like a stream, freely and randomly, finally arrive at the non-identity. "Stream of identities" and "non-identity" foreground his belief that human identity in postmodern society is a fluid process of constant becoming rather than a fixed entity.

Mosaic Law of identity centers on the fragmentation and collage characteristics of identity. Sukenick believes that the cultural diversity and heterogeneity in postmodern context pose greater difficulties in keeping a cultural centre and wholeness. When centre, wholeness and unity are demolished, individuals are just cultural shards. What they can do is to make meaning of parts and fragments. Mosaic Law of identity and psychosynthesis are just the strategy and psychological process through which we mosaic and piece together different parts.

In summary, Ronald Sukenick, in his fiction, makes a remarkable keen insight into identity crisis in the postmodern context. Moreover, he accurately grasps the characteristics of identity in the post-World War Ⅱ era: fluidity, fragmentation, changeability and dissolution. The three laws presented in his fiction, to some extent, summarize the struggles of individuals in their identity construction and the strategies they employ.

The "Death of the Novel" reveals the crisis of fiction in the 20th century. As man must find new ways to organize his existence, so must the novel and literature as a whole find new principles upon which to base its creation. Sukenick believes that the mainstream fiction of realism, which comes down from the 19th century, is inadequate to convey our experience in the 20th century. Sukenick's Surviving Law of Postmodernist Narratives is a diagnosis of the crisis that threatens the fiction and the necessity of dismantling the traditional way of writing, mainly the realistic way of writing. His challenge to established realistic tradition is based on his belief that the commitment of realism to formal verisimilitude fails to adequately express the facts of contemporary experience. Thus the obligation of fiction is to rescue experience from history, from politics, from commerce, from theory, even from language itself, from any system, that threatens to distort, devitalize of manipulate experience.

In order to catch the experience, all through his writing career, Sukenick has been working to push the fiction to its edges, with the purpose of opening up new spaces and searching for new possibilities. He is looking for a narrative alternative whose aim is to liberate potentials of fiction. Through his efforts of new fiction with no plot, no story, no character, no chronological sequence, no verisimilitude, no imitation, no allegory, no symbolism, no subject matter and no meaning, Sukenick challenges the established paradigms of traditional novels and redefines fiction. A fiction, to Sukenick, is not an ideological formulation of belief but a statement of a favorable rapport with reality. Fiction is not about experience, but is part of experience. Since modern experience is fluid and flexible, so the way we narrates experience should also change. Sukenick insists that narratives must be agonistic, sophistic, sophisticated, fluid, unpredictable, rhizomatic, affective, inconsistent, contradictory, improvisational and provisional.

Sukenick's Entropy Law of Postmodernist Narratives and the Mosaic Law of Postmodernist Narratives protrude his characteristics of self-reflexiveness and his improvisational technique. His postmodernist narratives emphasize his understanding of postmodern experience: fragmentation, fluidity, dissolution and mosaic. His typographical innovation, language play, patchwork and collage are made just to get fiction back to the truth of experience. His purpose is to free the writer to bring to bear the full resources of his experience, temperament and intelligence from any constriction. Composition is an ongoing interchange between the mind and the page. So a novel is a developing structure that from the first word has its own influence in determining its shape, and by the last has far more influence than its author.

Sukenick's fiction practice and his exploration in the theories of fiction valuably extend the way that we can consider and understand our world, and also the way that we can consider and understand fiction. All through his literary career, he has made unremitting efforts innovating many aspects of fiction: its form, typography and language, which make his books so deeply offend the average sensibility. However, by pushing fiction to its edges and by probing into every possibility of fiction, Sukenick greatly expands the potentials of fiction. Although the readership and research into Ronald Sukenick are rather limited, his achievement and contribution to American literature should not be ignored.

References

ADAMS T D, 1978. Obscuring the muse: the mock—autobiographies of Ronald Sukenick [J]. Critique, 20(1): 27-39.

ALFORD D F, 1991. The self in social theory: a psychoanalytic account of its construction in Plato, Hobbes, Locke, Rawls and Rousseau[M]. New Haven, CT, and London: Yale University Press.

ANDERSON L, WADKINS M, 1991. Japan—A Culture of Consumption? [J]. Advances in Consumer Research, 18: 129-134.

ASSAGIOLI R, 1965. Psychosynthesis[M]. New York: The Viking Press.

BELLAMY J D, 1972. Imagination as perception: an interview with Ronald Sukenick [J]. Chicago review, 23(3) :59-72.

BALLAMY J D, 1974. The new fiction: interviews with innovative American writers [M]. London: University of Illinois Press.

BARTH J. The literature of replenishment[J]. Atlantic, 1980, 245: 65-71.

BERGMANN L S, 1974. OT: a novel by Ronald Sukenick[J]. Chicago Review, 25 (3): 9.

BERNSTEIN C, 1986. Content's dream: essays 1975-1984[M]. Evanston: Northwestern University Press.

BLAKE N, 2003. What's your story: narration and "a new knowledge of reality" in The Death of the Novel and Other Stories [M]// ROBERSON M. Musing the mosaic: approaches to Ronald Sukenick. Albany: State University of New York Press: 65-73.

BOGUE R, CORNIS-POPE M, 1995. Violence and mediation in contemporary culture [M]. Albany: State University of New York Press.

BRADBURY M, RO S, 1987. Contemporary American fiction[M]. London: Edward Arnold Ltd..

BROOKS D R, WILEY E O, 1988. Evolution as entropy-towards a unified theory of biology[M]. Chicago: University of Chicago Press.

BROOKER P, 2003. A glossary of cultural theory[M]. 2nd ed. New York: Oxford University Press.

BUTLER J, 1990. Gender trouble: feminism and the subversion of identity[M]. New York: Routledge.

CALLEN H B, 1985. Thermodynamics and an Introduction to thermostatistics[M]. 2nd ed. New Jersey: John Wiley and Sons.

CARAMELLO C, 1983. Silverless mirrors: book, self & postmodern American fiction [M]. Tallahassee: University Presses of Florida.

CAVE T, 1995. Fictional identities[M]// HARRIS H. Identity: essays based on Herbert Spencer lectures given in the University of Oxford. Oxford: Clarendon Press. 108-122.

CLARKE D B, 1998. Consumption, identity and space-time[J]. Consumption, markets & culture, 2(3): 233-335.

CORNIS-POPE M, 2001. Narrative innovation and cultural rewriting in the cold war and after[M]. New York: Palgrave.

COWLEY J, 1987. Ronald Sukenick's new departures from the terminal of language[J]. Critique: studies in contemporary fiction, 28(2): 87-99.

CURRIE P, 1987. The eccentric self:anti-characterization and the problem of the subject in American postmodernist fiction [M]//BRADBURY M, RO S. Contemporary American Fiction. London: Edward Arnold:52-69.

DAVIS J E, 2000. Identity and social change[M]. New Jersey: New Brunswick.

DUNN R G, 1998. Identity crises: a social critique of postmodernity[M]. Minneapolis: University of Minnesota Press.

EAGLETON T, 1990. The ideology of the aesthetic[M]. Oxford: Basil Blackwell.

EKINS P, 1991. A sustainable consumer society: a contradiction in terms? [J]. International environment affairs, 3(4): 243-258.

EZZY D, 1998. Theorizing narrative identity: symbolic interactionism and hermeneutics [J]. Sociological quarterly, 39(3): 239-252.

FEATHERSTONE M, 1995. Undoing culture: globalization, postmodernism and identity [M]. London: Sage.

FEDERMAN R, 1974. In[J]. Partisan Review, 41(1): 137-142.

FEDERMAN R, 1975. Surfiction: fiction now … and tomorrow [M]. Chicago: The Swallow Press Inc..

FEUER L S, 1959. Theses on Feuerbach[M]// MARX K, FEUER L, ENGELS F. Marx and Engels: basic writings on politics and philosophy. Garden City, New York: Doubleday Anchor: 230-249.

FOLEY JR, 2009. Down as up, out as in: Ron Sukenick remembers Ron Sukenick[EB/OL](2009-03-26)[2011-05-11]. http://www. flashpointmag. com/downin. htm.

FREESE P, 1997. From apocalypse to entropy and beyond: the second law of Thermodynamics in post-war American fiction[M]. Essen: Die Blaue Eule.

FREUD S, 1949. An outline of psychoanalysis[M]. New York: Norton.

FRISBY D, 1988. Fragments of modernity[M]. Cambridge: MIT Press.

GERGEN K J, 1991. The saturated self: dilemmas of identity in contemporary life[M]. New York: Praeger.

GOVE P B, 1993. Webster's third new international dictionary of the English language [M]. Springfield: Merriam-webster.

GORDON M, 1964. Assimilation in American life[M]. New York: Oxford University Press.

HARMON W, HOLMAN C H, 1999. A handbook to literature [M]. New Jersey: Prentice Hall.

HARRIS C B, 2003. At play in the fields of formal thinking: Up and postmodernist metafiction[M]// ROBERSON M. Musing the mosaic: approaches to Ronald Sukenick. Albany: State University of New York Press: 39-63.

HARTMANN D, GERTEIS J, 2005. Dealing with diversity: mapping multiculturalism in sociological terms[J]. Sociological Theory, 23(2): 218-240.

HEISE U K, 2003. Sukenick's posthumans[M]// ROBERSON M. Musing the mosaic: approaches to Ronald Sukenick. Albany: State University of New York Press: 75-96.

HOLSTEIN J A, GUBRIUM J F, 1999. The self we live by: narrative identity in a postmodern world[M]. New York: Oxford University Press.

HORNUNG A, 1984. Absent presence: the fictions of Raymond Federman and Ronald Sukenick[J]. Indian journal of American studies, 14(1): 17-31.

HORNUNG A, RUHE E, 1992. Autobiographie & avant-garde [M]. Tubingen: Gutenberg-Universitat.

KATZ A, 2005a. Iconoclastic commitments: idolatry and imagination in Cynthia Ozick and Ronald Sukenick[J]. Mosaic, 38(3): 113-130.

KATZ A, 2005. Narrative thinking and experiential knowledge: the example of Ronald Sukenick[J]. Texas studies in literature and language, 47(3): 189-212.

KATZ A, 2006. A little direct intervention by the author is called for: textual identity in the work of Ronald Sukenick[J]. Angelaki journal of the theoretical humanities, 2(2): 63-80.

KELLNER D, 1989. Jean Baudrillard: from Marxism to postmodernism and beyond [M]. Stanford, California: Stanford University Press.

KLINKOWITZ J, 1972. Getting real: making it (Up) with Ronald Sukenick[J]. Chicago Review, 23(winter): 73-82.

KLINKOWITZ J, 1975. Literary disruptions: the making of a post-contemporary American fiction[M]. 2nd ed. Urbana: Univeristy of Illinois Press.

KLINKOWITZ J, 1981. The novel as artifact: spatial form in contemporary fiction[M]// SMITTEN J R, DAGHISTANY A. Spatial form in narrative. Ithaca: Cornell University Press: 275.

KLINKOWITZ J, 1987. The extra-literary in contemporary American fiction [M]// BRADBURY M, RO S. Contemporary American Fiction. London: Edward Arnold Ltd.: 16-25.

KLINKOWITZ J, 1992. Structuring the void: the struggle for subject in contemporary American fiction[M]. London: Duke University Press.

KLINKOWITZ J, 2003. 8 ½ Ronnies [M]// ROBERSON M. Musing the mosaic: approaches to Ronald Sukenick. Albany: State University of New York Press: 251-269.

KOCH S, 1967. Premature speculations on the perpetual renaissance[J]. Tri-Quarterly, (Fall): 5.

KUTZIK J, 1986. Fiction as performance: the fiction of Ronald Sukenick and Raymond Federman[M]. Carbondale: Southern Illinois Press.

KUTZIK J. Postmodern language-centered writing and the question of ideology: a polish perspective[J]. Journal of American studies of Turkey. 1996,4: 3-13.

LANDSBERG P T, 1984a. Is equilibrium always an entropy maximum? [J]. Journal of Statistical Physics, 35:159-169.

LANDSBERG P T, 1984b. Can entropy and "order" increase together? [J]. Physics Letters, 102A:171-173.

LECLAIR T. MCCAFFER L. Anything can happen: interviews with contemporary American novelists[M]. Urbana: University of Illinois Press, 1974.

LEITCH V B, et al, 2001. The Norton anthology of the theory and criticism[M]. 1st ed. New York: W. W. Norton &Company.

MCCAFFERY L, 1982. The metafictional muse [M]. Pittsburgh: University of Pittsburgh Press.

MEYER C M, 1982. An interview with Ronald Sukenick[J]. Contemporary literature, 23 (2):129-144.

MILLER P, 1956. Errand into the wildness[M]. Cambridge: Belknap Press of Harvard University Press.

NOEL D, 1976. Tales of fictive power: dreaming and imagination in Ronald Sukenick's postmodern fiction[J]. Boundary, 1(fall):117-135.

OLSEN L, 2003. Graphiction: technological reality in Ronald Sukenick's 98. 6, Doggy Bag, and Mosaic Man[M]// ROBERSON M. Musing the mosaic: approaches to Ronald Sukenick. Albany: State University of New York Press:153-179.

PUTZ M, 1979. The story of identity: American fiction of the sixties[M]. Stuttgart: Metzler.

RANDALL W L, 1995. The stories we are: an essay on self-creation[M]. Toronto: University of Toronto Press.

ROBERSON M, 2003. Musing the mosaic: approaches to Ronald Sukenick[M]. Albany: State University of New York Press.

ROSTON M, 2001. The search for selfhood in modern literature[M]. New York: Palgrave.

RUSSELL C, 2003. Explorations of postmodern time, space, and image: considering the works of Ronald Sukenick and David Salle[M]// ROBERSON M. Musing the mosaic: approaches to Ronald Sukenick. Albany: State University of New York Press:115-137.

SEMRAU J, 1983. Flying a kite: Ronald Sukenick's Up and Out[J]. Studia Anglica Posnaniensia, 16: 255-263.

SEMRAU J, 1986. American self-conscious fiction of the 1960s and 1970s: Donald Barthelme, Robert Coover, Ronald Sukenick[M]. Poznan: Wydawnictwo Naukowe Uniwersytetu im. Adama Mickiewicza.

SCHOLES R, 1974. Structuralism in literature[M]. New Haven: Yale University Press.

SUKENICK R, 1967. Wallace Stevens: musing the obscure[M]. New York: New York University Press.

SUKENICK R, 1968. Up[M]. New York: Dial Publishing Co., Inc..

SUKENICK R, 1973. Out[M]. Chicago: Swallow Press.

SUKENICK R, 1975a. 98.6[M]. New York: Fiction Collective.

SUKENICK R, 1975b. The new tradition in fiction[M]//FEDERMAN R. Surfiction: fiction now…and tomorrow. Chicago: Swallow Press:35-45.

SUKENICK R, 1975c. Twelve digressions toward a study of composition[J]. New literary history, 6(2): 429-437.

SUKENICK R, 1979a. Long talking bad conditions blues[M]. New York: Fiction Collective.

SUKENICK R, 1979b. Eight digressions on the politics of language[J]. New literary history, 10(3):467-477.

SUKENICK R, 1984. Autogyro: my life in fiction[M]// ZADRONZY M. Contemporary authors autobiography series. Detroit, Mich.: Gale Research Co.:283-296.

SUKENICK R, 1985. In form: digressions on the act of fiction[M]. Carbondale: Southern Illinois University Press.

SUKENICK R, 1986a. Blown away[M]. Los Angeles: Sun & Moon Press.

SUKENICK R, 1986b. The Endless Short Story[M]. New York: Fiction Collective.

SUKENICK R, 1987. Down and in: life in the underground[M]. New York: Beech Tree Books.

SUKENICK R, 1988. Experiment and experience: my life in fiction[J]. American Book Review, Nov-Dec:10-15.

SUKENICK R, 1994. Doggy bag[M]. Boulder: Fiction Collective Two.

SUKENICK R, 1999. Mosaic man[M]. Normal, Illinois: Fiction Collective Two.

SUKENICK R, 2000. Narralogues: truth in fiction[M]. Albany: State University of New York Press.

SUKENICK R, 2003. The death of the novel and other stories[M]. Tallahassee: Fiction Collective Two.

SUKENICK R, 2009. Cows [EB/OL](2009-03-26)[2011-05-11]. www. altx. com/

ebooks/download. cfm/cows. pdf

TAJFEL H, 1981. Human groups and social categories[M]. Cambridge: Cambridge University Press.

TRACHTENBERG S, 1982. The way that girl pressed against you in the subway: Ronald Sukenick's real act of the imagination[J]. The Journal of Narrative Technique, 12: 57-71.

WHETTEN D A, GODFREY P C, 1998. Identity in organizations: building theory through conversations[M]. Los Angeles: Sage Publications Inc..

WHITEBROOK M, 2001. Identity, narrative and politics[M]. London: Routledge.

WHITMORE D, 2004. Psychosynthesis counselling in action[M]. 3rd ed. London: Sage Publications Ltd..

WINKELMAN A, 1986. Authorial prescence in American metafiction: the novels of Coover, Federman, Sorrentino, and Sukenick [D]. Los Angeles : University of California at Los Angeles.

ZAMORA L P, 1989. Writing the apocalypse: historical vision in contemporary U. S. and Latin American fiction[M]. New York: Cambridge University Press.

杨仁敬，2007. 二十世纪美国文学史[M]. 青岛：青岛出版社.

杨仁敬，2008. 美国文学简史[M]. 上海：上海外语教育出版社.

周南翼，2000. 诺纳德·苏克尼克——不懈探索小说形式的美国后现代作家[J]. 外国文学，(4):3-4.

周南翼，2000. 令人陌生而又熟悉的虚构世界——评诺纳德·苏克尼克的创作风格[J]. 外国文学，(4)：10-17.

内 容 提 要

诺纳德·苏克尼克是美国二十世纪富有影响力的作家之一，出版了9部长篇小说、3部短篇小说集和三部理论文集，获得了1988年和1999年的美国国家图书奖等奖项。

本书深入研究了苏克尼克小说中关于身份危机和身份建构的主题以及苏克尼克为实现这些主题进行的后现代叙事的革新。本书主要探讨了苏克尼克在应对身份危机和小说危机时所采用的三种法则：生存法则、"熵"的法则和镶嵌法则。

本书是目前国内第一部全面深入研究苏克尼克的学术专著。本书的出版能丰富国内关于苏克尼克的研究成果。

图书在版编目(CIP)数据

诺纳德·苏克尼克作品的后现代叙事研究：英文/王海燕著.—武汉：武汉理工大学出版社，2017.9

ISBN 978-7-5629-5582-5

Ⅰ.①诺…　Ⅱ.①王…　Ⅲ.①诺纳德·苏克尼克-小说研究-英文　Ⅳ.①I712.074

中国版本图书馆CIP数据核字(2016)第221826号

项目负责人：王兆国　　**责任编辑**：徐　环

责任校对：王兆国　　**封面设计**：许伶俐

出版发行：武汉理工大学出版社

地　　址：武汉市洪山区珞狮路122号

邮　　编：430070

网　　址：http://www.wutp.com.cn

经　　销：各地新华书店

印　　刷：武汉天星美润设计印务有限公司

开　　本：787×1092　1/16

印　　张：9.5

字　　数：237千字

版　　次：2017年9月第1版

印　　次：2017年9月第1次印刷

定　　价：58.00元

凡购本书，如有缺页、倒页、脱页等印装质量问题，请向出版社发行部调换。

本社购书热线：027-87515778　87515848　87785758　87165708(传真)